LETHBRIDGE-STEWART

INTELLIGENCE TASKFORCE

Jonathan Blum

CANDY JAR BOOKS · CARDIFF
2024

Intelligence Taskforce © Jonathan Blum 2024

Characters from The Web of Fear
© Hannah Haisman & Lincoln Estate 1968, 2024
Lethbridge-Stewart: The Series
© Andy Frankham-Allen & Shaun Russell 2014, 2024

Major Bugayev created by Simon A Forward
Fiona Lethbridge-Stewart created by Gary Russell

Doctor Who is © British Broadcasting Corporation, 1963, 2024

ISBN: 978-1-917022-39-2

Range Editor: Andy Frankham-Allen
Editor: Shaun Russell
Editorial: Keren Williams
Licensed by Hannah Haisman
Cover by Adrian Salmon & Will Brooks

Printed and bound in the UK by
4edge, 22 Eldon Way, Hockley, Essex, SS5 4AD

Published by
Candy Jar Books
Mackintosh House
136 Newport Road, Cardiff, CF24 1DJ
www.candyjarbooks.co.uk

*For Marsha Twitty,
without whom it wouldn't have been
nearly as much fun.*

THE BEGINNING

SO ONCE upon a time and again, there was a brigadier.

Not *the* Brigadier yet, just *a* brigadier – he hadn't defined his article yet. Alistair Lethbridge-Stewart, if you're into names, but really he was what he did. And what he did was face the weird, and deal with it sensibly, and often explosively. His special talent, so they say, was being able to handle it all without understanding half of it. Cos he'd listen to his experts, and if it was a threat? He'd make sure the ineffable ended up well and truly effed.

Salt of the earth, that man was. With a lively wife and a kid on the way, even though he was the sort of officer who you could never imagine getting out of an upright locked position. Latest fruit from a long family tree of army men, all proud and upright and thoroughly conventional. Well, except for that business with his father, and his brother, and let's not get into his nephews and all, or Great-Uncle Archie's bit on the side, but somehow none of that ever stuck to him. Ask him, he was a simple man with a simple life.

Whatever this whole crazy universe threw at him, it wasn't Just Too Silly; no, he made it serious, just by dealing with it like it made sense. Chap with wings? Five rounds unflapped.

Which is good… cos once upon that same time there was me.

Call me Jonesy. Call us the Odds.

Whole family like me, stretching back to the days when the Lethbridges and the Stewarts were still killing each other at Culloden or somewhere. That's when the Oddfather fell from the skies. Hit the Himalayas and just kept walking. Quite a bloke, the family legends say, probably the salt of whatever not-Earth he was from. He started wandering from China to

India a hundred years before Alistair's great-greatish-grandad started pacifying the natives there, and kept going 'til he reached old blighty, scattering his seed behind him. Ten generations of descendants scattered around the world... and I'm the one who tracked us all down. The surviving us, that is.

I suppose that makes me the one to blame.

Anyway, all us Odds got different bits of what he could do. Some of us make unlikely things happen, sometimes even when we want to. We can squeeze and squint at the probabilities and make a random chance fall our way. Others, only the most normal things happen around them... or at least get noticed around them, cos them getting noticed makes even more unlikely things happen.

Course, every two-bit gangster or national intelligence service going wants to get their claws into us, the moment they know we're there. And the folks who *do* have their claws in us – who paid me to get us together – aren't gonna let us go without a fight.

All we want is a quiet life, really. All Lethbridge-Stewart wants is... Well, couldn't everyone else be sensible about the weird things as well? There's stuff out there that threatens the whole lot of us, can't we get the nations of the world to co-operate in dealing with them?

This has gone down about as well as you'd expect.

Right about now, we're both about as far as we can get from where we want to be. But together... there's a chance that'll make it all go right. If we can find it.

Toss your coins, everyone...

CHAPTER ONE
Nothing Important Happened Today

IT HAD all changed in a moment.

Captain Bill Bishop came to the Madhouse that morning expecting the Brig to give him their next move. Instead, he found Colonel Douglas making a terse announcement in the Ops room.

'I was informed this morning that Brigadier Lethbridge-Stewart has taken personal leave. I will be acting as commander until his return date, of which I have not yet been notified. We will have a more formal briefing shortly; in the meantime, carry on.'

But carry on doing *what?*

With all the suspicions they'd had about who was leaking information out of the Fifth, Bishop didn't know whether Lethbridge-Stewart had even let Colonel Douglas in on their investigations at all. And if he hadn't... The last thing Bishop wanted to do was blow the gaffe again.

Where could the Brig have gone? Bishop's guts tightened: he knew *why* he'd gone, without telling them. But that didn't leave him and Anne a way forward.

On a hunch, Bishop rang Fiona, on the conference-room phone. Wherever her husband had gone, she hadn't gone with him. She sounded brittle. 'He said he'd be "in the field", and that it was "need to know".'

'Well, if you can get him a message—'

'I'm sorry, Bill,' she said – sounding far too clenched to be sorry. She'd been shaken, and he could guess why, but it would still be a guess.

No one answered at Captain Kramer's safehouse either. Lethbridge-Stewart had announced days ago that she had gone back to the States; Bishop hadn't known whether that was misdirection to foil the leakers. And now that he knew that, however inadvertently, he'd been one of those leaks… No wonder he still wasn't sure. About anything.

Finally, furtively, he rang Anne at the Edinburgh University lab.

'The Brig's gone dark. He took leave. Told no one. Cut us all out of the loop.'

There was a long pause; was it sinking in for her as it had for him? That all their pieces had been knocked off the board, and the only moves left for them were bad ones?

'Oh,' she said. 'Well. To hell with him, then.'

When Bishop had told her on Friday night, Anne had been rattled. Shaken about how her moonlighting for Bryden Industries on that side project, plus his mistake, had left them exposed. She'd got defensive; 'Alistair's overreacting because he feels blindsided. But we didn't do that deliberately, we didn't know it was any of his business.'

And true, the offer from Bryden Industries had seemed completely innocent. Hell, perhaps it still *was*; not everything had to be part of a masterplan. Peyton Bryden, or more likely one of his middle-managers, had just seen a chance to make some money out of formalising and selling the detector system Anne had cobbled together for Operation Weatherballoon; just like he and Anne had seen an opportunity to put a decent nest-egg away in their savings. The thought that Bryden was any more than a nuisance around the margins – that he could have been the man using the Odds against them from the beginning – had never crossed their mind.

Over the last day or two, Anne's irritation had grown more righteous; 'Alistair knows I've been freelance for ages, I don't report to him.' And she'd rationalised it enough to more or less convince Bishop that their mistake was really an opportunity to take the fight straight to Bryden.

But now, suddenly Alistair's side of things was crystal-clear to him. 'With the Odds about, anything he told us could leak through sheer random chance…'

'We have plenty to be getting on with without him,' she insisted. 'My research with Dave and Nina. Working out what Bryden wants with them. When we get something, we take it to the Fifth.'

'If we can trust them.'

'Then we find out if we can.'

She was doubling down. She was so angry that Lethbridge-Stewart might not be trusting her, that she was determined to go it alone, and thus avoid facing the possibility that he might have been right.

'And when Alistair gets back?'

He heard her take a deep, cold breath. 'Assume that's not going to happen.'

'…What?'

'Or that he'll come back too late to make any difference. We can't rely on him. And we don't need to.'

He blinked. 'This is *the Brig* we're talking about.'

'Yes, it is. But we don't actually need him,' she said bluntly.

'He gave me my career.'

'Well, it's your career now. If he never comes back, are you just going to walk away from this? Abandon the Odds?'

Bishop made himself consider it seriously before answering. 'No.'

'Well, there you go. You didn't ask me for emotional support, you asked me what we should do now. So, of course, I'm being ruthless.'

Bishop gave a weary smile. 'Yeah, I could tell Ruth was nowhere in the area.'

'I do it to myself too, you know.' True, he'd seen this before. It was her way of dealing with loss, to stomp hard on any hope of things going back the way they were, as if that made it her choice to turn her back on whatever she'd lost. The anger blotted out the hurt.

When he rang off, he still had no next move of his own. Under the Brig's command, they were rarely at a loss for what to try next; he always made the way forward seem sensible and clear.

But now nothing was going according to plan, which was astonishing considering how little plan they'd had to go against in the first place.

Baby steps.

Anne focused on trimming Nina's photograph, to match the photo area of the security pass she'd retrieved from Abby. With an extra layer of lamination, she could make it look good enough to hustle Nina past the sentries at the Warehouse, the Fifth storage facility where her proper lab was located. Safer than trying to get Nina cleared properly, which would no doubt tip their hand to Bryden's pals in the hierarchy.

Behind her, Nina was trying to make the laser dance. 'Not having much luck,' she called out.

'Keep at it.'

They still hadn't been able to replicate the results of Nina's first trial of the two-slit experiment, though various other strange things had happened each time, from a weird rhythmic flicker to the laser randomly shorting out.

Baby steps. One goal at a time. Bill wanted a strategy, wanted action and leadership, but the only useful thing they could do now was to *learn more*. That was how science worked: let the facts lead them, and their direction would become clear.

And if Alistair was going to storm off in a fit of pique because he didn't think he could trust them…? After all they'd done together…? Well, they'd just need to have a nice big pile of knowledge waiting for him when he came to his senses and came back. Or not.

But what *were* the facts here? That was the biggest problem with the Odds: the scientific method was terrible at studying non-repeatable phenomena, and whatever was going on they didn't have enough control over to repeat consistently.

'I think I'm getting something!' called Nina.

Anne hurried over, peered at the wall, where the laser was passing through the two cardboard slits, producing the familiar but common-sense-defying quantum interference patterns. Which, defying even the uncommon sense of quantum physicists, were now wavering and contracting into a smoothed-out oblong blur.

Nina's eyes were alight with excitement. 'I'm thinking of ELP, that armadillo tank song, the bliddle-bliddle-bliddle bit, that's gettin' my head there…'

Quickly Anne squeezed the trigger on the 8mm film camera pointed at the wall, which she'd jury-rigged to run at a high frame rate. With the extra-large reels, they could get a couple of minutes of footage to measure. Then she knelt beside Nina, their grins spreading as the light contracted.

'That's it, right there, Mind over mass-energy. Nina, that has to be the most beautiful dot in the history of quantum physics.'

Bill and Alistair, bless them, could only see this work in terms of their immediate struggle, to get the Odds out from under Bryden's thumb. Neither of them had the patience to do science properly, not just lurch from crisis to crisis. But with the Odds, she could see so much more beyond that, and just how *exciting* it was.

Because that was one of the great debates still surrounding the core of understanding the universe; were the probabilistic effects at the centre of the quantum realm really random, or something deterministic which depended on variables as yet unknown to mankind? Was God really playing dice with the universe, or was the nature of existence actually understandable, predictable? She always felt it should be; if knowing the world wasn't actually within her grasp, it should be within *someone's*.

But could the Odds actually bend cause and effect straight to their will, or did they just load the dice somehow?

It was heady stuff: the Odds could show them the key to everything from the nature of the Great Intelligence, how it could choke the world in its web, to the question of what had happened to her father's mind as its neurons misfired through age and trauma. Or were those even one and the same thing somehow? All these huge answers felt just a little less beyond her reach than they had ever been.

The laser light contracted to a dot, like a turned-off television. Once Anne was sure Nina could hold it steady in that shape, quietly she went to the door, past the two soldiers slouching on guard, and motioned down the hall to Dave to come in. She switched on the second camera, by the door, so they could record his distance.

Stealthily, without disturbing Nina, they approached. As Anne saw the dot lose coherence, she waved at Dave to stop; she moved him back to see it focus again. In and out, till they could measure the range at which his abilities interfered with Nina's.

'So how am I doing that?' he whispered.

'I haven't the faintest idea,' Anne said, with a broad grin. 'You can let go now, Nina!'

Bishop could practically see the thundercloud hanging over Douglas' head.

The colonel had put him on paperwork detail, closing out and archiving the Weatherballoon files, as senior officer on the project in Lethbridge-Stewart's absence. Filing it all neatly under the carpet.

Now, as he handed over the final report, he tried to get a bit more out of Douglas about the Brig's disappearance. But Douglas was even more in the dark than he was.

'In the wake of the unpleasantness last Friday...' ...which was a striking way to refer to a Russian bomb threat on HQ and a firefight against Soviet agents... '...and the pending inquiry into his recent actions, he seems to have decided to keep out of the line of fire.'

'That doesn't sound like him, sir.'

Douglas pursed his lips. 'Don't I know it.' Whatever was bothering the colonel, he was being determinedly, almost vengefully, businesslike about it. 'Did he give you any warning?'

'I haven't seen him since Friday,' said Bishop, and every word he let out was true. 'He didn't give me any sign he was planning on taking leave.'

'So, you don't know where he's gone.'

'I didn't know he *had* gone, sir.'

Douglas frowned to himself. 'Did his behaviour seem odd to you?'

Bishop blinked at his word choice. 'He certainly had a lot on his mind. You don't think he's in trouble somehow?'

'More if he'd stayed,' Douglas said gloomily. 'But there's no sign of foul play, if that's what you're wondering.' He levelled his gaze at Bishop, politely challenging. 'If you know anything more about what he's up to, now would be the time to fill me in.'

'You know him better than I do, sir.'

Of course, that was exactly what was bothering Douglas. As a captain, Bishop expected his brigadier to be at least one step ahead of him on strategy; being surprised like this wasn't entirely a surprise. But Walter Douglas had been Lethbridge-Stewart's 2-I-C for years, and his friend for even longer; if anyone could expect to think of Alistair Lethbridge-Stewart as an open book, it was him.

But when it came to the leaks to Bryden, as arranged by the Odds... Bishop, Anne, Lethbridge-Stewart and Captain Kramer had kept Douglas in the dark, along with everyone else at the Fifth. It had seemed like such a small temporary thing, for the civilians' safety, but now there was no clear way out without making things worse.

And this inquiry… Officially it was about whether the blame for the Soviets' recent actions could be laid at Lethbridge-Stewart's feet, thanks to his attempts to deal with problems on an international basis. But since the Russian trigger-happiness – nuclear and otherwise – had been brought on by the same investigation which had led them to Bryden and the Odds… He'd have a lot of careful answers to give.

'Colonel. Captain.'

The shadow that had fallen over him was General Hamilton. He was standing in the colonel's office doorway, glowering. Bishop hadn't even known the general would be there today; it gnawed at him that what Lethbridge-Stewart was up to wasn't the only piece of the puzzle which he and Anne were missing.

'Dismissed, Captain,' Douglas said hurriedly as he stood.

'No, wait.' Hamilton paced in, looking at Bishop, but addressing the colonel. 'Get him to do it.'

Douglas calculated silently. 'Of course, sir.' He turned to Bishop. 'General Hamilton wants us to give him a full briefing on that American captain, Kramer. Get Dr Travers' input as well. Check whether Kramer or her people at the UN might have had an agenda of their own.'

Bishop played it cool. 'You think that's realistic, sir?'

'We've got to keep ourselves covered,' said Hamilton. 'In case this inquiry over the Bugayev mess goes ahead.'

So, there it was. Without Lethbridge-Stewart to hold everything steady, Bishop could already feel the hierarchy's focus shift: from investigating the problem, to investigating the investigators.

'There's still so much we don't know about the brain,' Anne told Dave and Nina over tea and sandwiches at the back of the lab. 'I can't be sure where a normal brain leaves off and yours begins.'

'Might be easier to start with me,' said Dave. 'If I'm more normal.'

He didn't sound normal, though. Dave was even more subdued than usual; now Anne was worrying how much of a toll the past few days had taken on him.

'But you're not. You're astonishing in a whole different way.' Anne put a hand on Dave's shoulder, as if trying to transfer her enthusiasm to him like static electricity. 'Like your dad. Can you imagine how many profoundly unlikely things had to happen for his life to stay so normal?'

'Jonesy said your dad could walk through a minefield and not get blown up,' Nina said gently, squeezing up close to him for support. 'Not even notice. It just wouldn't dare, you know?'

Anne picked up the thread. 'If you toss a coin twenty times and get all heads, you know that's unlikely, but it's just as unlikely to get heads-tails-heads-tails throughout, strictly alternating. Even though getting half heads is the most likely outcome in general. You and he just managed to take unlikely paths that *looked* normal.'

Now Dave looked bleak. 'Yeah, Dad was great. But he's still dead.'

'I'm afraid that's normal too,' Anne said gently.

It had been barely over a week since they'd lost Nigel Plummock. Anne knew just how much a loss like this could break your world; never mind that everyone had to go through it someday, there was still nothing that could prepare you for that sense of trying to keep walking after a bottomless hole had opened up beneath you. And Dave had been through even more since then.

'He was one in a million,' said Dave, and his voice quavered. Nina put an arm across his shoulder, her fingers through his hair, holding him to her. 'I'm a fraction of the bloke he was. All this normalising stuff... Didn't stop that Russian bloke getting to me.'

'You walked out of there with all your fingernails still in, and that night we had eggy chips for tea,' said Nina. 'Close to normal as you can get, isn't it?'

'Clearly it's not absolutely effective for you, but it's still amazing,' Anne added. Was Dave getting scared enough that he might pull out? Well, if Alistair wasn't going to bother being their inspiring leader – not like he'd inspired these two anyway – then it was down to her to get them excited about the way forward.

'Just think,' she went on, trying to charge him up. 'What if it's who you are that's saved you? What you bring to it? I wonder if it's not that this... this ability comes in one of two flavours, high or low, and shapes your life to fit. Perhaps the kind of improbability is shaped by who you already are. If you're down to earth, bit depressive even, the chances that come your way line up with that. If you're impulsive, or maybe manic like Jonesy, it skews the other way. And if you're like Nina…'

'Then it gets you from both sides,' said Nina, hunching inwards now.

'We could work with that, then. Nina. There's a medication, lithium, it's used to treat manic-depression, I could get you a prescription and we could see how it—'

Nina started, pulling back, retreating behind her hair. 'No. Not crazy pills.'

Anne put on her most sensible voice. 'It's just a medicine. Just like if you kept having an upset stomach. But it might help you in general too. I don't know if you've ever done a mental health evaluation…'

'No!' Nina stared furiously at her. Breathing shallow, fearful. 'I am *not* crazy. I've never done anything crazy.'

'Well not really crazy,' Dave said gently.

'It's not about that, I mean,' Anne stumbled, 'the human brain is a very complex system, and if things go a bit askew it's not—'

'No. *No.* You're not pinning that on me.' Nina backed away, eyes wide, then bolted for the door. 'This is not me, it's *it!*'

She didn't slam the door hard enough for the bulletin boards to fall off the lab walls. But they did anyway.

Anne immediately wanted to go reason Nina into submission, but Dave said to let him handle it. If Nina had got the wrong end of the stick – and it sounded like she'd really sunk her teeth into it – then she'd see anyone telling her she was wrong as a further attempt to lie to her.

She'd hit a wall with those two for now, but she still had one other line of attack to pursue. Even if Dave – and Bill – felt all wobbly because their daddy had gone away, she'd be damned if she'd let that stop her.

In the office up the back of the lab, she rang the Bryden Industries switchboard. Bryden had said his people would be in touch about scheduling the meetings for her consulting project. It was time to start taking the fight to them. No, it wasn't, really – she didn't know nearly enough of the right questions to ask yet – but at least it was better than standing still.

Nina got tea from the machine in the commons area. The cup

was soft plastic. The tea much the same. The lights were greenish fluorescent and the university building was brown. Her breathing, shallow and shaky.

The lobby was full of students passing through and they were all a million miles away.

Dave came in. He looked upset. She felt him hug her, and she remembered to put her hands across his back in return.

'I want to go home,' she said. Her voice squeaky tight. 'She thinks I'm a nutter.'

It was all too big. Fear and fury so fierce it froze her throat, 'til she could feel nothing but the immobility. Thoughts whirling so fast she couldn't even catch what was in her own head. Far easier to be small.

'Now, she's only trying to help—'

'She's gonna put me away!'

One of the students slipped. Stumbled, bumping another one, who bumped another. That one dropped their books, in the path of another, and the one who tried to squeeze past them jostled another's coffee cup. The chain wound through the room in seconds. She didn't know these people. Why did they and all their *things* have to keep happening?

'Mr Bryden told me personally this project was a priority.'

A rueful, patronising chuckle from the project manager on the other end of the line. 'Well, you see, miss... you were *Friday's* priority. Now he's got a contract, he figures all the rest of the work is just details. He's probably on his second big new idea of the day by now. I don't think we'll see him in the office for weeks.'

Anne wanted to kick herself. She thought she'd been so clever, telling Bryden she wanted his hands off her, but now there was no way to get her hands on him. As she rang off, she could feel her last clear way forward slipping through her fingers.

'No luck,' Dave said with a shrug, as he came back. 'She still wants to go home.'

Anne sighed tightly. 'You've got to let her know, medication's nothing to be scared of.'

'Yeah, but you've gotta understand... Before she met Jonesy, she lived her whole life not knowing about any of this.'

'And she got accused of being mentally ill? Or acting out?'

'No, it's more... All her life, she thought this was just how the world was. Weird stuff just happened. It wasn't her, it was bigger than her. It couldn't be all her fault, how could it?'

Anne nodded sympathetically. 'But she still got blamed, didn't she?'

'Then Jonesy told her. And now it *was* all about her… but in a way that wasn't her fault. It was like a superpower she'd been given. If she couldn't really control it, that's okay, it's just part of her secret origin story as she's learning it. It was even okay for her to…' He looked down. 'To screw up. It still didn't make her a bad person. It was just something else that happened to her.'

'But if she's superpowered *and* manic-depressive…'

'Then she's broken. You see?'

What Anne saw was years of therapy in this girl's future, which she wasn't qualified to give. 'If it helps,' she tried, 'you can tell her it's still not her fault, the way her brain's wired. What matters is what she does to deal with it.'

Dave sighed, stood up and headed for the door. Through the inset window, they could see Nina sitting back in the commons area, hunched, tear-streaked and furious.

'Yeah,' he murmured. 'Maybe we should give it all a miss.' He didn't just mean for the moment.

Alistair could have got them to come back. The same way he'd always ended up leading Anne back to him, even after all sorts of terrible friction, just by being so frustratingly upright and reliable. He could make anything feel sensible, acceptable. But her? She could speak the truth, but she couldn't stop it being scary. And so, they ran.

'I'll still be at the funeral,' she blurted, and he looked surprised. 'Your mum invited me. Maybe we can try again after that?'

'Maybe,' he said, saying no. And left to go to Nina.

Baby steps? thought Anne. Good luck with that, now the baby had fallen over and was having a tantrum. No, that was unfair: they were scared, hurting, and now she was lashing out too because she couldn't see any other way forward.

Oh, Alistair. Why did you have to cut and run?

CHAPTER TWO
The First Domino

IF THERE is one thing which sums up American overkill, thought Lethbridge-Stewart, *it's their TV dials.*

The tiny set in his modest Howard Johnson motel room in Queens – hardly the Algonquin – went up to thirteen, but with most of the channels empty. And then a second dial, with far more channels than one would need on most occasions – almost none of them serving up anything but static. Out of curiosity, he'd turned on Channel 13 while he was freshening up after his flight, and found himself watching a hypnotically frenetic children's show called *Sesame Street.* He rather sympathised with the conical-headed yellow puppet with the obnoxious roommate, and wondered how much of this he'd be seeing as the little one grew.

But now he stood on Twelfth Avenue under the grimy West Side Highway, feeling the trucks rumble overhead, as he squinted at the dumpy cargo ship moored at the pier opposite. The Hudson River air around him smelt of dead fish and diesel. Finally, he made out the ship's name – *Domino.*

Just as Jonesy had said, then.

Overhead a gap had opened up in the patchy layer of cloud, and a single beam of sunlight shone down on it from the bridge to the winch platform. All it needed was a rainbow. The only thing that kept it from looking utterly conspicuous was that it was so obviously random.

It was short work to get past the gates, and then up the gangplank. He crept around the deck, noting that once past the outer layer of boxy containers, the inner ones had been replaced with trailer-style prefabricated offices. No, not offices; he could see bunks inside. Not exactly cruise-ship standard, but noteworthy.

The hatches to belowdecks were all locked. No matter, Jonesy had said this mysterious gathering would be going on for at least another week, before the ship departed for wherever it was bound; he'd have plenty of time for a further recce.

But he couldn't resist pressing his ear to the metal. Deep inside the shell of the ship, he could hear a low rhythmic chorus of voices, the cold metal door buzzing against his ear in time with their words.

Chanting.

Part of what Jonesy had told him was checking out.

But Jonesy still claimed not to know what this gathering which Peyton Bryden had arranged was *for*. Even though he'd cheerily worked for Bryden all along, so long as Bryden bankrolled his search for his kin, in exchange for the odd probability-tilting favour from them. With this many in one place, this would have to be a big one.

But now Jonesy was willing to burn his protector? If what he said was true, about how Bryden and his man Nallers had engineered the death of Nigel Plummock, just to keep the Odds from being noticed by the authorities, well that was a plausible reason for betrayal… but not for the betrayal to stop there.

Because to a disreputable hippy like Jones… Lethbridge-Stewart knew he still stood for everything the man detested: the same power structures that he feared would use and abuse the Odds, on a scale far beyond what Bryden had done. Jonesy had Lethbridge-Stewart's word that he'd keep the civilians out of it… but why would that convince him? Lethbridge-Stewart was under no illusion that he was particularly special. And Jonesy was still willing to kill the ones he thought were threatening them, in a variety of unlikely ways. For now, they had a common cause, but here on the crowded streets of New York, with a thousand mishaps and acts of violence always happening just out of view…

Lethbridge-Stewart didn't have anyone's eyes to watch his back.

Next stop, the United Nations.

Literally the other side of New York: a shining modernist monolith which looked even now like an artist's sketch of a better tomorrow. Away from that decaying highway, and the workaday pier, here he could just about see why the Americans saw this place as the greatest city in the world.

Once through the layers of security in the Secretariat Building and the too-small lift to the twenty-fifth floor, he walked into the midst of a quiet maelstrom in the Field Administration and Logistics Division.

Knots of civilians were bustling about, having urgent conversations in hushed voices; clearly there was a bit of a flap on. But one voice was raised, and he could trace Captain Kramer back to her corner of the floor.

'Whadaya mean it's coming, the briefing's in half an hour, if we don't have sign-on on paper by then we're dead in the water. Get it done. Okay, Sam, the numbers look good, if you can tell me Somoza's boys won't have a hissy-fit then I'll run it up the chain. Kenny, where's that reduction-in-force report?'

There was rather a lot on her desk, quite literally. Lethbridge-Stewart stood by it as she strode up, scattering underlings on different missions as she went, then she barely broke stride as she circled her desk, retrieving a particular folder from the morass.

'Sorry, sir, it's a week full of Mondays here. The Reds have just said they're gonna veto the deployment to Afghanistan 'cause the troops are too Western, we're trying to rustle up a commitment from Egypt or Turkey or somewhere before the hammer comes down. And at the same time, our side wants to pull the plug on the Nicaragua mission, 'cause they think we'll be too soft on the guerillas. Sir Colin's busy playing nice, I'm just trying to salvage anything I can.' And she was off again, as another analyst scurried up. 'Thrill me…'

Lethbridge-Stewart stood back and watched until she had a moment. It was odd, he'd never seen her before in a situation where she could actually bark orders, and expect people – even civilians – to jump when she said jump. In her context, she even seemed like a bit of a martinet, actually. Perhaps it was compensation for all the times where she had to smile and talk softly and just hope people would listen.

Finally, things were under control for now, and she leaned heavily on her desk. He wondered how much use the chair behind it ever got.

'So, this is peacekeeping,' he said. 'I can only imagine this place during an actual war.'

'Oh, *that* they can handle in the field. Round here the first crisis is always whether we get to *have* our operations.' She shook her head ruefully. 'Anyone permanent on the Security Council can veto one, and they're split down both sides of the Cold War. There's *gotta* be a better way.'

No doubt, but that was a bigger problem than they could deal with right now. 'Well, I don't want to take up any more of your time than—'

'Right. The *Domino*. I got the papers.' Again, she unerringly found the right file on her desk. 'The ship's registered in Bolivia.'

Lethbridge-Stewart raised an eyebrow. 'Not much call for cargo ships in the Andes, I should think.'

'It's a flag of convenience,' said Kramer. 'Gets the owners out of paying taxes, safety standards, all that fun stuff. The actual owners are Panorama Chemicals, who are incorporated in Barbados, but they're a wholly owned subsidiary of Panorama Energy, an American company, and *they're* majority owned by an investment group—'

'—and it all leads back to Peyton Bryden,' finished Lethbridge-Stewart. 'Am I right?'

'Trust you to spoil the punchline. But you'll like this bit, Panorama's got an office downtown.' She slipped him a piece of paper. 'I think you'll like the neighbourhood, even if the construction noise is a bit loud.' She lowered her voice. 'And afterwards…? Meet me at the front door at six-thirty. There's someone I want you to meet.'

When Lethbridge-Stewart reached the address Kramer had given him, he paused a moment to take it in.

When he'd seen the Empire State Building with Sally, he'd been quite surprised at how unimpressive it seemed from just outside; it looked like any other building pressed against the pavement, and even staring straight up you couldn't get a sense of scale with nothing to compare it to. But this whole World Trade Centre complex had been designed to leave anyone who approached it in no doubt whatsoever: a wide fountained plaza giving them a clear low-angle view, all the way to the top of the twin fluted steel monoliths. Clean bold lines and honed precision. A skyline of lesser skyscrapers in the blocks behind them, all kept firmly in their place, as the twin towers loomed over… well… literally everything, everywhere.

It all evoked the same thrilling clarity as the UN building, he supposed: the Americans could never compete with a proper sense of the past, not when any random English stately home had a floor older than their entire nation, but they were experts at creating spaces which spoke of a gleaming hopeful future.

He craned his neck; from here he couldn't quite make out the gap near the top, where only the skeleton of the last few stories was in place under the roof. It wouldn't be properly finished for the better part of a year, but the lower floors of both towers were already occupied. Most importantly, by Panorama Energy, fifty-seven floors up.

He hurried across the lobby towards the bank of express lifts. This would just have to be a quick sortie, to get a sense of the layout and the scale of the problem. Later, he and Jonesy would work out a plan of attack. Always assuming that no one here recognised him, of course.

A woman held the lift door, and he squeezed inside, not wanting to delay them. They still had no idea how much information the Russians had gathered from their raid on Bryden's factory; they could be off on a wild-goose chase, or they could know more about the gathering here in New York than he did himself. Infuriating to be in a race where you had no idea if your competitors were ahead or behind. All he could do was put together what he could, from all his different sources, and hope that no one else would make the same connections.

Major Bugayev was standing next to him in the lift.

For a long moment, both he and Bugayev just stared straight ahead. Like everyone else in the crowded lift, they were more or less pretending that they weren't actually there. Lethbridge-Stewart shuffled his feet.

'Well, this is embarrassing,' he finally said.

Bugayev kept his eyes front. 'I'm not sure what the correct protocol is in these circumstances.'

Lethbridge-Stewart took stock. The lift was filled with six other civilians, from the young brunette secretary who'd held the door to the fat man with garlic breath standing right behind his neck. Bugayev was probably armed, but seemed to be dressed for business rather than mischief. There was no way off the express lift until it reached the sky lobby on the forty-fourth floor.

'I take it both our… firms… are pursuing the same project,' he ventured.

'It would appear so.' Bugayev gave him a sidelong look, around the secretary. 'Though I'd heard word your people had an inside connection.'

'Not exactly,' said Lethbridge-Stewart. It was infuriating that in this setting he and Bugayev couldn't even be as clear as their usual level of cryptic evasiveness. But this might be their only chance. 'In fact, I thought we might be able to arrange another joint venture,' he hazarded.

That took Bugayev by surprise, though all he gave away was a slight puzzled squint. 'I thought we were directly in competition.'

'It's rather more complicated than that. I don't think either of us understands the full situation. And unless we get a chance to talk it through, neither of us will.'

Out of the corner of his eye, he could see garlic-breath-man looking from one of them to the other, puzzlement giving way to nosiness.

'I'll have to check with my… bosses,' said Bugayev, and Lethbridge-Stewart flinched at the attention that pause could draw.

'Oh, of course,' he said hastily. 'I was telling my manager just the other day, the chemical business is far too cutthroat, we really should look at more partnership opportunities to broaden our market reach…'

Bugayev played along. The doors dinged, and he and Bugayev exited hastily into the sky-lobby, searching for the local lift serving floors fifty-three through sixty-one.

'I assume you're not planning on going in guns blazing?' murmured Lethbridge-Stewart.

Bugayev shook his head. 'Reconnaissance only for now. You could expose me, of course.'

'And you me. Seems like rather a lot of bother for no benefit.'

'Together, then? I suppose you could say we'll keep each other honest.'

Lethbridge-Stewart nodded. 'I'll follow your lead.'

When they finally reached the sleek faux-marble offices of Panorama Energy, Bugayev took visible pleasure in introducing Lethbridge-Stewart as his assistant.

He had an appointment, of course – to arrange a contract of some sort – and after a quick office tour (every detail of which they filed away for future reference) they spent a full hour in a conference room listening to a hapless middle manager give a sales spiel which neither of them had the slightest interest in.

Throughout it all Bugayev kept giving Lethbridge-Stewart dark sideways glances, as if daring him to start laughing.

He did get to ask a couple of useful questions, though. Speaking awkwardly, as if English were his second language, he did manage to get the manager to confirm that any export deals for plastics or petrochemicals struck with their subsidiary Panorama Chemicals, and their refinery in Barbados, would be able to bypass US law, and thus potential political entanglements. He saw Bugayev's ears prick up at the mention of their shipping capability; he hoped Bugayev would see that as a bone he was deliberately throwing him, but without telling him enough to jeopardise the Odds.

'We should meet again,' said Lethbridge-Stewart, as they finally exited the building.

'If the general approves…'

'How can I contact you?'

'You can ask for me through the embassy,' said Bugayev. 'I'm with the trade delegation.' He left him with an irony-laden but genuinely amused smile. 'This never happens to your James Bond, does it?'

'More's the pity,' said Lethbridge-Stewart.

Then back across town at the height of rush-hour traffic.

He'd been avoiding the underground, without even thinking about it – too many memories from last time, most likely – but now squeezing into a train was his only option to get back to Captain Kramer in time. Grand Central Station turned out to be hardly less gridlocked on foot, but finally, feeling rather the worse for wear, he reached the front entrance of the UN Secretariat building just as Kramer was emerging.

She looked bone-weary, but barely slowed down as she greeted him. He knew that look; she was running on the last of her momentum, and if interrupted she'd grind to a halt and never get started again. She led him across the plaza to hail a taxi.

'Afghanistan's dead,' she said. 'But we've still got a chance for Nicaragua.'

She'd protectively tucked a hefty briefcase under one arm. When a massive yellow taxi finally stopped for them, she gave him an address on 133rd Street and a significant-looking tip in advance.

'That's the big thing,' she went on. 'I'm supposed to be there to handle logistics when we deploy US troops as peacekeepers.

But every chance they get, the Russkies veto us from being able to put Americans in anywhere… And I betcha Colonel Braddock knew that'd happen when he assigned me here. So, I could sit on my ass being useless… but instead I help Sir Colin rustle up peacekeeping forces from other countries. And instead of representing my superiors to the UN, half the time I end up representing the UN to my superiors.'

The cab crawled through midtown, heading north. Brownstones giving way to brick-monolith housing projects, storefront churches and pawnshops, and the odd block of pure rubble which evoked childhood memories of the Blitz.

Kramer gave him an amused look. 'Thinking about putting on some shoe polish to blend in?'

'Hadn't crossed my mind.'

He didn't know why that made her look at him with respect. 'And don't you ever.'

She'd wriggled out of her uniform jacket, and tucked it and her hat inside the briefcase, laying its contents, a single file folder, on top. Now she could just about pass for a plainly-dressed civilian. Nevertheless, he had the sense that she was tooling up for enemy territory.

The cab pulled up outside a converted brownstone standing alone next to a vacant lot: what looked like a rather upscale bar by Harlem standards.

She spoke quietly now, fixing him with a guarded stare. 'Now, when we go in there, you let me do the talking, you don't speak 'til you're spoken to, and when I ask you to give me this—' she raised the briefcase '—you hand it over. You got that?'

He wasn't used to being given orders by a captain, but he nodded soberly. Whatever game Kramer was playing now, he knew he wouldn't get answers by asking direct questions. She was already serving multiple masters, at the UN and the Pentagon, and the more he thought it through, her actions didn't align perfectly with either one. Whatever her actual agenda was, she was keeping it close to her chest. She'd kept quiet, but all this time, he'd been watching her watching everything… and as their eyes met in the darkness, now he knew she saw him watching too.

There was only one way out from here, and it meant following her in.

CHAPTER THREE
Running On a Racecourse

INSIDE, THE first thing that hit him was the jukebox music; all bass and brass, and relentless conga drums, reverberating across the dark wood-panelled barroom. The second thing that hit him was the solidly muscled black man placing a hand across his chest. His face had a stony glower, and his jacket had a check pattern so large and pronounced that for a moment Lethbridge-Stewart wondered which clan's tartan it was.

Kramer stepped up, smoothly, taking the lead. 'We're here for Vern.'

'He expecting you?'

She looked up at him, unblinking. 'No. It's Adrienne.'

The man disappeared into the back, relying on the wary glares of practically everyone in the front of the bar to keep them pinned where they were.

Lethbridge-Stewart tried as best he could to fade into the background. He studied the yellow-and-black African mural behind the bar, beside the neon Miller High Life sign, trying to divine who they'd be dealing with from the upraised black fist in its centre. The air was thick with smoke and suppressed aggression.

Finally, the first man re-emerged with another, larger man, wearing a coat with striking fur-lined lapels, and an Afro so substantial that he idly wondered whether it might strain the fellow's neck. 'Come on,' he gestured.

The two men guided them into the back room, holding positions to block their escape. Street muscle or militants? Lethbridge-Stewart couldn't be sure; they didn't carry themselves with a Nallers level of professionalism, but there was a discipline there.

In front of the round table in the back corner stood a solid six-foot man, built like the other skyscrapers he'd encountered that day. Three voluptuous young women – all underdressed to the nines – clustered around him. Unlike the others, he dressed simply – in shirt-sleeves, the better to show off his biceps – and with a crispness that suggested the uniform of some unrecognised army. A neat goatee breaking up the curve of a cherubic face. Eyes sizing them up, relentlessly. He grinned: the smile of a hungry lion.

'Adrienne.'

He opened his arms, and Kramer came up close for an embrace; their eyes fixed on each other as if searching for signs of weakness. 'Damn, girl, you got to do something about that hair. Ain't natural.'

There was a knife-thrust under the words, but she met it with a honeyed smile and a murmur. 'Now how'm I supposed to do any good for you, if they don't think I'm tame?'

'Even Diana got a 'fro now,' insisted Vern, wide smile never wavering, teeth relentlessly bared. His eyes flicked over to Lethbridge-Stewart. 'Who the great white hunter?'

Kramer gave him nothing. 'He's carrying my bag.'

Vern was still holding her, looking into her eyes for rather longer than felt seemly. 'You got what I want?'

'Always,' she purred. 'But what you're getting's in that case.'

Well. Captain Kramer was certainly full of surprises. It was odd how natural she seemed, playing this role with this Vern; clearly Lethbridge-Stewart hadn't known her quite as well as he thought.

Vern motioned sharply to the others, and his two enforcers escorted Lethbridge-Stewart relentlessly to the round table, sitting on either side of him on the bench seat, blocking his exit. He set the briefcase conspicuously on the table. Kramer sat on the other side of the smaller large man; one of the women interposed herself between Kramer and Vern. Vern looked right past her. 'So lay it on me.'

Kramer gave Lethbridge-Stewart the nod. He gave her the briefcase. She slid the folder across to Vern.

'Herbert Chitepo, Solomon Nujuru and Josiah Tongogara,' she said. 'And their ADCs' details in there. Long as Tekere's still in jail, they're the brothers to talk to about ZANLA.'

Vern's gaze had gone cold. 'Now I want you to look me in the eye, and tell me when I call them, I ain't gonna be talking to some jive-ass CIA mother doin' a Rastus voice. Tryin' to hook me and reel me in.'

'They're the real deal,' said Kramer, without even blinking. 'Chitepo's a hustler. Political arm. He'll hook you up.'

Vern leaned in, bearing down on her. 'And you tell me how the hell they ain't throwing you in the stockade just for talking to them?'

She widened her eyes, self-mocking. 'If we goin' in for peacekeeping now, we gotta talk to both sides.'

'And then you telling me this?'

'Well. I'm just making introductions.'

A smile well below his eyes. 'Yeah. You real sociable.'

'Now they know you, what you get up to's your own business.'

He raised an eyebrow ironically. 'Sho 'nuff?'

'Don't you sho-nuff me, you never lived south of Arlington.'

That got her a surprised look from the entourage, but Vern took it gracefully. She wasn't talking back *much*, and she was careful not to make him lose face, but Lethbridge-Stewart still got the sense that it was more than any of the others ever got away with.

'All I'm sayin,' purred Vern, 'is you know how much your Uncle Sam wants to burn my ass.'

She rolled her eyes. 'I ever want to burn you, Vern, I ain't gonna have to sit on the phone to goddamn Lusaka for an hour to do it.' She turned to the enforcer sitting between her and Lethbridge-Stewart. 'I forget, were you boys with him when he tried to go Black Muslim?'

'Didn't stick, you know that. Ideological differences.'

'And you liked your Natty Boh too much.'

Lethbridge-Stewart didn't quite know what to make of the situation, but he gathered that no one there knew quite what to make of Kramer. The women in particular, all wearing what he guessed was high fashion, aiming to look both voluptuous and thin at once, trying to get the measure of this plain-dressed heavyset woman who didn't feel the need to compete with them. Who just assumed any contest they were imagining, she'd already won.

She leaned in now, going on the offensive. 'Now your turn. What's new with Unsteady Eddie?'

Vern leaned back, casually stretching. 'Same as I told you

last time. He got a new deal. Out of the life. Damn, even his luck wasn't gonna hold. Workin' downtown now.'

'That all you got in three months?'

Vern shrugged. 'He funny, you know that. Talk a whole lot of crap.'

'Any of it about a boat?'

'Yeah. Part of his new gig.'

Kramer frowned, decided. 'Take me to his place tomorrow. We gotta lean on him.'

Vern showed his teeth again. 'Roger that.'

'And something else.' And now Kramer turned the room's attention to Lethbridge-Stewart. He felt all the eyes lock on him. 'This is Alistair. We're working together on this.'

Vern took his measure, warily. 'He Culp to your Cosby?'

'Something like that.' Kramer paused for breath; she was keeping up her front, but now Lethbridge-Stewart could see a real tension behind it. 'I just want you two to know each other. If anything happens to me 'cause of this… you find Vern. He'll see it through.'

'Ain't nothing short of an A-bomb gonna take you out,' said Vern. And this time the smile looked genuine.

'I mean it.'

She wasn't smiling, and now Vern took it seriously. 'You gonna need protection?'

'I might…' She met his eyes soberly. 'I don't know if I can afford the price.'

'I getcha,' said Vern gently. He levelled a serious look at Lethbridge-Stewart. 'You watch her back, y'dig?'

'*M, bi siɛ*,' Lethbridge-Stewart said.

Vern blinked, suddenly on guard. 'The hell was that?'

'Mende,' said Lethbridge Stewart. 'I was agreeing to do so.'

Now Vern was glowering. 'You pick that up off your houseboy?'

'From Chief Yembe in Royoke. Sierra Leone. I did him a rather good service once.'

If anything, Vern's expression got colder. 'Now who the hell you think you're impressing with that.'

'It was meant to be respectful—'

'In Mende? Hell with that crap, man, I'm Yoruba.'

Kramer leaned herself in between the two of them. 'Yeah, sugar, and that means your great-granddaddy probably sold my great-granddaddy to the white man in the first place, so I wouldn't lean on the history.'

Vern motioned for her to be quiet, and Kramer took it. Vern leaned slowly across the table to Lethbridge-Stewart, his eyes glowering, but his voice restrained, suddenly even professorial. 'It is incumbent on any man wishing to support the African cause – and by that I mean pan-African – to understand the range of us. That great American melting pot, which tried to boil us all away, has left us with no grasp of our own differences, and how we must respect them while still working for our common goals.' He paused for effect. 'So up yours, honky.'

'Always liked that speech,' Kramer said quietly, with a hint of regret. 'You was so good.'

She got a sudden flash of his smile. 'And you never known how good, girl. But I ain't letting him disrespect us for nobody.'

Lethbridge-Stewart could still feel himself bristling; probably much the same way Vern had. He took a breath and kept his voice as level as possible. 'I can apologise if you like.'

'Oh, you can. Limey come in here thinking he can flash a few words of Mende and all the restless natives gonna fall at his feet?' Vern was only building up more of a head of steam as he glared at Lethbridge-Stewart. 'We been talkin' bout *Rhodesia.* Three thousand miles away from any of the crap you been coming out with. *Parlez-vous* Estonian?'

'Still closer than you've ever been,' Kramer said simply. 'He's been there. And he's trying.'

'The hell you kissing his ass for?'

She smiled sweetly. 'Same thing I'm so tantalizingly close to kissing yours for, sugar.' The smile iced over. 'I just want to get the job done.'

After a moment, Vern's own smile looked rather rueful. 'Eyes on the prize,' he said, accepting it, and she nodded. Then he followed it by blatantly checking her out, in a manner that made both of them laugh. It had the ring of an in-joke, but Lethbridge-Stewart was very aware of how much he was outside of it.

'Yes, well, if you're quite finished scoring points off a failed attempt at courtesy,' Lethbridge-Stewart narrowly stopped himself from saying. Instead, he said 'I apologise unreservedly for the offence.'

Vern nodded. 'All right, we cool. But you get uppity with

me again, you gonna be looking for your shiny pink ass three blocks up on the corner of Shit and Go Blind. You dig?'

'Somewhat,' said Lethbridge-Stewart.

'Right on.' Vern leaned back and stretched – owning the room – then got up. 'I'll get you a cab,' he told Kramer. 'When it's me calling 'em, they come.'

'Don't be a stranger,' said Kramer with a sultry lilt, but, from their eyes, Lethbridge-Stewart could tell it was far, far too late for that.

As Vern and his entourage filed out, Kramer called after the young women. 'Oh, one thing, girls. You keep him honest.' Her gaze went back to Vern. 'I ever hear a bad word outta them about you, all our deals are off. You got that?'

Vern took that with guarded grace. 'Copy that, Captain.'

Kramer waited until they were gone, then sagged, staring listlessly at the table. Performance over. 'I ain't never gonna hear any kind of word out of those girls.'

'I did wonder about them,' Lethbridge-Stewart said.

She shook her head. 'Vern ain't pimpin'. He get that for free.' She swallowed, grimaced, as if trying to force her voice back into her more usual register. 'But you know, he never really made a pass at me, not a serious one, all these years. He and Donald, they're like brothers. He respects that.'

'Donald?'

'My husband.'

It was all rather a lot to take in at once. He had just seen a wildly different Adrienne Kramer than the one he'd fought alongside, and he wasn't quite sure which one was more real.

'Is Vern actually Yoruba?' he asked.

She snorted. 'Not for a hundred and fifty years. But it's kind of a Jewish thing for him; you know, never forget.' She stood, and slowly led him back to the main part of the bar, taking in their surroundings as they went. 'He's from Glen Burnie. South of Baltimore. When I met him, the only team he followed was the O's.'

'Where exactly do you know him from?'

'He was Donald's roommate back at Howard. Three of us against the world.' They had entered the front of the bar, passing back through the loudest music, loudest clothes, and all the extravagance the regulars could afford. She was quiet in the midst of it all. 'We went to the March on Washington together. Almost missed it, couldn't get a bus down from campus. Ended up back by the Washington Monument, squeezing up to try to hear. Only caught about every other word from Dr King. But we were there.' Now she stood at the front window of the bar, looking out into the Harlem night. 'Nine long, long years.'

'I take it he took a different path,' said Lethbridge-Stewart.

'Always did.' Kramer had her back to the crowd, kept her voice under the radar. Right now, he wished he had her skill at fading into the background. 'He never got it. That I could fight for the America that set us free, that doesn't mean I forgot the one that chained us up in the first place. But this country right now gave me a better life than my daddy, gave him a better life than his daddy. Without that GI Bill he got, he could never have sent me through Howard. Yeah, he was one of the lucky ones. I owe it to them to keep making it better.'

'Passing on contacts to a Communist-backed guerrilla group is a rather unconventional way to serve your country,' Lethbridge-Stewart observed carefully.

Kramer turned to look at him, warily. He was beginning to recognise that look: the one weighing just how many of her thoughts to let out. 'That's the other bit Vern never got,' she said. 'Compromise.'

CHAPTER FOUR
Improbable Cause

LETHBRIDGE-STEWART HAD the taxi drop him off in midtown, followed by a quiet dinner alone in a dimly-lit Italian restaurant. He needed time to think, and work out how much to say to who.

Then his last stop of the night was on the south side of Times Square. He worked his way through the late-night throngs, dodging pedestrians and random scraps of litter. Everything seemed to be overflowing: rubbish bags piled around the street signs, washes of music and exhaust spilling out of passing cars, young women spilling out of their outfits. Vast arrays of lightbulbs on theatre marquees, grabbing for any passing eyeballs, hawking what appeared to be art films, with titles which ranged from the clearly suggestive to the rather too cryptic for him.

Not exactly the well-integrated neighbourhood of humans and puppets which the television had promised him on arrival. This was about the fourth or fifth wildly different New York he'd been in today, and none of them felt like they had any connection to him or each other. Major Bugayev might have something to say about Western decadence, were he in the neighbourhood… Then again, for all he knew Bugayev could be inside one of those theatres right now. After today, Lethbridge-Stewart wasn't inclined to make assumptions about how well he knew anyone.

He reached a low-rent hotel, made his way up the grafittied stairs, and knocked on a second-floor door.

'Ah, the Brigadude!' Jonesy threw the door wide. He was grinning loosely and looked rather unsteady on his feet. 'Awright, so we're finally getting on the case! Come on, come on in.'

The room beyond him was smoky and underlit; the faded

stripey wallpaper was peeling away in one corner. Beneath it, a TV was pumping out more background noise.

He kept chattering, as if compelled. 'Great to have the old act back together. Like Eric and Ernie. Nah, Ernie and Bert.' Jonesy gave a wheezy little chuckle, like that overenthusiastic puppet from that show Lethbridge-Stewart had seen earlier. 'So what you been up to, ol' buddy ol' pal?'

'Talking to people who you don't want to talk to.' *Most of whom don't particularly want to talk to me either*, Lethbridge-Stewart thought.

'Aw, I spent all day talking to the family. On the boat, making introductions, teaching them all sorts of Odds and ends.' Jonesy bustled about, vaguely trying to sort out some tea in the plug-in kettle. 'Since then, I've been killing time, lying around in the tub, trying to see if I can levitate the soap.' He grinned and gave the sort of shrug where you didn't care where your arms ended up. 'I mean there's gotta be a chance, right?'

Narcotics of some sort, thought Lethbridge-Stewart. He studied Jonesy's eyes. Possibly narcotics of every sort.

Jonesy turned on a dime, continuing to burble. 'Ooh, when I got off work, I saw this amazing soap opera. This fella's long-lost brother was actually still alive, but it wasn't really him, he was another version from somewhere in parallel time, and his adopted nephew's best friend turned out to secretly be—'

'That's enough.'

'I mean come on, it knocked *Dark Shadows* for six—'

'I said, that's enough!'

He hadn't meant to bark it so loud. Jonesy was clearly very skilled at getting under peoples' skin. But he always seemed to be making a point with it: in this case, that Bryden clearly had an alarmingly detailed file on his life and past missions. Which Jonesy had read. The man was crazy like a weasel.

And now Jonesy was slinking up to him: in control, something dangerously sober beneath it all. His grey eyes were still, clear, and knowing.

'Seriously, man. How the hell can you even pretend you've got a normal person's life?'

'Shall we get to work?' Lethbridge-Stewart said bluntly.

Jonesy paused, then shrugged. 'Good an answer as any.' He cleared off the tiny table, save for one blank piece of paper. 'So did you get into the office?'

'Yes. Though I ran into Bugayev in the lift. Not the usual sort of thing that happens, even in New York. Your doing, I suppose?'

Jonesy shrugged. 'Could be me rubbing off on you.' *Perish the thought.* 'But I think this whole town's infected now. You gather enough of us in one place, the going gets weird.'

'Either way. He's probably after the same information we are. I'm trying to persuade him to co-operate, but if he finds out what you're capable of first...'

'I know, I know. You got the layout of the place?'

'Yes, but so did he.'

'Ah, but I know where our files are hidden. And I know how to get us in.'

Jonesy started explaining his plan. It involved scrawling an elaborate diagram of the building on the piece of paper. By the time he finished, Lethbridge-Stewart thought he must be mad.

'You must be mad,' he said.

'Well. Only a little bit,' said Jonesy. 'If I massage the chances for you? Safe as houses.'

Ask my wife how safe our house feels.

'There must be a simpler way,' Lethbridge-Stewart insisted. 'All we need is an excuse to get me in through the front door...'

'And past all the closed-circuit TV cameras Bryden's got installed out front?' Jonesy shook his head. 'I've tried to short them out just by looking at them funny, but no dice. The mean-time-between-failures must be too long. No, the only way we can stay off his radar is if we go straight to the executive offices. And I do mean *straight.*'

'No cameras in there?'

'Course not. And that's where the answers on this whole project are. Come on,' insisted Jonesy, grinning a little too enthusiastically. 'It'll be a brigadoddle.'

Jonesy was selling it as hard as he could, giving this mix of plausibility and transparent rubbish a sheen of convincingness. Heaven help them all if the Odds went into advertising.

'You're sure there's no other way of finding out Bryden's goals?' said Lethbridge-Stewart. 'You haven't learned anything on the ship?'

Jonesy shook his head. 'They keep me busy. Meeting new arrivals at the airport or the ferry terminal, settling them in on the boat, then a crash course in every training technique I've worked out.'

'I heard chanting.'

'Oh, just some basic meditation. Turn on, tune in, try not to bring the chandelier down. I pair up high- and low-improbability Odds, to try to get 'em in sync with each other, keep each other stable. But where do I go from there? The bosses aren't telling.'

'You don't even know why a ship?'

Jonesy exhaled hard through his pursed cheeks. 'I've got ideas. None of 'em good. Lovely way to get hidden people past customs, for a start.' He shook his head, and for a moment that skittery energy dropped away, overshadowed by something serious. ''Cause it really doesn't matter what they're planning to do. What matters is what's gonna happen no matter how well they plan. Sooner or later.'

He got up, motioned towards the little TV. To his mild surprise, Lethbridge-Stewart recognised that Marty Feldman fellow, mugging away. But that wasn't what Jonesy was drawing his attention to, instead it was the overlay of grainy, whirling static, the faint tuned-out hiss woven through the signal.

'It's already like that all over Manhattan,' he said. 'And it's only gonna get fuzzier, the more of us turn up. Even with all the control I'm teaching them, this many of us in one place… How long d'you really think it's gonna take, before someone rolls snake-eyes?'

Major Bugayev was on deck when the groaning noises started.

He'd slunk past the night watchman and up the gangplank, and was ducking between the converted container-cabins as scattered people began to return to their quarters for the night. He was trying to spot any of the scattering of Russians, Czechs, and Bulgarians whose travel visas his people back home had linked to this gathering of Panorama's, but so far he'd had no luck.

What he heard was the low groan of creaking metal, like the boat was being twisted and wrung out. Grinding up against the pier, perhaps. The passing civilians on deck noticed enough to look around, but didn't seem too concerned. He decided to blend in and slouched past the assorted civilian passengers, as if he'd just gone up on deck for a cigarette.

The hatch to belowdecks was open. As he descended, he took in the hold: another improvised tower-block of containers, and a large open space, with scattered knots of people awkwardly talking. A few dozen of them, more than he'd expected, but with space for even more.

The slow wrenching noise shrieked to a peak. And the ladder tilted beneath him.

Now the crowd began to look around in confusion, swaying as the ship listed. A few edged uncertainly towards the exit ladders. Others hastily sat down in circles, joining hands, chanting a low steady mantra. Its pitch and speed climbed shakily while the deck continued to waver, as if they were frantically trying to reach inner peace as fast as they could.

Nothing steadied, and as the hold lurched further their nerve finally broke. The circles stampeded towards the exit ladders. Bugayev hurried back up to the deck, slipped into the growing throng squeezing down the gangplank towards land, shouting in a babel of languages around him.

There was no sensible way the *Domino* could have been holed beneath the waterline, not while sitting safely in port, the odds against a hull plate just randomly bursting at the seams were—

But the ship didn't seem to agree, and Bugayev was left standing on the pier, guiding the last bewildered civilians to safety, while the *Domino* settled against the pilings at a jaunty angle and continued to groan its way slowly downward.

By the time the men from Panorama arrived to take charge, he had long since melted into the shadows.

You wanna know why I'm making you do this the hard way?

Well gather round, kiddies, and let me sing you the story of Walter J Jones.

Dad was a Fool. Capital F, like the Tarot card. Who am I kidding, you don't know Tarot, you probably figure I Ching runs your local laundry. I mean he had a gift not just for blundering into extraordinary situations, but blundering out of them again with his skin intact. Tarot guards with mystic hands, so they say.

Wandering off to Paris to make a few quid wasn't the craziest thing he'd done so far in his life. Getting stuck there when the Nazis moved in, well that might qualify. He'd meant to get out before then, but his papers got destroyed in that unfortunate incident with the goose in the *boulangerie*, so like everything else he ever did it got complicated.

So, for the next year or so, he sort of half-heartedly backed into working with the black market. Picture George Formby trying to play a spiv. He knew a few people who knew a few people, but he never managed to be a proper villain, or a proper anything really.

Then Elsa fell into his life. Pretty much literally; it took a wobbly bannister in a hotel and a bowl of vichyssoise across the face of a prominent financier to knock him off his feet. They spent the rest of the night running away from assorted people together. Ended up in a nightclub drinking champagne out of her shoe, and I'm pretty sure they meant to do that.

She'd been living in Paris as a German expat, and when her country caught up with her she stumbled into a job as a file clerk with what passed for the occupying authorities, being bilingual and all. A head full of romantic ideas about passing stuff on to the Free French, but no actual contacts to share it with.

So, Walter, still hoping to impress this mad dervish who he hadn't even dared to kiss yet, spun a tale about how he knew a bloke, and then was astonished to find out that a bloke he knew actually *did* know a bloke, so they had someone to pass whatever they got on to. And he hatched a plan that, for him, actually had a fairly good chance of success.

'Cause one thing he was, was really lucky with locks. Not always sure he knew what he was doing, mind, but if he jiggled it around enough, nine times out of ten they'd just open. The tenth he'd break something, of course, but usually he could get away with it.

Elsa sweet-talked old Phillippe the night watchman into letting her boyfriend into the building so they could have a bit of, you know, private time after hours. Spun a whole story about how her stuffy flatmate and officious old aunty of a landlord wouldn't let a girl have a minute to herself, and this was the only place she felt safe and private, what with him guarding the place and all. A little light bribery, a special knock on the door, and she whisked Walter off to the records room for some down-and-dirty ravishing of the files.

But wait! Phillipe, that old perv, was playing peeping tom. Peeking in through the door at the far end of the file room. When they spotted him, well, they realised they'd have to wing it. Cue a mad clinch where she nearly bit his tongue off – trying to whisper to him at the wrong moment – and they ended up ripping all their clothes off to give Phillipe a good show, and pantomiming the whole thing with her bent over the filing cabinet she was busy rifling through while he upstaged her with his bum.

You may laugh. Remember this is my mum and dad we're talking about.

And they laughed too, afterwards, from the sheer glee of it all. Cos it worked. They made it out of the building with the confidentials tucked in her unmentionables, and he passed it on to good old Pierre who passed it on to Colonel Chestbridge, and they said thank you very much do you have any more? And they were off and running.

It was the best game ever for them. Loudly murmuring sweet nothings while she copied bits out of the files. Cracking the office safe naked, knowing Phillippe could walk by at any moment and they'd have to strike a pose.

And then after a while, they stopped play-acting.

Yeah, they'd fallen for each other. Lifetime kind of hard. I think what clinched it was when they compared notes and realised their families each had the same legend: that their one crazy parent had an even crazier one, who liked to talk about great-grandad coming from the stars. They figured it was destiny. Yeah, our kind are drawn to each other. How could we not be? Turned out nice again, hasn't it?

So it was all kind of idyllic till the Nazis started losing. Then came the day when she ran to his apartment, tears streaking her makeup, and told him that the sensitive staff were all being forcibly evacuated to Berlin; she's on the next Army lorry out in the morning, she doesn't know where she'll be, oh and by the way she thinks she might be nearly two months gone.

So yeah, Liberation Day and he's left mooching round Paris with a broken heart. And she's somewhere behind enemy lines trying to keep her bump from getting bombed.

Things got fun again after that, Philippe ratted him out and he almost got done for horizontal collaboration. Only escaped the mob after a chase across a rooftop, hiding under the bed in a stranger's apartment, and slipping out on a food truck disguised as a sack of flour.

But did he shuffle off back home and become a nice sensible desk worker? No, he did not. Fast forward to '45, and after V-E Day he's moving heaven and earth to find her. He slipped on into Berlin by schmoozing his way up the military chain, first in the French zone then the British one, leaving a trail of bewildered servicemen in his wake who couldn't work out whether he was a hero of the Resistance or an utter prat. Till the day he managed to do a good deal for an American intelligence major – y'see, round Walter, things actually *did* fall off the backs of lorries – and finally had someone who would listen to his whole sad story.

Major Hardison was interested all right, in the two luckiest idiots in the whole of Europe. And he managed to trace Elsa to an address in the Russian zone of East Berlin… a scientific research institute, which had taken as much of an interest in her as Hardison had in him.

In those days before the Wall, it wasn't too hard for Hardison to contrive an excuse for Walter to go into the Russian zone. So, he whistled his way past the checkpoints, and then blagged his way right into a psi research centre run by the KGB.

He found her in their dormitory. She'd had her head shaved, for the brain tests. Captain Lusenko had tried her on drugs to see if they could amplify her effects, then other drugs to control them. When Dad walked into her room, she wasn't sure he was really there.

You've heard about what the KGB's scientists were doing, right? These were the blokes whose idea of psi research was to give electric shocks to newborn kittens just to see if their mums would react out of earshot.

I've got no idea what they did to me. I wasn't even a year old.

Anyhow, once Mum and Dad finished crying, they gathered me up and made a run for the border. Didn't really have a plan, they were trusting to luck and each other.

But that's the thing. We don't have good luck, we don't have bad luck. We just have *luck*. And this time, their luck was that out of all the back alleys in all the towns in all the world, Captain Lusenko himself walked into the exact one they were escaping through.

They ran. His men ran harder.

When they finally grabbed her, Dad says Mum threw me to him, a real Hail Mary, 'cause she knew he'd catch me. And he did. He fell over, but he made sure his body took the hit for me.

By the time he made it back to Hardison for help, carrying me the whole way, they'd already shipped Elsa off to God knows where. All these years, we've never been able to trace her.

Real big shame, old buddy, said Hardison. But, of course, you know, if they think you can do all these crazy things, of course, we're going to have to run some tests on you ourselves. Just you come with us. For your own good, you understand…

The only reason Dad got away with me was because of a pothole, a bent axle, a sudden intrusion by a drunken shopkeeper waving a bratwurst, and an abandoned bicycle with a basket. He pedalled off speedily into the night. And then spent the rest of the night in a rubble-filled bombed-out basement, trying to figure out how to get food for me. God knows which one of us was crying more.

How could you do that to a man like him? And a woman like her?

Anyway, he got me out. Tiptoed on home back to the British Isles, spent the next eighteen years trying to be a nice sensible desk worker at a whole string of short-lived desks. Oh, how he tried. But the whole thing broke him. Scared of his own shadow, now. I remember growing up, Dad always looked like he'd seen a ghost and that ghost was him.

When you hear these stories as a kid, you just think they're normal somehow. Took me years to get a sense that other people never had to flee a country even once.

And I was a handful. I'd got Oddness from both sides of the family, so I was even more of a weirdness magnet, but I also had more of a sense that it could be managed. Kind of by instinct, and then consciously. See, I channelled all my teenage rebellion into not accepting that stuff just happened to me. Because he never had control, that's why I swore to get it. I had the skill, 'cause I had both of them in me. But he never had control. Least of all of me.

Anyhow, we muddled along, him looking out for me if he could, 'til that tragic day nearly ten years ago now when he made that fateful choice, and accepted a job at an import-export company in Melbourne.

I didn't go. That age, I don't think I trusted him not to sink the ship.

I haven't seen him since then. I wrote, trying to patch it up, but I could never be sure it even reached him.

So, you see, Mr Brigadier, sir, if you're telling us Odds that we should trust the government, any government… you better think long and hard about why I'm even trusting you.

Hang on, gotta get that, if they're calling this late it's gotta be… Yello? What? Oh God. Christ on a pogo stick, I *warned* you! Look, where has everybody got to…? Oh, to hell with it I'll be right there…

CHAPTER FIVE
Dead Man's Hand

'**AND ALISTAIR** thinks we could collaborate internationally,' muttered Anne, over a despairing dinner with Bill. 'We can't even keep *him* on board. Let alone Dave and Nina.'

'Well, it's like the Russians when the Engineers landed,' said Bill. 'Turned out we went off and made a nuclear-level call, without agreeing on it with anyone.'

Bill, bless him, really was trying to argue Alistair's side. Pity Alistair himself couldn't have bothered. That was the bit that actually *hurt,* no matter how much she tried to pretend it simply angered her.

'So, he went off and did the same?'

'Well, if I hadn't already compromised us to Bryden, he might have…'

'I don't think you did,' she said simply. He stared, and she went on. 'At worst, I think you only confirmed what he already knew.'

'But I was the one directly liaising with him, on Weatherballoon.'

'As if you're the only person in the government who ever talked to Peyton Bryden.' She sliced through her fish, dissecting it as cleanly as the evidence. 'Bryden's people started going after Nigel long before we went to Peel. He knew about the original incident, even before we got Weatherballoon off the ground.'

'There's still another leak.'

'And if Alistair wasn't scared to talk to us, I'd tell him that right now.'

Early the next morning, she kissed Bill goodbye and caught a plane to Ronaldsway, then the bus to Peel, on the Isle of Man. She'd promised to look after Edith on the day of the funeral.

'And I'm staying over in town till tomorrow,' she told her firmly. 'It's the days after I want to keep an eye on you for. That's when the whole "what do I do now" thing really gets worse.'

She was speaking from experience; if nothing else she wanted to guide Edith through this particular underworld, the way Bill had stood by her when she lost her father. He'd known that no one should have to do this alone.

'Oh, it won't be so bad after,' said Edith. 'I've already talked to Mr Kendall at the bookshop, he needs someone to help keep track of their stock. And Ben Higgins' son needs tutoring in his maths. I'll have enough to be getting on with.'

'Oh, good.'

Edith was sounding much better than a few days ago; the world around her was pulling her back together. But Anne knew how fragile these moments could be; further study was recommended, as they say.

They bustled around, preparing the house for guests, and chatted about the town around her. Edith Plummock was a keen storyteller about the people in her life, with an eye for detail. Calling it gossip would be unkind; her subjects, even the ones she didn't like, emerged from her tales sympathetic and human. Even if Dave would be mortified that Anne had heard that one about him, his old girlfriend, the local tough, and the poison ivy.

These chats were a relief for both of them, she suspected. She'd been ringing Edith every couple of days, partly to check up on her, more basically for the pleasure of spending half an hour rabbiting on about nothing. People gave Anne stick sometimes for being able to compartmentalise her emotions, but the sheer blessed freedom of getting a break from it all was a lifesaver.

Then Dave and Nina arrived, and the atmosphere turned sharp and brittle. Nina was glaring at her like a cornered feral cat. Anne took Spotless for his walk and faded into the background as best she could.

At the cemetery, Anne ran an eye over the mourners.

A knot of Nigel's workmates, younger folks from the kipper smokehouse, some old war buddies, friends from down the pub and their wives. Neighbours clustering round Edith and her son. Amazing how many people a quiet life could still bring together.

But no sign of the lanky, black-denim hippie Bill had described. Surely Jonesy would be lurking here at least? Only something huge could make him miss this.

Edith sobbed but kept herself from disintegrating, and Dave held his mum up in a way that helped hide when he was crying too. Nina was wound tight, staring daggers at Anne throughout. Whatever was going through her head, it wasn't fear, it was fury.

Anne kept bracing throughout for another shoe to drop. But all that dropped were those first shovelfuls of damp earth onto the coffin, that same dull crump that always seemed to echo through time. She supposed that was the last thing Nigel could do for Edith: make this no worse than any other routine tragedy.

She wished she'd met him.

When it was his turn, after the shovel, Dave gazed into the grave and produced a well-worn pre-decimal half-crown. 'Jonesy called heads,' he murmured, and sent it flipping down into the earth.

Anne peered at it. Tails.

Afterwards, Anne kept things moving in the kitchen, working with Mrs Kincaid from up the street to keep the mourners fed and watered, and look after anything Edith needed.

There was chatter and even laughter, as the house grew smoky and the drinks flowed far more than the tears. Anne made her first move with Dave, as the crowd began to thin out around teatime. She'd brought a couple of rather good bottles of wine with her and offered the first to him as an apology.

'Honestly,' she said. 'We're lost without the two of you.'

'I can't make her trust you again,' Dave said, resignedly. But he took the bottle and wished her luck.

So, she left Mrs Kincaid to look after the roast and went out the back, where Nina was watching the sunset, almost chewing on her cigarette out of raw nerves. Next door Anne could hear a gaggle of kids kicking a football around in their garden.

At the sight of her, Nina backed away down the steps, breathing hard, staring harder, in aggressive terror. 'Keep away from me! I'm not gonna let you put me away!'

Anne blinked. 'I never said—'

'You want me drugged up or locked up before I hurt someone—'

'—I'm saying I'm sorry—'

'Well I'm *not* crazy! I would *never!*'

'Heads up!' cried a voice from next door.

The football flew over the fence and thumped into the edge of the vegetable patch.

And exploded.

Then the back steps hit Anne in the face.

Nigel's prize rosebush took the worst of the blast, she realised later. And her own body shielded Nina from most of the dirt and debris, but they were both knocked off their feet. There were more shouts from inside, and a screaming wail which had to be Edith.

Anne hauled herself to her feet and hurried inside. 'You're bleeding!' shouted Nina, scared for her, not of her. She could feel impact wounds on her back, but a quick feel around told her there was far more bruise than blood. That could all wait.

Edith had sunk into Nigel's big chair, howling like it was just too much. Anne held onto her hand, brushed back her curls, spoke calmly and insistently to her. 'It's all right,' she murmured. 'We're all right. It was just the gas main.'

Dave ran with the lie, soothingly. 'Yeah, remember, Mum, you were having trouble with the gas lines months ago, they had to replace the heater, but it never did work right...'

And now Nina was beside her, adding her voice to theirs. 'It's okay. The house is still here. We're still here.'

They weren't the only ones rallying around her; Mrs Kincaid and Mr Finch and the other remaining guests all joined them, saying little but reassuring her they were there. They held on as the sound from Edith's mouth tipped back from shrieking to simple healthy crying. Anne saw Edith gulp hard, squeezing her breath into shape, clutching the armchair until she pulled herself back under control. She grabbed onto their hands, deliberately holding them to her. Without Nigel, her world may have been blown to bits, but she wasn't going to let it take her with it.

After that, Anne could busy herself with the practical stuff; making a big show of calling the fire brigade even though there was no fire, get the nicks on her back cleaned up and bandaged, then help Mrs Kincaid serve their tea, even persuade Mr Finch to replace the rosebush for Edith by Tuesday, free of charge as a gift.

'Thank you,' Edith finally managed over dessert. 'I had to decide... Without Nigel, I had to be a bit more tough. But it's easier to be tough when there's someone else to lean on a bit, you know?'

In another stolen moment as they cleaned up the plates, Dave told her as much truth as he knew. 'That thing Jonesy said, about Dad being able to walk through a minefield…? I think he meant it. That the blokes trying to kill Dad planted a landmine, and he just kept missing it.'

That did sound like it could be Nallers' style; Bill had told Anne that Bryden's man was a blunt instrument with an explosive tip. A small mine rigged to explode straight upwards, directing all the force right at the man who stepped on it… Her stomach shrivelled. But it would explain why she and Nina were alive.

'And the ball just happened to land on it,' Anne said pointedly.

Dave was looking fairly slumped himself. All his trying to keep things together for his mum, and the space he kept together didn't even stretch as far as the back of the garden. And Nina looked shaken to her soul. No matter how hard she clung to her belief that what happened around her was down to chance rather than choice, that medicating it would somehow make it a reflection on who she was, she couldn't shake the fact that the only person who could have brought this chance on was her.

Later that night, after they'd put Edith to bed and started the final tidying-up, she tried again with Nina, and the other bottle of wine.

A lot of the fight had gone out of Nina, and she clung to Dave as he tidied the lounge room.

'It wasn't fair,' Nina said shakily. 'You called me a crazy bitch. Wanted to put me away…'

'That's not how I remember it,' Dave said gently. Trying to be the calm one again, for her. He reached out for her; she shook free. 'Now think about it, does that really seem plausible?'

A shaky pause. Nina shrugged, helplessly threw her hands wide: look at my life. 'How would I *know*?'

In a way it made sense, thought Anne. She'd made Nina feel soul-breakingly terrible, so something really awful must have happened, it had to be that harsh to explain how bad she felt, so that's how she remembered it. And she couldn't rely on questioning her memories to be sure of the truth, because a lot of the answers to what happened to her wouldn't be sensible ones anyway.

'I came here to say I'm sorry,' Anne said. 'What I said – what I *actually* said – was really hurtful. Even if I didn't mean it to be, it still hurt you.' God, even being sincere didn't stop it sounding awkward. 'Does that help?'

A wounded glare. 'Maybe.' As if it still wasn't in Nina's control how she felt or what she did.

'Well, is there a chance?'

Nina held up thumb and forefinger a fraction apart.

Anne had thought about what to tell her next, but hadn't wanted to go into it unless she had to. She had to.

Before you can take baby steps, you have to crawl.

'Did I tell you why I think medication is so important?'

'No.'

'Were you on some?' Dave asked sympathetically.

'Just for a little while, after… After I lost my father,' Anne said.

She took a deep breath and slowly let it out, trying to release as much of the knot of tension growing in her guts as she could manage.

'But it's actually because of my father, himself. He was prescribed something, but he wouldn't take it, oh no. Oh, he knew he still had all his marbles. He had no idea I'd been picking them up for him for years.'

Nina reacted to feelings, Edith had told her. If you were ever in distress, she was really sympathetic. Trying to stoke empathy wasn't always the first tool Anne reached for in her toolkit, but if it would work, she was willing to share this.

'There was a moment… He was complaining about me mothering him, and he called me by his wife's name. And he meant it. Mother had been dead nearly thirty years.'

Nina was still staring warily; she must think Anne was faking it. And she was, really; she was trying to talk about what happened without feeling it. She closed her eyes, made herself reach for the truth of it.

'If he'd only listened, it could have…' A sudden stab of anger, surprising her. 'No, it couldn't have saved him. But it could have saved him from the worst of it. Or at least saved me.'

Even that wasn't quite true. The worst of it had to be the moment when she'd seen the sheer *earthliness* of his growing dementia. All those years, every time she'd glimpsed a shadow over her father's thoughts, she'd seen it as a relic of the unearthly *thing* they'd known as the Great Intelligence, which he had encountered over all those years, that force which had horrified him, obsessed him, even possessed him for a time, and left him forever changed since before she was born. Having something like that weigh on him, she could accept. But something so human as a simple decaying brain?

'It was so unfair,' she whispered tightly. 'He had such a mind. Taught me so much about how to think. And to have that eaten away…'

'Was he a scientist too?' murmured Dave.

She nodded. 'He did such… important work.' Anne choked back the details, even as she tried to express the truth of him. 'Facing up to the big unknowns. He could stare into the abyss and drag bits of sense out of it.' Where was that smile she could feel on her face coming from? 'If that was what took him away, I could more or less deal with it. Like a hero falling in battle; you can't argue with that.' And in a way, he had. 'But if he… If he let his brain rot away through sheer stubbornness… then that's what broke him. Not even the disease. His choices.'

The last thing she needed right now was actual pain. She sat down on a discarded chair, feeling herself rocking slightly back and forth. Dave was no longer holding Nina back; instead, she was holding on to him, looking at Anne with wide eyes. If she wanted her feelings, well, these were them.

'And it was so bloody pointless! He shouldn't have been so…' She ran out of words. 'The universe should make more sense than that.'

She kept blinking to clear her eyes. When she looked up, Nina was crouching near her. Nina hugged her, then looked her sternly in the eye. 'I'm not a nut. But I'm dumb sometimes.'

She let her body sag against Nina's. 'Aren't we all?' So, there was a way forward for them after all. Finally, she rallied, and offered them the wine. 'Come on. These bottles aren't going to drink themselves.'

CHAPTER SIX
Odd Man Out

AFTER THE two bottles, and a couple of partial ones which happened to be left over from the day, they'd settled in a heap in the loungeroom.

Just like my student days, thought Anne, only she'd always been much more cautious about drinking then. Now she had a better sense of her limits, so she could go a little further. They drank one more toast to Dave's father, and then to her father, and she found herself telling more of his story. Not the alien-supernatural bits, but the parts she thought anyone might be able to understand.

'Oh, that's not the half of it. I said I lost him. That doesn't quite mean he's dead.'

'You're not making sense,' said Nina, eagerly somehow.

'It wasn't just the dementia. There were other things going on with his mind, his life. I can't explain it, it'd probably be classified if I did. But there's a man, right now, out there, living with my father's face. And all his faculties, as far as you can tell. Except that he…' How *not* to explain time travel and alternative lives…? 'He has no memory of the past thirty-odd years. None of it. He didn't have me, he didn't raise me. He's got his studies, and he seems healthy and content. Oh, we can work together sometimes, be basically friendly… But I'm just not a part of his life.'

'Least he's alive,' murmured Dave. 'I wouldn't knock it.'

And she had to swallow a spike of anger, for their sake. 'Some people might think that's a miracle,' she said, forcing her voice to be steady. 'They've never had to look into their father's eyes and see he doesn't love you. Has never loved you.'

That hit home for all three of them. She felt something bubbling up, halfway between a laugh and a sob. 'And I'm happy for him. Really. Just, not for me.'

'It's okay,' murmured Dave. 'I get it.'

'No, you don't.' The words felt hot and tight in her throat. 'There isn't a human being alive who can understand what that feels like. I'm the only one it's ever happened to, and *I* can't understand it. Not *here*.' And here she pointed at her heart.

Sure, she understood the mechanics of time travel, of temporal duplication, parallel lives, all that, but knowing there was a man out there who was both her father and not him at the same time...?

'So, the dementia, it was only the beginning,' she mumbled. 'And I still don't know why. I don't know where choice ends, and chance begins.'

Alistair, damn him, could slide right off that sort of wrongness. He could face something that insane and just get on with what he had to do. But to her it had to *mean* something, and there was no understanding she could reach.

And yes, she really wished he was here.

Nina tried to give her a hug, but ended up bumping chins with her. They fumbled about a bit for a while trying to make the hug work. Anne felt exhausted, grappling with huge emotions that she couldn't make sense of... Good Lord, this must be how Nina felt most of the time.

Dave joined in, patting her on the back. 'It's all right. Hey... You're not one of us, are you?'

'Oh God no,' she said hastily, then laughed. 'I literally checked; stared at that laser for ages. Not a blip.'

Dave escorted her the few streets back to her room over the pub, and the following morning – once she'd reassembled the more widely scattered parts of her head – Anne rejoined the others at breakfast.

Edith was in fairly solid form, getting ready to head to Mr Kendall's bookshop to see how she could help out. She stayed and chatted while Dave and Nina left early for the police station, to explain why they'd need a minesweeper around the back of 10 Tynwald Road.

'We're flying out at noon,' Anne told Edith, as she tidied up from breakfast. 'And I'll see if I can come back with them after that. Maybe next week.'

'Will they be around past Wednesday, then?' Edith went

on. 'Only Dave said they had to leave by Wednesday. Wouldn't be able to come home for quite a while. Something big on.'

Had he now. 'Well, I'll have to check that with him, I guess.'

To her surprise, Dave had no trouble getting the police to co-operate. She'd volunteered to back up their story – tying it to That Business with the Escaped Fugitive – but they hadn't needed her. He seemed to be rather good at convincing people of innocuous half-truths.

The truce with Nina was still holding after the flight back, when Anne escorted them into her secure lab in the Warehouse. With her right there, the sentries at the gate didn't look too closely at Nina's altered pass; she'd told Nina to dress like Abby just to make sure. Dave's pass was already correct from his previous work with the other students. Now they could get to work on some more serious experiments, using equipment which she could never have justified bringing to the university.

'We've got a whole stack of tests to get through,' Anne began, then slipped the stiletto in, 'before you disappear after Wednesday.'

'Uh, yeah.' Dave shifted uncomfortably. 'Jonesy sent us a couple of tickets to New York. Some sort of gathering of the tribe. We don't know much more than that.'

'Uh huh.' They must have been arranging this for months, just to sort out visas. 'Any idea when you'll be back?'

'Could be ages,' said Nina. 'He said we'd be back for the autumn term, though.'

'Well, say hi to Jonesy for me,' Anne said pointedly. Probably they were playing dumb, but she had a few days to get more answers out of them. (Minus the time she'd have to spend in meetings at Bryden's complex.) During which time, she also had to learn as much about how they worked as she could. Why did this have to be cut short when she was so eager to sink her teeth into understanding them? If they wanted, the Odds could be her life's work – as opposed to understanding the Great Intelligence, which was simply the work which had dominated her life.

'Now,' she went on. 'For this experiment, we're using a small amount of radioactive material—'

'Erm.'

'Oh, don't worry, I'm not putting Nina anywhere near anything that could chain-react, an experiment like that would be rather difficult to replicate. It's just a little sample of technetium.'

In the shielded chamber, Anne positioned the Geiger counter over the isotope, letting its steady ticking fill the lab. 'Now, this has a fairly high specific activity and short half-life, so we can predict the number of decay events that will probably occur per minute... all other things being equal.'

She returned to the control area, where Dave and Nina waited with their mugs of sweet tea.

Nina was pondering her cup. 'I keep waiting for the milk to form some kind of mystical sign. Not 'cause it'd mean anything, just 'cause it would *look* like it means something. That's what it does to me. Chaos looking like order. But it's just Brownian motion. Does that mean the brownies are doing it?'

'The hash brownies, more like,' Dave put in. Then glanced guiltily at Anne out of the corner of his eye.

'Wee elves stirring everyone's tea.' Nina's eyes gleamed. 'Only round me they get all frisky.' She shrugged wryly. 'It makes sense if you're me.'

Anne finished checking the gauges. 'So far, so normal. Nina, will you step up close to the glass?' She did so. 'And Dave, would you leave the room please?'

With a shrug, he headed out. 'Well, I know when I'm not wanted...'

The ticking from the Geiger counter began to surge. She watched Nina press her nose against the glass, fascinated as the needle climbed just from her presence. Like a rush of static: the sound of a thousand random chances all happening at once.

And over it now, a high-pitched beeping.

Anne froze, following the sound to a cupboard in the corner. No way anything in there could be plugged in, but something was still drawing power, from nowhere that made any sense. She flung it open, dug through the tangle of wiring and half-dissected electronics inside, knowing before she laid eyes on it what it would be.

Then she ran straight to the door and shouted at the top of her lungs. 'Dave? Get back in here *right now!*'

When Alistair and Fiona Lethbridge-Stewart had gone on holiday to Egypt, he ended up tracking down a lost alien desert city and a creature imprisoned in it for thousands of years.

When Walter and Penny Douglas had gone on holiday, they went to Southend. *Somehow,* thought Bishop, *that sums it all up.*

It wasn't that Colonel Douglas was a bad commander, but he didn't have Lethbridge-Stewart's instinct to get out in front of a crisis somehow. The moment of strangeness which led to the Weatherballoon investigation, which led to them finding the Odds, would never have troubled him. Give him a goal, he'd achieve it without missing a beat. Give him a threat, he'd form a solid strategy. Give him a mystery, though… That was where Lethbridge-Stewart had the edge. Throw him into a strange situation, and no matter how much mumbo-jumbo he professed not to understand, he'd still be able to get on top of it.

That was a whole extra skill, and right now as Colonel Douglas sat behind his desk reading his carefully neutral report on Captain Kramer, Bishop couldn't shake the feeling that no one else at the Fifth had it.

On the other hand, as the Brig himself would admit, throw him into a strange *political* situation, and he'd blunder through a minefield. And Bishop had the sinking feeling that *that* might be going on just out of their view now.

'I suppose I might as well tell you,' Douglas muttered.

Bishop straightened up as the colonel stood, meeting Bishop's eyes as a fellow officer rather than an acting CO. He kept his tone neutral, but his face had the troubled look which Bishop had seen Lethbridge-Stewart himself wear many times.

'This inquiry's not going to hurt the Fifth as a unit; realistically we did everything we could. But some of this mud could stick to Lethbridge-Stewart, personally.' He lowered his eyes, considering his desk. 'Hamilton hasn't just assigned me as a caretaker. He wants me to evaluate future directions for the unit. Figure out what we do now. I'm supposed to proceed on the basis that Alistair may not be coming back.'

CHAPTER SEVEN
Long Shot Straight Drop

MORNING IN New York, and Lethbridge-Stewart got an early call from Kramer. 'I need you at Unsteady Eddie's place. Dress official.'

In uniform, complete with regulation pullover, cap, and swagger stick, he went to the address she gave: a cheap rented room in midtown, where one of Vern's boys opened the door. Kramer and Vern were busy standing over a young black man, while another of Vern's bulky followers held him in place with a hand on his shoulder. Kramer, in full uniform, was wheedling in his ear. 'Now don't you worry, we're all cool with Jonesy, we just gotta know what he's up to with you on that ship.'

Unsteady Eddie had a thin, twitchy face; acne scars, poorly shaved, a jittery expression like Nina's. Lethbridge-Stewart could hear his breath shake as he tightened up and looked at Kramer.

'I ain't much, but I ain't no snitch.'

Kramer turned to Lethbridge-Stewart. 'He won't talk, sir. We might have to push him harder.'

'Just give me five minutes with him,' said Vern, glowering heavily.

Kramer nodded decisively, then hustled Lethbridge-Stewart back towards the door. He could just glimpse Vern closing in, and hear Eddie's wavery cry. 'Oh no, man. No no no—'

The door shut.

Lethbridge-Stewart stood in the dimly lit hall, staring at Kramer with disbelief and low outrage. 'What the devil have you dragged me into, Captain?'

'We just needed someone to play the heavy—'

'So, you brought him in to do the dirty work?' He glared at her, trying to impress on her the sheer force of his disgust. 'This is unworthy of the officer I know.'

'Oh, so now you think *that's* me?' Rather than being shamed, she was bristling right back at him. 'The moment I get a bit sneaky, you figure I'd…'

'I've never treated you as anything less than the officer I knew you were. Thought you were.'

'Long as I behave,' she said. 'Every single day back in England. I knew I was on display. God help me if I was any less than perfect.'

And that stung him in turn. 'So, you only bring in thugs when no one's looking,' he retorted, which made her hackles rise even higher.

'You think Vern's a thug? You wanna know him?'

'Enlighten me.'

A sudden sharp pride in her smile. 'Vern holds his streets together. He helped fit out the People's Ambulance. He's headed off turf wars, revenge killings, 'cause they respect his people; better justice than the courts. He's dealing with all the gangs, the pushers, keeping random crime down, making it safe for everyday people. Least round a few blocks.'

'An effective strongman,' Lethbridge-Stewart said curtly. It didn't change whatever was happening on the other side of that door.

Kramer paced in the hallway, genuine fire and frustration in her words. 'You know what it takes to run a Neighbourhood Watch in Harlem, and have it *work*? Vern could be one of the best damn leaders we got, if he'd just drop the lefty revolutionary crap. But he's too busy falling out with his brothers 'cause they can't agree if Che Guevara's just another white boy or not.'

'And the Rhodesian guerrillas?'

'Funding proxy wars is kinda the American way,' said Kramer with heavy irony. 'Less escalation than weighing in yourself. Yeah, the US is neutral, but a buncha good-ole-boys who read *Soldier of Fortune* are over there in Rhodesia right now fighting for their whites. Private citizens. Can't a brother do the same?'

He placed a hand on her shoulder, pinning her where she stood. 'You're supposed to be a *peacekeeper*.'

'There's only so much peace I can keep!'

Her own outburst clearly startled her, as well as him.

Lethbridge-Stewart could feel the righteous anger boiling out now, as she shook his hand off.

'I can't fix it all. And the Army won't let a girl like me shoot the bad guys. So, I gotta use anything I can to beat 'em.'

He nodded coldly towards the door. 'And if you can't beat them…?'

'Then I make the choices that do the least damage.' She turned away now, quieter, bitter. 'What I do, every day, is all about the compromise.'

'So, you expect me to turn a blind eye?'

'Nah, just *open* it.' She wheeled to face him again. 'What do you think I'm doing?'

A sharp knock from inside the door. Kramer opened it to reveal Vern. Beyond him, Eddie wasn't visibly injured, but wide-eyed terrified.

Lethbridge-Stewart paced in, stood over the skinny little man. 'Whatever they've done to you, I'll make full restitution.'

Eddie blinked. 'You ain't done nothing yet.'

'Tell us about the boat,' said Kramer, deflecting it. 'You been living on it?'

Now Eddie was positively desperate to please. 'Yeah. We shippin' out to the tropics on the man's dime.'

Vern shook his head knowingly. 'I'm telling you, man, that's how brothers got sent to Haiti, one way.'

'But the boat just sank, didn't it,' said Lethbridge-Stewart. 'What's the plan now?'

'Got me a plane ticket,' said Eddie, smiling nervously. He reached for the coffee table and removed the ticket off it: Barbados, dated two weeks from now. 'Jonesy booked us all this morning.'

'All on different flights, no doubt,' said Lethbridge-Stewart.

'I got a buddy. We travel together, it's gonna keep us stable.'

He hopes, thought Lethbridge-Stewart.

'And is that all they've been teaching you on the ship?' asked Kramer. 'How to be stable?'

'It's just hippie shit, man. Opening our inner eyes. And a poker game that's been running for two weeks straight…'

Unsteady Eddie didn't know what was in store for them in Barbados, and all they got out of him basically confirmed what Jonesy had already mentioned. Still, everyone was going to come out of this room in one piece, and Lethbridge-Stewart more or less considered that a victory.

When they finally left Eddie in peace, Lethbridge-Stewart stopped Vern, with a quiet challenge. 'I have to know. What did you do to him when we left the room?'

Slowly Vern beamed, purring. 'I just told him what *you* were gonna do to him when *I* left the room.'

And Kramer smiled out of one side of her mouth. 'You thought it was *Vern* we brought in to play the heavy, didn't you?'

'You didn't tell me.'

'You didn't *trust* me.'

As they left the building, they were each still scowling, in their own thoughts. Lethbridge-Stewart replayed their conversation in his mind, trying to find the moment where she'd stopped trying to tell him what she was up to, and instead left him to twist in the wind with his misconception.

'Sir. I just want to say... We're outside of channels here. If you want me to get things done, you're gonna have to be okay with me lying my ass off.' He shot her a look. 'Not to you. But we gotta play it loose here.'

'Do you seriously expect me to take it on faith when you bring in a "community leader" who's working with Communist-backed Rhodesian guerrillas?'

Kramer signed hollowly. 'Know why I thought it was okay, to give Vern those numbers?' she murmured. "Cause in the big picture it's not gonna mean a damn thing.'

He said nothing. The brownstones towered over them both.

'He's got this vision that he's funding a peoples' uprising over there... not round here, that's why I can talk to him, he's cleaner than the Panthers. But those gangs and pushers? They keep him sweet. Paying their dues to the hood, through his pockets. Most of it's gone to the community centre... Now some of it's going overseas.'

'Rhodesia.'

She nodded. 'But he doesn't know how penny-ante his whole thing is. If the UN gets called in there, he's not even gonna be a fart in a thunderstorm.' She grimaced at the grimy street around them. 'Even the gangs still have their wars, over in the barrio now, just off of Vern's turf. It's not gonna change anything... Except in how it stains his soul.'

'And yours.'

She didn't argue. 'Vern says he's in it but not of it,' she muttered. 'Well, I know just how well that works.'

She slowed her pace, heading for the subway station entrance. 'This is what I do,' she muttered. 'I hustle. I spend my days talking to people who never want to talk to each other. Like you and Vern. I give everyone a little of what they want, so they don't try to take too much. And I take what I can right back. I will smile, and kiss ass when I can't kick it, and go along to get along, and I do damage and I take damage every goddamn day. All in the name of doing what I gotta so we can *win.*'

He almost said something sympathetic, after that. But he only wished he could be clearer on who *we* meant in this context. It was getting harder to be certain that Captain Kramer was reporting to people who had everyone's best interests at heart.

'All right, Brigadaddy!' called out Jonesy. 'In his combat jumper, no less!'

'If you've quite finished,' said Lethbridge-Stewart.

Jonesy emerged from the service lift, arms wide. 'That's what makes us such a great pair, y'know. No nonsense meets all nonsense.'

Around them the bare concrete floor — the one-hundred-and-eighth — stretched uninterrupted to the bare steel columns of the World Trade Centre's external frame. Bars all around like a flat wide birdcage. The glass of the windows hadn't been put in yet, so there was nothing between them and the sky. And from there onwards, nothing else this high up until you hit some mountains in upstate New York.

They walked to the edge and looked down at the sun. It was setting dark red, so New Jersey was on fire.

'Give it another few minutes,' said Lethbridge-Stewart.

Jonesy looked askew at him. 'Don't want to be able to see how far down it is?'

'I don't want anyone else to look up.'

He went back towards the concrete core of the lift stack and started wheeling the first of the two laundry bins towards the edge. After a moment, Jonesy took the hint and followed him. The bins were full of the equipment Lethbridge-Stewart had spent most of the day gathering, then smuggled up in the construction lift with the access key Jonesy had slipped him.

Behind his sunglasses, Jonesy looked very much the worse for wear. 'I was up all night. Rehoming all the Odds we had stashed on the ship. Mates who barely even spoke English, and I had to get them into cheap hotels in the middle of the night. And now I've just been stuck in the office downstairs very patiently explaining the whole concept of *critical mass* to Peyton Bryden himself. Oh, he thought we were all stable, but get that many of us on the boat...? It's a wonder we didn't bring down the West Side Highway along with it. Whatever Bryden's planning, there's no way we'll be ready for it.' Jonesy gave a huge, almost theatrical yawn, swaying slightly on his feet, looked down over the edge again, and clapped his hands together enthusiastically. 'Right! Let's get on with it!'

'Are you *trying* to shake my confidence in you?'

Jonesy gave him an innocent look. 'Me and Bryden were the last ones in the office,' he said. 'The coast'll be clear by the time we get down there.'

Assuming there weren't any windows lit up between this floor and that one. Lethbridge-Stewart checked the building plans for the Panorama floor, counted the pillars from the corner of the building, made sure they were standing in the right place.

'Well, come on, man...'

'I'm not going to rush this,' Lethbridge-Stewart said implacably.

'Ooh all right. Yes, Brigadear...'

Lethbridge-Stewart ignored his new 'nickname'. He'd had so many over the years, and not all of them well meant. Ali-stare, Grimnod... What was one more?

He opened the laundry tubs to reveal the harnesses and carabiners, and two vast coils of rope. 'Three hundred fifty feet each,' he said. 'Should give us a reasonable margin for error. Nowhere near the ground, though.'

He pulled on a thick pair of leather gloves and offered a matching one to Jonesy. He'd bought the latest figure-8 descenders, and helmets with small caving lamps, just in case the cover of darkness was too great.

'Figures, doesn't it? This building, it's supposed to be ground zero for the secret world government, they say. Built by the Rockefeller fellas so they and their friends the Rothschilds can run everything from one convenient address.'

Jonesy finished tying one end of his rope around one of the external columns at the edge of the floor, and slapped the steel beam just to see if it would echo. 'Well, here I am, up to my neck in a secret conspiracy with a rich global industrialist working out of the World Trade Centre, and I have to tell you we're bloody winging it. Bryden doesn't know what the hell he's doing. None of them do. They just want to see how far they can get.'

Jonesy had slung a bulky backpack across the front of his chest. Poking out of it was the industrial-strength glass cutter he'd need at the other end of the journey, and a long piece of twine running all the way from it to his wrist. He adjusted the zipper to hold the tool firmly in place. He was utterly nonchalant, as if nothing could go wrong – for him.

'You have done this before?' Lethbridge-Stewart asked.

'Oh yeah, sure, loads of times.'

'You've got your harness on backwards.'

'Do I?" said Jonesy, clutching at his chest in shock, then grinned. 'Nah. It's Australian style.'

'What do you mean?'

'You'll see.'

They each threaded their rope through their descender, then Lethbridge-Stewart tied his securely around the pillar next to Jonesy's, on the outer face of the open floor. The columns were load-bearing, so at least they only had to worry about the ropes coming loose rather than the building. At the other end of their coil of rope, they each tied a bulky knot, as a last line of defence.

'We could use the same line, you know,' said Jonesy.

'I'd rather not have us relying on just one support.'

They each lowered their rope off the side into the gathering dark. Jonesy whistled casually. Lethbridge-Stewart tightened, as if clenching would keep the distracting sounds from wriggling into his ears. He rechecked each clip in his harness. Finally, their lines were all played out.

Jonesy looked at him and grinned. 'Well, as General Custer would say, Geronimo…'

And he charged straight off the edge and started running face-forward down the World Trade Centre.

Lethbridge-Stewart clutched onto the pillar, staring down at Jonesy's shrinking back, until he was sure that blasted man was controlling his descent and not actually plummeting to his death. He felt his own heart pound, and willed himself to breathe slowly. Jonesy was braking himself with an arm across his chest, taking big comical bouncing strides down the windows. It was far easier to focus on him than on the tiny, dotlike cars in the darkening street so far below.

Lethbridge-Stewart had run out of things to double-check now. Nothing left to do but do it.

He triple-checked the knots around his pillar regardless, then faced away from the sheer drop and carefully leaned back into it, playing out the line. One step backwards, tipping onto the glass. Keeping his eye on the rooftop above him, the blackening sky higher up. Feet squeaking on the window, scrabbling to keep his balance. Pushing against the steel columns – good, a bit of extra bracing. The columns here were only about eighteen inches apart, keeping him and Jonesy both in the same neatly defined groove.

He'd wound the rope around his backside for a little extra braking ability. Belt and braces really, but right at the moment he didn't want to take any chance of any kind.

He loosened his grip on the descender and pushed off.

The first drop was a bit wobbly, but he let himself get his balance before trying the next. It became a series of swinging jumps, dropping ten or so feet each pace, landing back on the window and braking. A natural pendulum motion.

The wind was whipping up from the ocean. He hadn't expected it to feel so cold.

And then it hit him exactly where he was. Spasm in his chest, breath blocking his throat, *Good Lord, man, what do you think you're doing? You've got a child on the way—*

He fought down the urge to try to swim his way upwards through the air. Steady now. Halfway down the outside of the world's tallest skyscraper was neither the place nor the time to reconsider one's choices in life. It was either too early or too late, but there would be no way to know until later, so there was Just. No. Point.

Focus on the floors. From the blueprints Jonesy had shown him, the maintenance level was on the seventy-sixth floor, so once he passed the big bank of louvred vents he had nineteen more to go. Seventeen. Sixteen. *None of the floors below that count – yes, there's enough space down there to kill you, beyond that it doesn't matter how much there is. The only bits out of all of it that matter, are the rope through your hands and around your back, your feet on the glass and the buckle on your harness, because those are the pieces you can control.*

Four. Three.

He risked a glance down. Jonesy's head was coming up beneath him. There wasn't room for the two of them between the same set of columns, so Lethbridge-Stewart dragged himself to a stop and stepped over to the other side of the column he was fastened to, before shuffling down the last few feet. His hands were starting to ache on the line.

Jonesy had braced himself between the two columns to work, and switched on his helmet lamp. The air around them filled with a shrieking buzz as he dragged the cutter back and forth across the glass, over and over again. Tracing a pair of nearly-eighteen-inch squares, one atop the other, across the surface of the window.

'This is the tricky bit,' he said.

Lethbridge-Stewart chose not to comment on how the other bits so far had compared with this. He gathered up the remaining rope beneath him, looping it around him, then tied it off a bit below his descender, blocking him from falling any further. Finally, his cramping hands could uncurl.

'Get your hands in,' said Jonesy through clenched teeth. 'We don't want them popping out and falling.'

Lethbridge-Stewart placed one hand on the traced part of the window. Even with the knot, he couldn't quite bring himself to take his other hand off the line.

Jonesy took a breath, bent his knees, then pushed off hard from the window, swinging outward into the air. Hurtling back inward, he kicked, hard, and with a crunch the scored glass panels cracked inwards—

—the bottom corner popping out—

—his own hands lunging, holding it in place as Jonesy skittered off sideways, almost kicking him in the face—

—Jonesy scrabbling for a hold on the steel pillar beside him, slowing his swing, grasping for control…

Lethbridge-Stewart took a slow shaky breath. Nothing had fallen. Neither of them was dead.

The two squares of glass were squeezed half inside the gap, pushed up against the inner pane of the double glazing. With stiff fingers, Lethbridge-Stewart pried the top panel loose, then the bottom one, and Jonesy stowed them carefully inside the backpack tucked across his chest.

'Right,' he exhaled. 'Now we do it all over again.' He pulled the glass cutter back out and started attacking the inner pane.

Lethbridge-Stewart steadied himself against the adjacent window and forced his muscles to relax. They had it under control. He had taken every precaution. And when he returned home, perhaps it was time to start taking the extra precaution of not letting himself get into these mad situations in the first place. Let the younger men, the ones without children, take point on operations like these. Surely by now, he had done enough.

His rope lurched.

A skewer through his heart. Sheer reflex made him clutch the slick steel column. Useless. That lurch could be his weight tugging the knotted loops up top an inch or so round the pillar – or it could be those knots fraying, the rope chafing against the edge of the floor till strand by strand it tore. Just something happening far above, out of sight and out of reach, that might kill you at any moment—

'Hurry up, man!'

He reached out to grab the edge of the hole in the outer pane. His fingers wrapped around it. It wouldn't make much difference if the worst happened, but never, ever let it be said he hadn't done every last thing he could.

Another little lurch.

—Fiona—

'Got it!'

And he and Jonesy both swung round into action, two sets of boots kicking hard at it, the glass giving way and his leg thrashing wildly to keep it from falling outward, pushing it into the office beyond. He felt himself sway sideways in the wind.

'After you,' said Jonesy.

Lethbridge-Stewart wriggled himself through the narrow gap. He had to loosen the knot in his line to give himself enough slack, but he didn't remove it entirely until he had both feet on the ground, on the plush carpet in Bryden's darkened office, and the world was steady again under his feet.

Jonesy slithered in after him. He was grinning, face-splittingly wide. 'Ohhhh man. Man, oh man. Now tell me truly.

Have you ever felt more alive?'

'Frequently,' said Lethbridge-Stewart. He was fairly sure his heart was still beating. He looked around the office. 'Is that the cabinet we want?'

Applause from the doorway.

Peyton Bryden was watching from the dark.

CHAPTER EIGHT
The Turn of a Friendly Cardsharp

LETHBRIDGE-STEWART BACKED away defensively as Bryden advanced on them.

'Well done, both of you. Tell the truth, Jonesy, I thought it was a rotten plan, but you pulled it off.' He turned to Lethbridge-Stewart. 'Shall we bother with the bit where you deny that you're here to find out about the Odds, or skip on to the next part where I tell you?'

Lethbridge-Stewart turned to look at Jonesy, but he was shrugging fecklessly. Oddly unconcerned. 'I told you the answers were in here,' he said. 'Didn't say they were necessarily in the files.'

'You set this up.'

'Well yeah.' Jonesy nodded. 'I told you that first night, I had to be sure about you.' He prowled coolly over towards Bryden, standing beside him. 'You figured 'cause I told you I was testing you, that meant it was over. Nah. Today was your final exam. You passed.'

'What do you mean?'

'Tell me,' Bryden said. 'You just did something extraordinarily foolhardy.' He moved towards the gaping hole in the window, looked down theatrically. 'How exactly is it you think you're still alive?'

'I took every precaution,' said Lethbridge-Stewart. 'And I know about Mr Jones' abilities. He was stopping any unfortunate mischances.'

Jonesy's voice was quiet. 'Actually, I was trying to get you to fall.'

Silence. Lethbridge-Stewart turned towards Jonesy, his breath caught in his throat. He couldn't be serious. He was serious.

'But I couldn't. I knew it wouldn't work.' Jonesy grinned, genuinely awed. 'This just finally proved it. You're stronger than me.'

'Stronger than…?'

A whipping noise from outside. Lethbridge-Stewart turned to the window just in time to see the loose end of his rope plummeting past the window. Reflexively, he grabbed hold of the other end he'd just untied.

'See, I can do it *now*,' said Jonesy airily. 'But not when you were hanging in the balance. You, my friend, have a charmed life.'

Lethbridge-Stewart felt the rope whip-crack against a window far below. Mutely, on automatic, he started hauling it back in.

'You really have the most extraordinary record, Brigadier,' said Bryden. 'You've found yourself at the centre of all sorts of spectacular incidents. And yet they've all worked out for you.'

'I'm good at what I do.'

'Oh, indeed you are. You are in fact the perfect man for it.' He was circling around Lethbridge-Stewart, forcing him onto the defensive. 'Sort out the alien menace and home in time for tea. The next morning the world's still there, and you get to have a proper English breakfast before facing the unimaginable all over again.'

And Jonesy from his other side. 'And no one ever knows. Keeping a little bubble of normal going for everyone? That's your job description right there. You never wondered why you were so good at it?'

'…No.'

Two minutes ago, he'd been clinging to the outside of a skyscraper, without feeling his knees go weak. Now the urge to sit down was overwhelming. He refused to give way, but Jonesy kept chipping away at him.

'And your family tree? Huh. More like a mangrove. You've got weird crap going back generations. How can you even pretend you've got a normal life after all that?' His grey eyes met Lethbridge-Stewart's, and they were unnervingly sincere. 'But you do.'

'And now you know why,' concluded Bryden.

'…Impossible.'

Bryden smiled. 'You and I both know how little that word means.'

Lethbridge-Stewart felt his hands tightening on the harness he was still wearing. 'Nonsense. This is *nonsense*.'

'Oh, possibly. But even if you don't believe it yourself… If our little project with the Odds gets exposed to any of the authorities, Mr Jones and I will probably end up mentioning your name.'

'Your mate Kramer, her bosses, maybe even your bosses. The Russians who got my mum. They'll all want a piece of you. Whether you believe it or not.'

'So. Blackmail. Over something that isn't even true.'

Bryden spread his hands wide. 'It doesn't need to be.'

'But it is, we made sure. That's what it was all about all along,' Jonesy murmured. 'All those attempts on you. Testing your resistance. We wanted Kramer dead, but if you were one of us, you'd pull through.'

That, at least, Lethbridge-Stewart had some idea how to respond to. He gave Bryden a sharp look. 'Are you confessing to attempts on the life of an American officer?'

Bryden shrugged. '*He's* confessing. But to what? Trying to think someone to death, and it didn't work? Tell that to the judge.'

'And the death of Mr Nigel Plummock?' Lethbridge-Stewart looked to Jonesy, to see how he would react. Jonesy was giving nothing away. 'There must have been some more direct intervention there.'

But the question was like water off a duck's well-oiled back.

'I see you've been telling some tales, Jonesy,' Bryden chuckled. Jonesy gave an evasive, deferential half-smile. 'Well, I'll tell you the same thing I told young Mr Jones here. If he can find any evidence that Mr Nallers was responsible for Nigel dying of… I believe it was listed as natural causes?… then I'll be sure to act on it. But all I did was say I wanted him out of Peel.'

'You're saying you don't know what happened.'

'Not really my department.'

'I was under the impression you thought everything was your department, Mr Bryden.'

'Ooh, very good. But I also believe in giving highly motivated employees a good deal of latitude to make their own decisions. There is nothing to connect me to whatever happened to Mr Plummock.' And he'd made sure of that, of course.

'You're asking all the wrong questions, mate,' murmured Jonesy. 'You should be asking why we've gone to all this trouble to get to you.'

'I should have thought that was obvious,' said Lethbridge-Stewart, rallying. 'Mr Bryden's wanted things from the Fifth Operational Corps for quite some time now. The answer is still no.'

'You don't seem to understand, Alistair,' Bryden said gently. 'The Bryden family has spent years building an international empire, spent untold amounts of money on developing cutting-edge technology, expanding the frontiers of science... just so we never have to hear that word.' He smiled, relentlessly. 'A no is just a yes that's still in development.'

'Then what are you after?'

'For now? Just for you to know where our interests coincide.' Bryden's smile was high-grade oil. 'You know what's at stake now. Not just for you... For your family.'

Fiona, in the nursery, those paint-splattered overalls covering the swell of her belly. That wind had chilled him to the bone.

Bryden went on. 'And that is why you're going to continue to work with Captain Kramer, until she's called in to report to her superiors about the Odds. We've arranged that. At which point you're going to completely undercut her. We need her discredited. Humiliatingly so, if possible. I want her fantasies about the Odds to be a career-limiting manoeuvre.'

'She's a friend.'

'It's self-defence, man.' Jonesy locked eyes with him, urgently. 'She's hunting us. She's been after us all along. That's why we aimed you at her car in the first place.'

You might've told me you had one in the oven, he remembered. All sorts of words, moments, tumbling through his head, looking different in a new light. Everything felt off-balance, dissociated, like that concussion he'd never got checked out.

'So, that's why you want me to think I'm one of your...' *Freaks.* 'People. To convince me to backstab my friends and look after my own.'

'Oh no, much more than that, Alistair.' Bryden was shifting smoothly into sales-pitch mode, playing the business visionary. 'If you can harness your abilities... This will benefit both of us. It's your chance to reach your personal potential.'

Bryden was being unusually affable. Perhaps for the first time, the man was seeing Lethbridge-Stewart as something other than an obstruction, blocking him from strip-mining the resources of the Fifth. Now he was a resource in his own right; someone to be persuaded rather than browbeaten. He clung to that thought; it was something to focus on other than this *fantasy…*

'But what's it for? What do you want with… us?'

A showroom smile. 'What's the point of exploring any new technology? To make peoples' lives easier.'

'Especially the Bryden family's,' deadpanned Jonesy.

'Everyone's, really.' Bryden sat down in the chair behind his desk, with the self-satisfied look of the master of his own universe. 'Easier… and more controllable.'

'You're training them to work in concert. What for?'

'Oh, great things, great things.' Bryden settled back in his chair; Lethbridge-Stewart had a sense that the audience was over. 'You'll be told in due time. In the meantime, Mr Jones here will make arrangements for you to join our little training sessions, in between your engagements with Captain Kramer.'

'I don't think he'll need much,' said Jonesy. 'He's a natural. More stable than anyone I've seen.'

'Then I hope to be seeing you soon, Alistair.' Bryden smiled. He clearly still had something more to say, and was just as clearly saving it for a final comment to deliver as they walked out the door.

Lethbridge-Stewart started out, then paused, bracing for it.

'Oh, and next time… take the elevator.'

'Okay,' murmured Jonesy out the side of his mouth, once they were safely away in the express lift. 'You do realise that about a third of what I said in there was rubbish, don't you?'

'That little?' Lethbridge-Stewart said curtly.

'Just the bits where I played nice with him. Yeah, you're one of us. No, I don't know his big plan. He swears it's nothing violent, but then he would. Bryden's still a nutter, and we've gotta get out from under him. But now you know you're not just saving me, or all the little people out there. It's you and yours too.'

'Impossible.'

'Wish I could hand you proof. I've been trying, all this time, to figure out where you fit into our family tree. Haven't spotted the link yet. Unless someone had the Odd bit on the side somewhere.'

Great Uncle Archie rushed unbidden to Lethbridge-Stewart's mind. Allusions made over the years, whispers barely heard between brothers – Uncle Archie and Grandfather… Could it be…?

'But don't you doubt it's real,' Jonesy continued. 'I can feel it, every time I'm around you. Like the world's buzzing.'

'No. I'm not like you,' Lethbridge-Stewart declared flatly. 'Not… random. Accident prone.'

'That's cos you're special.' Jonesy grasped his shoulder, and his eyes were shining; something was making him earnestly *happy* about all this. It felt obscene. 'It's like you're a combination of the two sides of us. Weird things happen round you, but the outcome tends to be normal-ish. You get what you want. The chaos becomes ordered. You're like the missing piece of us. The one who makes the Odds even.' He actually slapped Lethbridge-Stewart on the back. 'It's why we make such a good team. The irresistible force meets the unflappable object.'

'No!' Lethbridge-Stewart snapped. 'We don't make a good team. I make a good officer.' He knew what he was feeling now, and it was a cold proud fury at the whole idea. 'I handle these situations because it's my job, I've been trained, I know what I'm doing, not… mystic mumbo-jumbo.'

He says he's in it but not of it, he heard Kramer's voice echoing in his head. *Well, I know how well that works.* He shook his head sharply, trying to dash that thought away.

Jonesy was looking at him, quietly, with an infuriating compassion. 'Look, I get it. I know it's a lot to take in. But the more you think about it, the more a lot of things will make sense.'

Rather the reverse, thought Lethbridge-Stewart.

No room to pace in this wretched lift. He needed to move, to put distance between himself and Jonesy and everything. This weird little man – slouching, slippery, unkempt, unreliable – was almost the definition of what he was not. Jonesy had been nothing but infuriating all this time, and it was even worse now that he was being kind.

When the door finally opened, Lethbridge-Stewart stalked across the vast deserted lobby. Jonesy still kept pace. He sounded gentle, even respectful. 'You're a better Odd than I am. Probably a better man than I am.' *Not a high bar to set,* thought Lethbridge-Stewart. 'You wanted to protect us even when we weren't your own. But now…' He caught him at the door, and spoke gently. 'You made a home. Like Nigel's. I envy that. Don't screw it up.'

Lethbridge-Stewart went straight to the address Kramer had given him. A modern midtown tower of flats. Hers looked spartan and temporary, with no sign of that husband she'd mentioned. She looked puzzled at his arrival.

'You knew all along.'

'Knew what?'

'When you asked Vern what he'd uncovered. You said, "Is that all you got in three months?" You'd been investigating the Odds before you came to Britain. You already knew.'

To her credit, she didn't deny it. 'I knew a little,' she confessed. 'Now you know more than me.'

The flat was small, but the distance between them was now huge. 'You got our co-operation under false pretences. If you're not willing to come clean about the interests of the US military – or its intelligence services – in this matter, you may consider our arrangement at an end.' He glared at her across her table. 'I will not be used.'

Captain Kramer looked at him, astonishment giving way to hurt, giving way to a slow-burning emotion which he just couldn't read. She turned, walked slow and alone through her loungeroom, listening to the traffic noise below.

She spoke quietly. 'You know what it's like, to be really damn good at doing something you *hate?*' She turned to him, and her eyes were old. 'I keep secrets. I hate secrets. I've made my career out of not just telling people what I think of them.' A step towards him. 'But when I tell you I respect you, sir, then that's for real.'

'Then don't lie to me.'

He left the words hanging in the air for a long moment. *Do it,* he thought. *Give me one clear reason not to trust you. Show me you're a threat to Fiona, to the little one, and it will all be so much simpler. Or just walk away before I have to bring you down as well.*

Then, decisively, she picked up her phone and dialled. 'Kramer 064-972. Get me D.IntOps.' Lethbridge-Stewart waited. 'Sir, we gotta bring him in tonight or we're gonna lose him.' He tensed, ready to run, or fight. He kept an eye out for Kramer's gun. He didn't like the thought of fighting a woman, but then Kramer had made herself an exception in rather a lot of ways.

'Right, half an hour.' She hung up, turned to him. 'I got some people who might give you answers.'

'Do I have a choice?'

'It wasn't my call, not to tell you. But it's your call to come and listen.'

She took him to the UN plaza, then the General Assembly Hall. She had to give a nod to the security guard to let them into the locked, darkened building, and he checked a list before giving her an internal key.

She opened the ground floor doors to the great hall. The rows of national desks were lit only by their footlights, like the world's largest movie palace, with similar low lights picking out the Secretary General's desk in the front centre. Kramer led him up the aisle to the central dais.

'You sit up there,' she said. 'Centre seat. They want you to know, you can leave at any time. I hope you won't.'

He knew no more answers would be forthcoming, so he climbed the steps and sat in the Secretary General's chair. It all felt deeply presumptuous.

He waited, but nothing continued to happen. Kramer had disappeared into the dark.

The last lights went out.

A single spotlight stabbed into his eyes. Like the movie theatre's projector, with him in place of the screen. No: the world's largest interrogation chamber, with him on the business end.

A voice from the dark.

'Brigadier Lethbridge-Stewart. You are in possession of information which is potentially of tremendous strategic importance to Her Majesty's Government. Why have you not reported it to your superiors?'

The voice booming from the speakers was British, a bit plummy, with the testiness of assumed authority.

'I refuse to divulge this information to an unauthorised party,' Lethbridge-Stewart said crisply. 'Please identify yourself.'

'You do not need to divulge any classified information,' put in a second voice. This one had a pronounced accent – Swiss? French? – and a smooth, soothing cadence carefully calculated to allay fears. 'We are looking not for the specifics of the matter, but the philosophy of the man.'

'You have a duty to the State,' reiterated the first voice. 'Why have you not executed it?'

There were answers to be gained, Kramer had intimated, if he played along. He could interpret the rules judiciously; it wouldn't be the first time.

'The information I have uncovered has sensitive international implications. I feel it is my responsibility to ensure that when I do pass on the information I have gathered. I do not do so in a way which makes the situation worse.'

They pushed and prodded him on that. At least three voices, different accents, each challenging him from their own angle. Was he disloyal? Did he think he knew better than the proper authorities? Whose side was he on? Was he just acting to protect himself?

That last challenge made him pause. But not for himself: he thought of Fiona readying the nursery for the little one, the one all these vultures would descend upon if ever they thought Bryden and Jonesy were right. Damn every last one of them for putting a child in the firing line.

'You didn't swear an oath to the whole world,' the first voice cut through. 'You are an instrument of Her Majesty's Armed Forces. Your duty is to serve Great Britain, not salve your conscience.'

Lethbridge-Stewart kept his gaze level into the light. 'I wasn't aware that it was impossible to do both, sir.' He leaned forward. 'When I started my investigations, I saw a threat to my country. Now what I see is a threat to vulnerable civilians. Including, but not limited to, citizens I am sworn to defend. The threat comes from them being exploited. In matters like this one, I see no reason why I cannot both serve my country and the rest of the world.'

'Oh, for the good of all mankind, then,' the first voice said drily.

He thought about demurring. But no. These people had literally put him on the world stage and were forcing him to justify his choices. If he was to be damned, he would be damned for the right thing.

Honesty, then.

'Yes.'

The voices were silent for a moment. Then the first one spoke crisply, taking charge. 'Captain Kramer, you told us this man would make a valuable asset for us, if he could be recruited. What is your assessment now?'

Kramer now, echoing through another microphone. Giving a low and rueful laugh. 'Oh, you don't know what you started,' she said. 'I don't get to speak my mind. Even when you guys ask me my opinion, you do *not* want to know everything that's in my mind. But here we go. Real talk.

'Every guy I ever talk to…? Well, every guy but Donald. I'm just waiting for the bullshit to kick in. But with the brigadier here? It never does.' Her voice rang out. 'Every day of my life I'm waiting for the condescending bit, the little digs, the smackdown if I dare to stand up. But not him. You have any idea how refreshing it is not to worry, and to just get to do your job?'

Which was all rather flattering, but he wasn't quite sure he'd earned all that. Truth be told he still didn't think he had any idea how to relate to a black American woman like her – just how to relate to a junior officer. With respect.

'And how did I repay that? By spying on him for you. Not even for the Army – for *you*. Using him to find out about the Odds. I couldn't even tell him you already knew a bit about them, and the whole point of what we were doing was to try to keep them out of anyone's hands! But I did my job. I pumped everyone around him for information – from his top staff down to a jerk of a corporal. I even got his old GI buddies to report back on him. Oh, they hated me for trying to put him through the wringer. Every one of them said he was a model officer and such a decent guy that I felt like a heel for pushing it. Truth, sirs, he's a far straighter arrow than I am.'

Then he could almost hear Kramer straightening up in the dark as she spoke. 'And I know that's part of the problem for you all, you figure he might blow your identities and cripple the whole operation. But he gets the reason to keep quiet. You've heard what he has to say, and you can be sure he means every word of it. You shouldn't be asking if he's a good enough man for us. You should be asking if we're good enough men for him to trust us.'

A long silence.

'Well,' said the second voice, amused.

'Quite an endorsement,' said the first.

Then the second voice turned on a dime. 'Brigadier, you are aware that you now hold Captain Kramer's career in your hand? A word to her superiors about what you have seen and heard tonight, and she is compromised in their eyes and useless in ours. You do understand that, Captain?'

Unbending. 'Yes, sirs. I do.'

A career limiting manoeuvre, thought Lethbridge-Stewart. Exactly what Bryden had said would guarantee his safety. But the captain must have known she was in danger of this the moment she had asked for a chance to tell him the truth.

'Trust has to start somewhere,' he said.

'Very well then,' said voice number one. 'Captain Kramer, you have permission to brief the brigadier on the nature of our joint operation, and our efforts to contain the situation with the Odds. Standard security protocols still apply.'

He could hear Kramer exhale. 'Thank you, sirs.'

'We are a group within the United Nations which investigates such matters,' said the third, African voice. 'We share information – intelligence – and work to get our nations to cooperate. If they do not... we still do what we can without their blessing.'

'We are all patriots, to our own peoples,' said voice number two, and Lethbridge-Stewart wondered again which people that was. 'But we also recognise the need for collaboration. That this world faces threats which cross national, political, and even planetary boundaries, and that it is necessary sometimes to look beyond national interests to stand together against them.'

And the first. 'There are those who would consider our actions treasonous, for not putting our party or our nation first in all things. But the principle which guides us, is the principle of this hall: that we act for the good of all mankind.'

Abruptly the lights flared on. As he blinked, he could see his interrogators sitting at the last row of desks, distant suits and uniforms, getting up and filing out before he could get a good look. One figure among them walked the other way, towards him, as he descended from the dais.

Adrienne Kramer approached him, looking every inch the

perfect soldier, until the moment when her reserve finally cracked to reveal a huge beaming smile.

'Congratulations, sir. Welcome to UNION.'

CHAPTER NINE
One Chance Out Between Two Worlds

'**UNITED NATIONS** International Operations Network,' explained Captain Kramer over a questionable-looking slice of pizza. 'IntOps for short. We wanted a name that gave away as little as possible.'

'And who exactly are "we"?' asked Lethbridge-Stewart. 'Professionally, not personally.'

'We're what's left of the original international taskforce,' she said. 'When UNIT was strangled at birth, some of the folks kept working at it. But underground. There's a little group of us, mostly in the Field Administration and Logistics Division. The peacekeeping forces,' she clarified. 'And anyone in other departments who's willing to share notes.'

'Unofficially, I take it.'

'Depends on the official. I don't think this goes all the way up to the Under-Secretary General. Brian Urquhart's a great man, I mean seriously, but he's always got to make it clear he respects national sovereignty, otherwise the peacekeeping missions would never get off the ground. The guys running this, above me, they make sure he knows what he needs to know, without knowing how we found it out.'

Lethbridge-Stewart folded his hands. 'So. A UN intelligence network so secret even the UN doesn't know about it.'

'And one specifically set up to deal with the unknown. And the things normal people would find difficult to believe. Me, I asked a few too many questions after that first time you and I worked together… They had a quiet word with me.'

It seemed utterly mad to talk about such things here, in an unprepossessing street-level pizza parlour on the East Side. The tiny black-and-white TV blaring in the corner, the old Italian man behind the counter, the thin pine panelling and plastic check tablecloth – they were all a world away from what had unfolded just an avenue or two from here. And that was why Captain Kramer had insisted on going there for their private chat: in New York, she said, the best security was obscurity, and the best way to avoid the people who should never know about UNION was to go a few blocks away into a completely different world.

It still left a sour taste in his mouth, though, and the thin, oily pizza was the least of it.

'I wanted to call it UNCLE, y'know,' she went on. 'Thinking that, if anyone did hear about us, they'd never believe it. They'd figure it was a joke, someone'd watched too much TV. But then they told me just how many people a year ask at the desk about UNCLE, or try to find that damn tailor's shop…'

'I'm afraid I have no idea what you're talking about,' said Lethbridge-Stewart.

'Right, you never got parked at a desk job. Never had time to waste watching TV like I did. Anyway, I could never make the acronym work, so UNION it was…'

'You've done remarkable work, Captain,' Lethbridge-Stewart said. Regretfully he drew breath. 'And I do wish I could be a part of it.'

A long pause. He could see her retreat, pulling back within herself. 'I get it, sir. Queen and Country.'

'It's not just that.' He had the urge to reach out, however awkwardly, across the table. 'You are doing exactly the work I've wanted to do for years,' he said. 'But I can't. Not properly. Not unless it's aboveboard.'

She put down her slice of pizza, studied the pool of oil gathering on it. 'So, is that it, for the Odds?'

'Oh, I can work with you on this investigation. It won't compromise the security of my country. But to take part in an arrangement like you're proposing… sooner or later that would.'

'…So, don't call you, you'll call me. Is that it?'

'Well, perhaps don't make it clear who you're calling me for.' He contemplated his pizza, awkwardly, as if hoping it could turn into something more appetising. 'Unless we could find a way to make it official.'

'There's no goddamn way, sir,' she snapped. He could hear the disappointment curdling in her voice. 'It's your own guys who pulled the plug in '67. I asked around; the pushback came from the Royal Army.' Her eyes gave him a sideways look: probing how much of this he already knew. 'That's why Hamilton brought you in, to head up the Fifth. Cause they knew you were their man. You wouldn't give the game away to the rest of the world, even if you wanted to. Not if it was your duty.'

'They never told me that.'

'But they were right.'

He nodded, accepting that. 'And in turn, that's why your people wouldn't trust me.'

'Well. 'Til a few days ago, they weren't sure you weren't the one doing the pushback yourself,' she acknowledged.

General Hamilton, he thought. Dressing him down the other day. *I didn't back it then and I won't back it now.*

'But it's not just your guys. We'd have to rebuild the coalition. Anything we try to set up, it goes to the Security Council. And any of the big five has a permanent veto. Us, you, France, Russia, China. You need all five of them or you're dead in the water. And none of them are gonna sacrifice the advantage they get from going it alone.' She scowled. 'That's why my department never gets to do anything major. Nobody wants peacekeeping when one or another of us is backing most of the wars.'

'I served with the UN in Korea,' he said gently. 'It does happen.'

Kramer had the look of a woman who'd seen too much. He watched her round, dark face, the way it creased in a bitter, rueful smile. 'I forget. Some people are used to the system just working for them.'

'It's not perfect. But it's our duty to make it work. We have to do it right.'

He looked at her, and remembered sitting in another cheap restaurant with her and Sally, a few long years ago now, sharing a drink to celebrate having survived. Kramer was shaking her head now, and smiling wearily, but there was respect in those eyes.

'Sir… You're a hell of a soldier, and a terrible spy.'

'I'll take that as a compliment,' he said, and she took that as praise right back.

The next morning, Jonesy phoned him with meeting details for a gathering of Odds.

'We gotta get you trained up, you know? See if you can surprise yourself.'

'That is categorically the last thing I ever want to do,' muttered Lethbridge-Stewart.

Fortunately, Kramer called shortly afterwards, telling him her superiors had summoned her to the Pentagon tomorrow, to account for her extended time overseas. 'Convenient, huh?'

'Yes...'

Bryden had hinted he had this in the works. His friends in the US Army must have applied pressure to call Kramer to account; this must be when he expected her to report to her superiors about the Odds, and for Lethbridge-Stewart to do his Judas bit and hang her out to dry. So, his session with the Odds would have to be mercifully curtailed.

Jonesy's meeting turned out to be in a run-down dance studio, closed for business until the afternoon. Jonesy was already there with ten other Odds; a mixture of white, black, and brown, from their twenties to their fifties, all regarding Lethbridge-Stewart with sceptical stares. He kept to himself and glowered at them. He had nothing to say to these people.

Jonesy cocked a smirk. 'Welcome to Wonderland, Alistair...' He raised his voice. 'Right all, this is Alistair, he's a bit of a square but we'll round off his corners as we go. Now, this is a remedial exercise, just for those of you who need a bit more practice on your focus, somewhere where you're not quite so likely to sink any ships. Everyone assume the position...'

Jonesy sat cross-legged on the floor. A formidable Hispanic woman in her thirties, with a ponytail which snapped like a whip when she turned to glare at Lethbridge-Stewart, translated his words for those who needed it.

Gradually the whole group formed a circle, sitting the same way as Jonesy.

'Right, keep your knees touching, you'll need your hands free for this one.' At which point he and the translator stood back up. 'Okay, now. Turn off your mind, float downstream, and for those of you who've never turned on your mind, just imagine you've had a stiff whiskey and are feeling no pain. Olivia?'

The translator picked up a basket, containing a dozen long-stemmed roses. Jonesy put some droning sitar music on a cheap record player. They circled the group, and one by one handed each of them a tightly closed rosebud.

You can't be serious, thought Lethbridge-Stewart. Nevertheless, Jonesy actually was doing it.

'Consider the rose,' he went on. 'No really, consider it. Look at every detail. Picture it so clearly you can still see it when you close your eyes.'

Lethbridge-Stewart kept his eyes on the other Odds in the circle. One of the faces, staring across at him in undisguised terror, was Unsteady Eddie. As Olivia reached him, he muttered something anxious and Spanish to her. Olivia looked over to him, and her face grew hard. He glared right back at them.

'Got the rose in your head now? All right, now close your eyes and hold it there.'

Shan't, Lethbridge-Stewart thought petulantly. He kept his eyes open to see Olivia take Jonesy aside, mutter to him fast and low. Jonesy was raising his hands, trying to placate and reassure her, but she was still shooting Lethbridge-Stewart suspicious looks. None of the others had seen.

Finally, Jonesy spoke, continuing his even spiel. 'Okay, so some of you are worried about the new boy? You think he's a narc? Well… he was. But then he found out he's one of us. Funny, huh? And he's got real good reason not to blow our cover. But don't you worry, I'll be keeping my beady little eyes on him.'

The Spanish translation sounded much less conciliatory, or perhaps it was just the look Olivia kept aiming at Lethbridge-Stewart.

'Now. We're gonna start, and on each time round, I want you to picture the rose opening in your mind. Breathe it open, kay?' Jonesy let the words hang there for a moment. *'Ommmmm… Ommmmm…'*

The chant was slow, the rhythm of unforced breath. The group took it up in chorus. Lethbridge-Stewart stayed resoundingly silent. Jonesy circled the circle, checking their form, leaned down to whisper in a couple of the Odds' ears. To Lethbridge-Stewart, he just murmured, 'C'mon. Pull out the pole you're sittin' on.'

Om for God's sake, he thought.

Jonesy took his place in the circle beside Olivia, then kept staring pointedly at Lethbridge-Stewart, pulling increasingly ludicrous exasperated faces, until finally Lethbridge-Stewart closed his eyes. He knew he was being childish. It only seemed appropriate, given how childish the whole idea was.

'We're not gonna stop 'til after you start…'

'*Om.*' Lethbridge-Stewart sighed. '*Om.*'

The *om* ran on long enough for him to pass from tight anger to boredom, and then into plain old not-caring. He pictured the rose, just for something to do. It kept pulsing, opening and opening, the bud unfolding to reveal another bud inside, his mind moving inwards until the new one filled the space of the old. Each *om* a slow out-breath blossoming, each inhale pulling him deeper.

Slowly the tempo quickened. He didn't feel it change, only noticed afterwards how much it had sped up. Walking pace now, almost march time. The throb of the rose demanding more. His mind pushing into it, prying further, harder, deeper…

Now Jonesy's voice was quieting, all hushing to hear him as he slowed. The sound faded to nothing. The rose in his mind came to rest, both closed in the centre and open in its glory at once.

Lethbridge-Stewart looked.

And the rosebud in his hands was wide open.

He shuddered, nearly flung it away.

It must be the others, he thought. The effect of so many of them around him. Every single one of their flowers had opened, his must have been swept along for the ride. Unsteady Eddie's had outright exploded, a pile of petals scattered on the floor. But Jonesy, the blissful idiot, was rounding the circle collecting all the roses and smiling.

'Now how can you argue with that?' he murmured.

At least Kramer had given him an excuse to duck out of Jonesy's gathering as soon as he could. He took Jonesy aside and explained, then headed out the door.

And slammed into a stone wall of a man, who efficiently shoulder-checked him just as he stepped through. Hard enough to send him stumbling backwards. The man's leg swept his own out from under him, and he landed in a heap on his backside, staring.

Nallers was looming over him.

'One back for the hospital,' he said bluntly.

Jonesy helped Lethbridge-Stewart to his feet as he dusted

himself off. 'Bryden had Nallers fly in this morning, as a troubleshooter,' he murmured. 'As in, we make trouble, he shoots us.'

The three glowered at each other for a moment. He'd expected something of the sort, Lethbridge-Stewart told himself: Nallers was the fist at the end of Bryden's arms-length distance.

'I'm off to Washington,' he said curtly. 'Mr Bryden knows why.'

Nallers made a show of stepping aside to let him go. Lethbridge-Stewart realised that Nallers had positioned himself outside the door, waiting, just to make this point. Just what they needed: a thinking thug.

He tried to put it out of his mind. The man had just blindsided him. But then, hadn't they all?

CHAPTER TEN
Uniting Nations Intelligently

BRYDEN HIMSELF phoned Lethbridge-Stewart back at the Howard Johnson's, once he'd booked his train tickets. Bryden wanted to recommend a good hotel in Washington, one more befitting a general officer.

'And you know what to do when they ask you about the Odds, of course?'

'Deny her three times, I take it,' Lethbridge-Stewart said, which amused Bryden no end. But, of course, since those superiors weren't the ones who had sent her to investigate the Odds in the first place, and had no idea they even existed...

He had to wonder just how much of a grip on the situation Bryden actually had. He knew from experience, the man was an opportunist who liked to believe he was a strategist; he may have managed one big idea about what to do with the Odds, but he didn't have the imagination to be a full-scale megalomaniac. But even if he didn't know what he was doing, what did he *think* he was doing?

By 5pm, Lethbridge-Stewart and Kramer were settled on an Amtrak Metroliner, rattling its way across the marshy fens of New Jersey.

'You gotta come by our place,' Kramer told him. 'Donald always picks me up at the station, we can have a late dinner.'

'I take it you do this a lot?'

She smiled. 'Pretty much every weekend for seven years. Either I go down, or he comes up.'

'I'm surprised he hasn't moved up to join you.'

'He's an architect, got a good job. Not easy to find. We can't really afford to look for a new one, while he's still making a name for himself.' A rueful shrug. 'So, until I get a DC posting, or he pulls up stakes and moves up here… kind of hard to settle down and have kids.'

For a moment Lethbridge-Stewart just watched the barren-looking fens rocket past.

'Well then we'd better get a move on, hadn't we?'

'What d'you mean?' she asked.

'If we're going to get UNION set up legitimately before you resign to have children.'

She blinked. 'What makes you think I'm gonna resign and… What am I *saying*? You think we could pull that off?'

'You said it'll take five Security Council votes. That means we need five people who can make a persuasive case to their governments.'

'The UN delegates are dead set—'

'I don't mean political channels. I mean military and intelligence. We need to talk to our opposite numbers, and work our way up from there. Find people on the shadowy side of things, because they're the ones who will be guarding their national interests in that area the most fervently. They're the ones who need to know we have common interests as well.'

'And you think maybe the Odds are a good case for that?'

'The likes of Bryden aren't beholden to any government. Even the people who might want an arms race wouldn't want a new competitor to win it.'

'So, you're thinking, make it like a security council veto of *him*?' A slow, cunning smile began to grow on Kramer's face. 'Oh, that's good. The Russkies'd really hate the idea of the arms race getting *privatised.*'

'Exactly. We don't need to shift the whole government, we just need to push a few people who know where to push.'

She knitted her brow. 'We've got contacts at Groom Lake now, after the Engineers business…'

'And if we can manage the Odds, I'll be in a better position with Hamilton.'

'Like they said, only Nixon could go to China.' Kramer frowned. 'You really think all your old Empire types are gonna go for this? I can't see them accepting a world authority.'

Lethbridge-Stewart looked out of the window, at the greenery shooting past as they rocketed along. They said to an American a hundred years was a long time, while to an Englishman a hundred miles was a long way.

'I don't think you quite understand what the British Empire *was*,' he said. 'We were quite all right with the thought of a world authority. We just thought it would be us.'

'Five people,' mused Kramer. 'Four if we skip the French. I figure if we manage to work out a deal with the commies on this the French will be too startled to even think of vetoing it. Hmm. My Rolodex isn't great on China…'

'We can make a start on the Russians, then.'

She turned to him in her seat, her eyes serious. 'You really think we can do this?'

He didn't want to answer yes. If he actually thought about it, cold-bloodedly, it still all seemed terribly far-fetched. But wasn't that exactly what Jonesy and his Odds were all about, making the unlikely possible? And if they were right and he (no don't even *think* about that)—

He steadied his own gaze and met her eyes.

'It's a good goal.'

Three hours of strategy later the train sighed into Union Station in Washington, and Kramer led him towards the end of the platform.

'I'm just gonna pretend you're not here for a minute, okay? Don't worry, I'll get back to you.'

And she bustled up to a tall, heavyset black man waiting for her, looked into his eyes with a wide deep smile, and kissed him like she meant it.

'Donald, this is Brigadier Lethbridge-Stewart,' she said, once Lethbridge-Stewart finished averting his eyes. 'He's got my back.'

'Pleasure to meet you, sir.' Donald shook Lethbridge-Stewart's hand, firmly. 'I hear you took good care of her while she was away.'

Of course, they hadn't seen each other since she'd first travelled to the UK. That explained why Captain Kramer was still hanging off him and beaming at him like a newlywed.

'She's been a great help to us,' Lethbridge-Stewart said.

'Your daddy's already at the house getting dinner ready,' said Donald, hefting her suitcase. 'Welcome home, honey.'

George Donald Kramer was tall, heavyset, and easy going, one of those men who brought down the ambient stress level just by being present. Round face, round glasses. Around him,

Captain Kramer was light on her feet. Odd, in all the years Lethbridge-Stewart had worked with her, he'd never actually seen her relax, not like this.

Donald drove them through the warm Washington night in a well-worn Plymouth Valiant. After the looming monoliths of Manhattan, it felt oddly free to be in a city designed for a panoramic view, full of low buildings and spreading parkland. To one side he caught a glimpse of the Capitol Building, gleaming in its night-lights as they cruised past. The radio was playing a song which he gathered was called *What's Going On*, judging by the call-and-response vocals which the Kramers ai-yi-yi-ed their way through in wildly diverging keys. She had her window down, her arm resting casually on the edge, and her head bobbed gently in time with the music as she echoed Donald's phrases. Lethbridge-Stewart got a powerful sense that she was already home.

'How'd it go with the Venusians?' asked Donald.

'Oh God,' she said. 'They spent all day arguing with us about not infringing on their territory, and refusing to concede that they were causing the problem in the first place. Refusing to let go of even a single, uh, laser photon torpedo. The whole bargain fell through. Sometimes I could strangle the little green bastards.'

'Erm,' said Lethbridge-Stewart hastily, quietly horrified by Kramer's loose lips. 'Where did you two meet? At university?'

'Summer before I went to Howard,' she said, smiling freely. 'It was on a protest, desegregating the swimming pool at Glen Echo Park.'

'Well,' said Lethbridge-Stewart.

She shrugged. 'I was seventeen, I held a sign.'

'And I brought a couple of bottles of Coke with me, from Peoples Drug,' put in Donald. 'Thought I'd give one to this cute girl.'

'How's that working out for you?' she said, patting his hand. 'Quite a summer,' she told Lethbridge-Stewart. 'Set up the next four years. Him, me, and Vern. The Three Musketeers.'

'Oh, he's met Vern?' said Donald, grinning fondly. 'Still brave and crazy.'

'He says hi. And he says you're still wrong about Mr Spock.'

Donald chuckled. 'I told him, the actor himself—'

'He doesn't see the Jewish. He figures they're writing him

to be like the Chinese or something, all calm and inscrutable, you know?'

Donald shook his head. 'Just cause that old TV of his made him look yellow...'

'So you two have been together... about twelve years?'

'Married for seven. At Rankin Chapel, right after we graduated from Howard,' Donald said. 'By then we knew she was going to go in for officer training, down at Fort McClellan in Alabama—'

'We do *not* talk about Alabama,' Kramer put in, with dangerous precision.

'—and we wanted to get hitched before she shipped off.'

'So, all these years,' mused Lethbridge-Stewart, 'you've only been able to live together when she's been stationed in Washington?'

'Keeps it fresh.' Kramer shrugged.

'And they're always bringing her down here to report in. We get maybe half a week at a time. Here we are...'

Donald pulled up to a simple brick bungalow in North Michigan Park. As he hauled her suitcase up the path of steps through the ample front lawn, Lethbridge-Stewart took a moment to buttonhole Captain Kramer by the car.

'You have some very odd ideas about operational security.'

'Whadaya mean—'

'Just telling him about the Venusian incident.'

'What? Oh, that's how I redact things,' she said. 'When I want to blow off steam about what some assholes from a foreign delegation got up to, and not blab anything classified, I tell him they're aliens from another planet.'

Surprised, he weighed the idea. 'Inventive.'

'Lot easier than keeping it bottled up,' she said. A quick furtive grin. 'The one time it had to do with real aliens, I just told him they were Japanese.'

He was genuinely rather amused by that. 'Good to know,' he said as he headed indoors. 'An incident like that would be most unlike the ambassador from Venusia.'

'Thanks—wait, *what?*—'

His moustache twitched slightly, when he was sure she couldn't see.

Vigorous frying sounds were coming from the kitchen, where Frank Harris was cooking with the enthusiasm of a man who just loved to eat, and fancied himself a chef. Lethbridge-Stewart recognised his type: the big stick who walked softly. Six-foot-five, greying, imposing in form but gentle in his movements and speech. He put down the wooden spoon, stood to attention and snapped off a credible American-style salute.

'At ease, Sergeant,' said Kramer, and he gave her a hug and went back to stirring the pot.

'Proudest day of my life, when my daughter outranked me,' he told Lethbridge-Stewart. Apparently, he'd left the Army in '48, but had returned to Fort Meade as a civilian employee once he'd got a degree, and had been there ever since. He'd kept soldiering in his blood, and it looked like he'd passed it down to her.

'Ma's off with Mabel tonight. Fixing everybody's business. You know how they are. She'll come by after supper.'

Dinner was meat and potatoes – literally, a profoundly filling meatloaf with heaping portions of vegetables and potatoes on the side. Donald and Harris went out of their way to make Lethbridge-Stewart feel at home, and took turns telling him amusing tales of what a law unto herself young Adrienne had been.

'When she was seven, there was a riot at our swimming pool in Anacostia. That was back in '49, white folk pushing back against desegregation.'

'Years before Glen Echo,' she put in. 'White boys and their swimming pools…'

'Little Adrienne, now, she was so *furious*. It was Not Fair. Oh, she didn't even get the segregation. It was those mean people picking fights, they got the pool closed for everyone, so she couldn't swim there for the whole rest of the summer!'

Captain Kramer, laughing, shook a finger angrily and imitated her childish squeak. 'You oughta be *shamed!*'

'And when the city listened, and opened it again to everyone the next summer… I swear to God, she wrote them a thank you note.'

'My little crawler,' said Donald delightedly. Kramer positively whooped.

Lethbridge-Stewart was seeing yet another face of hers; he was beginning to get the sense that she really did have to switch selves all the time, but this was the most open of the lot. He'd spent a fair bit of time wondering which one was the real her;

now he was reckoning that they all were.

'You've done a very good job, then,' said Lethbridge-Stewart. 'Taking that and moulding her into an excellent soldier.'

'They still won't let me go shoot the bad guys, though,' mock-pouted Kramer.

Harris leaned back contentedly, patting his stomach. 'I didn't teach her to fight, her mama did that. I just taught her how to win.'

'I used your rule while I was over in England,' she told him, spearing a potato pointedly. 'Corporal with a chip on his shoulder, thought he was the only one who ever bled.'

'Wright?' Lethbridge-Stewart asked, trying not to smile.

'How'dja guess? I coulda just given him what he deserved, but I used it to get him to see where we had some common ground.' She pointed her fork at her father. 'Like he always said. It's not just about what they deserve, or about what you deserve—'

'It's about what you need to win,' Harris finished sagely.

'Wright is all right,' said Lethbridge-Stewart, which earned him a sideways eyebrow from Kramer. 'He may not want to learn, but he does. He's become rather a better soldier since I've known him.'

'Yeah, well, you tend to have that effect on people,' Kramer said drily. 'Rather a lot. You ever noticed that?'

And there it was again, that feeling of something clenching around him. Why did they have to think of him as exceptional? Even here?

'I wonder what the odds are of that,' he murmured.

Later that night, the taxi dropped him off at the Watergate Hotel, a soft curving building overlooking the bend in the river. Rather more luxurious than he was used to, but Bryden had insisted on picking up the tab: a way of asserting ownership, he suspected.

He was weary enough that tonight it didn't matter. Relaxing had allowed exhaustion to creep in. From his room, he could see the water and the woods of Roosevelt Island, a scattering of lights in the night beyond. All was quiet.

His first phone call was to the Soviet embassy. It took a bit of a struggle to communicate, but he finally did get them to take a message for Avakoum Zahov, of the trade delegation, or if he wasn't available just get it to Grigoriy Bugayev, blast it. He couldn't tell if the night operator's ignorance was down to a careful espionage veil of silence or just ordinary obliviousness.

Then he lay on his bed fully clothed, flipping a Kennedy half-dollar he'd picked up on his travels. Keeping count and wondering.

The results never strayed much from fifty-fifty. But they wouldn't, would they? If there were anything to that idea of Jonesy's which kept gnawing at him, he'd have to find some way of skewing things away from the norm. Only then, if it stayed stable, could he be sure that the wrongness was in him.

Finally, when it was late enough, he picked up the phone and dialled.

'Hello, Fiona? Good morning.'

'Alistair!' He heard her voice light up with shock. 'Where are you?'

'Washington DC now. Reporting in at the Pentagon, had a bit of a quiet night. How are you holding up?'

'Oh, fine, aside from Mr Pennington next door threatening to take a chainsaw to one of our trees if we don't prune the bits that are growing onto his property...'

'The elm in the back corner?'

'The elm, yeah. Miserable old buffer...'

It was as if he'd placed a phone call back to the real world. What a delight to speak to someone who didn't want to talk to him about how exceptional he was, or see him as a threat from outside their everyday world. Someone who didn't see him as an inspiration or a freak or even an officer, just as the man he was when he wasn't anything else.

'Alistair...' she said, and he could hear the edge of tension in her voice now. 'There's nothing wrong, is there?'

Even her.

He'd thought about telling her some whimsical little story about what the Martians were up to. But the whole idea felt so forced now. Not when she was braced for him to bring more danger into her life.

'I just... rather wanted to hear your voice.'

CHAPTER ELEVEN
Never Tell Me the Odds

TWO AND a half hours and several lifetimes after the start of her first Bryden Industries consultancy meeting, Anne was escorted by her project manager into the records room, where she was allowed carefully supervised access to the Weatherballoon schematics. On this first glance, the most useful bit of information she was able to gather was which filing cabinet they were stored in.

Eight hours after that, Corporal Wright whispered to Bishop as they both pulled on their balaclavas. 'So, this is all completely off the record, is it, sir? I'm not a corporal, you're not a captain, none of that then? Right then. Have you gone completely bloody daft, butt?'
Minutes later they cut through the chain-link fence around the Bryden Industries complex.

Twelve hours after that, Captain Bishop stood in an office in that same complex, blandly telling the managers that the Russians had done a very professional job on their second visit, they hadn't left a trace.
The spool of microfilm with the pictures he and Wright had taken was still in his jacket pocket, and butter remained unmelted in his mouth.

Six hours after that, Bishop handed the film over to his wife, as she had asked; full of every record the complex had about the Odds or Weatherballoon, along with the bodged-together control box and a snipped-off strip of the balloon fabric. Anne looked weary and haunted and couldn't tell him why.
'You know that effect where if you observe something, you

disturb it? Even without intending to; the very fact that people know what I'm looking for could affect what I find. I hope it has absolutely nothing to do with any of this. I hope I'm chasing a wild goose that's just caught a red herring. I hope I'll look back on this and gladly say it makes no sense at all.'

That was just the part she thought she *could* put together. Then there were the bits that she couldn't make fit at all. Bubbly little Nina just sat there in her lab happily breaking science. What if every tool Anne had was useless, and she was trying to make sense of something for which the scientific method didn't even apply?

And that night, Corporal Wright stood knotted at a payphone, getting halfway through dialling an international number and hanging up, over and over again. 'Cause Captain Kramer had taken him aside, hadn't she, that night when it all went funny. Right after the brigadier had left with his missus.

'Okay, boy, you remember that nuke I got aimed at your ass? Well, I'm just gonna ask you to let me know if Captain Bishop gets up to anything shifty while I'm back home. Here's the number to call. Ask for I.C. IntOps.'

Not that he'd ever thought he'd call it, oh no; that was the kind of mistake old Evans would've made, passing on the family secrets, and he wasn't gonna be Evans now, was he? But this wasn't an official secret, was it? More like kept secret from the officials.

Bishop had said even the rest of the Fifth couldn't know, he'd picked Wright cos it was need-to-know, but he didn't even bloody well know what he knew, did he? Something to do with Kramer and Weatherballoon, he guessed, but was this going on behind Lethbridge-Stewart's back too? What the hell was Bishop up to, and why was he in the middle of it?

Wright had his head in his hand and let out something shaky like a sob.

Colonel Braddock's office in C Ring of the Pentagon was unpretentious and a bit nicotine-stained. Kind of like the colonel, who prided himself on being a regular guy, or at least a regular guy's boss, and who couldn't understand why simply treating you like one of the guys wasn't the same as treating you with respect.

'Okay, Kramer, I just want this in your own words. What the hell have you been up to, with this Scotland thing?'

'I did put it in my reports, sir.'

He widened his eyes innocently. 'Oh yeah, you did. Security consultation following the events of an American–Soviet–British exchange of data, incident number blah blah blah, all as generic as you can get. You just left out the sentence where you mentioned you were away from your desk for goddamn weeks on end.'

'I did say I'd gone to Edinburgh on assignment. In the first one.'

'Oh yeah, and just never quite mentioned that you hadn't come back.' And he'd only just spotted this, or been tipped off, weeks later. She didn't want to fault him for his inattentive reading, that would only get him more pissed off. Let him have his head. 'I don't like it when my people try to pull a fast one on me.'

'I'm not trying to be difficult, sir.'

Braddock smiled wearily. 'Yeah, well, somehow, Captain, you keep managing it.'

'I was running my team from the field, over the phone—'

'Well, if they can get by without you being in the office for weeks on end, it kinda makes me wonder what we're paying your salary for.' He switched his tone to something more cajoling. 'Come on, I found a good place for you. Why you gotta keep asking for so much?'

Kramer shrugged, smiled politely. 'Well, if you got better things for me to do, I hear there's a war on…'

'C'mon, hon.' She tensed. 'You know I could palm you off on the Pacific Theatre command, but you know what they'd do to you?' *The secretary speech*, she thought. 'You'd end up in a file room in Saigon, playing secretary to some high-up redneck who wants to know why you're not scrubbing his floors. You know I've been keeping you away from that for years, now can't you at least be a little bit grateful?'

She was grateful he took the bait, at least. If he thought she *wanted* to be reassigned, that'd make him less likely to yank her out. Though he'd never really hand her over to any unit anywhere near Nam; that would mean a reduction in his manpower, and here on the domestic administrative side the only wars the colonel ever got to fight were turf ones.

'Seriously, sir. I went across the pond to ask questions for FALD. The British specifically asked me to stay on, FALD approved the mission.'

'Yeah, well, what I'm not hearing is the word "America" anywhere in there.' Now he was leaning in close. 'Your job is supposed to be about serving our interests, not just the UN's. So come on, what have you done for us lately?'

Here we go. 'Well, sir, I figure it's better if you hear the story from someone who's cleared to talk about it.' She turned and pushed the outer office door open a crack, raised her voice. 'Brigadier?'

And Lethbridge-Stewart took his cue to enter. He'd persuaded the secretary outside not to announce him, just to maximise the look on Braddock's face as he scrambled to his feet.

'Is there something I can clarify for you, Colonel?'

Best possible start, thought Kramer. Now it would get tricky.

Introductions out of the way, Lethbridge-Stewart dove into the explanations.

'Earlier this year, there were three simultaneous incidents around the globe. One in Siberia, one on the Isle of Man, and one at the US Air Force base at Groom Lake—'

'Whoa, whoa. You mean, Blue Book country?' Colonel Braddock's eyes narrowed. 'Is this gonna get weird?'

'Only somewhat,' said Lethbridge-Stewart, and Kramer still flinched. 'But Captain Kramer's part was perfectly routine.'

'Kinda my job to decide that,' said Braddock. 'So, what did you need Kramer for?'

Kramer's right here, she thought.

'We needed a co-ordinated international response. Captain Kramer and her office helped provide it. And it was all smoothly resolved.'

'And I got a couple of one-liners buried in a report. Why wasn't I given a full brief?'

'Air Force classified,' Kramer put in. 'Last I checked, they're still American.'

Braddock gave them both a funny look. 'You're telling me the Area 51 guys clapped a lid on it?'

'It doesn't particularly matter to Captain Kramer's part in this. No need to trouble yourself,' Lethbridge-Stewart said smoothly. Which was a mistake. Braddock didn't trust smooth.

'Now hang on. These incidents. Level with me. Were you chasing aliens?'

'The problem turned out to be earthly in nature.'

'Turned out, huh.'

She didn't like the way this was going, and tried to salvage it. 'It's Brigadier Lethbridge-Stewart's job to consider all possibilities—'

Braddock talked right across her. Far as he was concerned, she was irrelevant to her own interrogation now. 'Look, Brigadier, I'll believe in anything if it helps get the job done. But this is not the job.'

Lethbridge-Stewart was unfazed. 'Then perhaps, Colonel, it *should* be someone's job.'

Braddock gave a dubious smile. 'With all due respect, Brigadier, I'll believe it when I'm briefed on it. By *my* people.' Kramer could see Lethbridge-Stewart being pushed into the box marked 'fruitcake'. 'So then what, you kidnapped her for a few weeks?'

'This part's out of the Air Force's jurisdiction, so I can be open about it. There were concerns about a security breach, at the Isle of Man site. Captain Kramer's superiors at the UN sent her to find out whether we contained it successfully. She arrived in the middle of an ongoing investigation that I was conducting, and stayed to help get the results. And deal with the incident when the Soviets tried to, shall we say, investigate on their own.'

Braddock ignored most of that to seize on the one bit Kramer didn't want him to dig into. 'Security breach? What was it?'

'It went into the press as an unidentified flying object,' Lethbridge-Stewart admitted grudgingly. 'Of course, to us it was thoroughly identified.'

Identified as alien, Kramer thought. She just prayed Braddock couldn't hear the tapdancing.

Braddock wasn't deterred. 'Brigadier, I'm gonna ask you a straight question. And let me warn you, if you beat around the bush, I'm throwing a grenade into it.' He locked eyes with Lethbridge-Stewart. 'Did you drag Captain Kramer away from her duties for all those weeks to chase little green men?'

Lethbridge-Stewart took a long moment to respond. But when he raised his eyes to meet Braddock's, they were clear and unblinking.

'Nothing of the sort,' he said. 'The only enemy alien involved was the Russian agent.'

'Then what the hell were you doing—?'

'You may recall that earlier this year, there was a nuclear alert.'

'Yeah, Russian sabre rattling.'

'Do you know exactly why?'

She could see the penny drop for Braddock, in slow motion. '…That was you?'

'They were responding to the three incidents I mentioned. The Soviets took them very seriously.' Lethbridge-Stewart was implacable, in command of the facts. 'And what we found was that those incidents were down to a third-party extremist using advanced technology to prepare a simultaneous strike against all the superpowers.' And again, that was a pretty good summary of the Earthbound side of the Engineers crisis, if you left out what planet the tech had come from. 'The actual threat we found was not aliens. It was political.'

'And the whole thing was hushed up?'

'Check the dates,' Kramer said. 'Something else went down in Nevada round then.'

Braddock didn't even turn to her, he looked to Lethbridge-Stewart for confirmation. 'Third party…' Braddock was calculating the dates. 'This was the Arabs, right? The ones who took out Harrison Bailey.'

'I couldn't possibly confirm,' said Lethbridge-Stewart, and Braddock took that as a yes.

Good, thought Kramer. Because if they had confirmed, they'd have had to tell him that Harrison Bailey, golfing buddy of the President, had been a crazy-ass John Birch type aiming to use the Engineers to make himself king of the world, and the Arabs were a made-up scapegoat for when they had to frag him. But never mind that.

Braddock turned away to the window; Kramer could see his world rearrange itself in front of him. 'Damn,' he said, stretching it to two syllables.

'We spent those weeks chasing down whether what happened to Harrison Bailey was only the tip of the iceberg,' Kramer told him. 'Sorry, I can't say more.'

Lethbridge-Stewart picked up on her words. 'Our remit at the Scots Guards Special Support Group is not aliens, it's the unknown. The *uncertain*. We investigate whether an unexpected occurrence is mischance, or enemy action, whether it's technological, biological, or just inexplicable. And those investigations are ongoing. That's what Captain Kramer was dealing with.'

When Braddock turned back from the window, his shock was hardening into something stronger. 'We should know.' There was a sort of bewildered anger in his eyes. 'Something like this is going down, the US Army should damn well know.'

'I fully agree,' said Lethbridge-Stewart. 'And if we can set up a formal programme through the UN, for the sharing of such intelligence, I would be happy to read you in.'

Braddock stared, then managed half a chuckle. 'UN, hell. I was just wondering how we could pry the story out of the Air Force.'

'Could be a good opportunity for you, sir,' Kramer put in.

Now Braddock turned to her, still bewildered. She was winging it now, but there might just be a sales pitch that could work.

'You may not think the freaky stuff is worth it, but a lot of countries out there take it seriously. If we formalise this kind of arrangement... It gets them thinking, when something off their radar happens, they could use some good old American know-how. Gets us intel out of countries who wouldn't share it otherwise. Maybe makes 'em more comfortable about our boots on the ground.'

He still looked dubious, but at least he was talking to her now rather than about her. 'One of your outreach programs, huh?'

And Lethbridge-Stewart was following her lead. 'If we were to get UN backing for this, that would require an inter-service force for dealing with these matters. The Air Force would have to be part of that. There'd be channels to go through, and you could be in them.'

Braddock still looked sceptical, but that was a big step up from hostile; now that there was an opportunity for him, he was interested.

God damn, Lethbridge-Stewart had pulled it off. He'd taken the whole crazy mess, all the intrigue and just plain coincidences, and found the bits in it which made a simple true story, one which even Braddock could get on board with. This was Lethbridge-Stewart's superpower; stripping out all the bits that didn't make sense, and just dealing with the bit that did. He made it sound normal.

'Captain Kramer, ma'am,' said Braddock's secretary. 'Phone call for you.'

A bit after 5pm, Edinburgh time, Wright's nerve had finally broken – or pulled itself together, he didn't know which.

He loaded up his pockets with 10p pieces and set about feeding the payphone around the side of the barracks. 'Get me I.C. Intops,' he told the American operator. 'And make it snappy, it's nearly a quid a minute.'

But it wasn't snappy, oh no, they took so long to transfer him to Kramer that he had to wave down Jezza as he passed and get him to go break another fiver.

'I.C. IntOps,' said Kramer's voice. 'Go.'

'Wright here, ma'am.' He looked around furtively. 'Got a message.' Christ, he could hear his voice shaking, and his mouth had gone dry. He took a slow breath and tried to straighten his shoulders. 'But I'm only gonna give it to the brigadier,' he said.

A pause. 'What do you mean?'

'Been working it out, see,' said Wright. 'Saw you two before you left. You disappear, he disappears. I reckon he went off with you.'

'Okay,' said Kramer, measuring her words all careful-like. 'You told anyone else about this brainwave of yours?'

'Well not yet,' said Wright. 'But if you don't put him on right now, I might just.' To make the point, he called out to his mate. 'Oi! Jezza!'

'Now don't do anything hasty,' Kramer said hastily.

'I mean it.' He tried to make his voice strong. 'I got something to tell him. And I'm not telling you.'

'What?'

'I mean it. Put me on jankers, knock me down to private, I don't care. I don't trust you, see. And Lethbridge-Stewart done right by me.'

She sounded almost impressed. 'I'll see what I can do. Hold please.' Then it took another two pounds before she picked up again. 'Okay. Here he is.'

'Corporal?'

'…I was right, then!'

'Apparently. And if you tell anyone—'

'I know, sir, more'n my neck's worth. Only it's Captain Bishop, sir. He's acting all squirrelly-like. Had me break into Bryden's offices with him, get pictures of some files. All hush-hush.'

'I see,' Lethbridge-Stewart said thoughtfully. 'Did you see which files?'

'Might have been Weatherballoon, sir.'

'Interesting.' Lethbridge-Stewart thought for a few more really pricey moments. 'If you need to tell me anything else, you can call my hotel directly.' He read out a number, which Wright had to scribble on a cigarette paper. 'Oh, and… Keeping it for my ears only. Finding me. Very commendable. Your sister would be proud.'

Wright's eyes widened. He hadn't expected a lump in his throat, on top of his dry mouth. 'You mean it, sir?'

'Of course.'

'Thank you, sir. I'll let you know, sir.' He moved to hang up, then remembered. 'Oh, and I'll want paying back for this call! It's a fortune.'

'Fair enough,' said Lethbridge-Stewart.

'Okay, I gotta ask,' said Kramer, as they left Braddock's office. 'His sister?'

'Half-sister.' They had just discussed a bit of international conspiracy over a Pentagon phone line, but for this Lethbridge-Stewart still felt a strong urge to lower his voice. 'I assume Sally told you, what she found out about her mother's little adventure?'

Kramer's eyes widened. 'He's Sally's half-… That jerk?' For once, her unreadable professional mask had fallen clean off, and she was straight-out floored. 'I thought the last name was just… There are a lot of Wrights out there, but how come…?'

'After she passed on, he took her family name instead of his father's. A sort of tribute to her.'

Slowly Kramer shook her head. 'I mean, is this like a British thing? I mean, you, him, the Traverses… Do all you guys over there have family trees that make no kind of goddamn sense?'

And that did gnaw at him. As far as he knew, the fact that they all had such complex family backgrounds was an utter coincidence, but right at the moment, that was the exact opposite of reassuring.

Ahead lay the southeast exit, with a throng of Pentagon visitors queueing at the security gates. But as he looked, one man in the queue just happened to drop his umbrella, while the person in front of him advanced a couple of paces, and the stream of people leaving for lunch scattered in exactly the way to give him a clear view of the two black-clad figures waiting just beyond them. One burly and brick-shouldered, the other skinny and spider-haired. Both staring straight at him.

'I think perhaps you'd better go back to the office,' he murmured to Kramer. 'We'll meet later.'

Kramer's eyes moved to look at him, while her face stayed impassive. 'After dinner,' she said. 'I got a lead on all the airline tickets Bryden's people booked to Barbados. By tonight, we should know how many of them we're up against.'

'Well?' demanded Nallers.

'The colonel didn't even ask about you,' said Lethbridge-Stewart. 'Kramer didn't volunteer anything. There was nothing about you for me to contradict.' It was, in fact, a minor point of pride that he'd made it through the entire debriefing without once actually having to lie. And he could hardly convince the Army to abandon an investigation they weren't conducting in the first place, could he?

Nallers scowled. 'Crap.' Lethbridge-Stewart wasn't sure if it was directed at the situation, or at what he had told them.

'Well then,' said Jonesy, twitchily cheery. 'If they haven't clapped her in irons, that gives you about six hours to stop the *next* crisis. You know what she's after now?'

That was a test, he was sure. 'Something about following up on your plane tickets.'

'Oh yeah. That means, she's getting a list of all us Odds, ready to hand over to the Army. Or the highest bidder. Whoever she's really working for. If that list falls into *anyone's* hands, we're all marked men.'

And Jonesy had a point. Even if Lethbridge-Stewart trusted Kramer's people, such a list could easily be found by someone less trustworthy down the line, and effectively hand them instructions on how to build an atomic bomb. Jonesy had already spent years tapdancing, to try to keep such a list even out of Bryden's hands... Though once Bryden had them all in Barbados, even that would be a lost battle.

Jonesy paced round Nallers, whose glare remained fixed and threatening. 'Your mission -- whether or not you choose to accept it – is to stop her getting it.' He grinned snakily. 'And just to make sure you're really strongly motivated… we made sure your name's on the top.'

CHAPTER TWELVE
Mission: Not Bloody Likely

__SUBMITTED FOR__ your approval: this fine potato of a man is Mr Rosenberg, a civilian employee at the Navy Yard, and under-the-table contact of Captain Kramer. He's been doing the legwork on the list. And you've got to get the papers out of his hands before he can pass them on to her tonight.

Through the miracle of modern phone-tapping, we know where and when he's having dinner tonight, talking things over with his ex-wife. He's gonna meet Kramer there right after that. Bonus points if we can keep him from noticing that we've lifted the list until well after we get away.

And the assets available to you to make this possible: one low-improbability Odd and three high-improbability ones, namely your old mates Dave and Nina, fresh off the plane from the UK, plus Olivia Suarez, who you met in the Big Apple, and yours truly. Direct from New York: the Odd Squad. All present and approximately correct, sah!

Sorry. You know if I had to do it all straight, I'd scream.

The other point of the exercise, surmised Lethbridge-Stewart: Bryden and Nallers wanted to see how he worked as a commander. Whether he had the skills not just to devise a strategy using the Odds' abilities working in concert, but to convince a rag-tag group of malcontent civilians of marginal competence to follow his lead.

So far, it wasn't promising. David Plummock merely looked like he didn't want to be there, but Nina didn't look like she'd trust him as far as she could throw him, and Olivia looked ready to do the throwing. As far as she knew, he'd been interrogating Unsteady Eddie, and was at the very least playing both sides.

And the more he tried to put Jonesy in the position of his sergeant – since he thought they'd respond better to commands from him – the more feckless and casual Jonesy seemed to get. It was entirely deliberate, too; he made a crack about 'Odds' Army' which made it clear he knew just what he was doing.

It wasn't working with the uniform, Lethbridge-Stewart decided. They'd hustled him straight from the Pentagon to this meeting, at the back of a sandwich shop called the Psyche Delly, without even giving him time to change. Pointedly, he stripped off his jacket and even loosened his tie.

'Now we all know, some of you would rather be protected *from* me than by me. I know we've got very little in common, but one thing we do agree on is, none of us want you to be exposed. So, let's stay focused on that.'

And, he didn't add, Mr Nallers wasn't lurking on the scene just to mark his performance. If they didn't retrieve the list, no doubt he'd step in… as of yesterday his boss may have preferred Kramer discredited rather than killed, but now she'd dodged that, all bets were off.

So, strategy. Plan A: if Rosenberg left the list in his car, Jonesy – the one with the best instinct for locks – would extract it from the car and/or boot during the dinner. Plan B: if Rosenberg brought it with him to the table, they would need a small, deft distraction to allow them to snatch the papers.

Trying to brainstorm potential distractions degenerated rapidly. To keep things practical, he had them decamp to the restaurant for a recce, in Nallers' unmarked van. *The Old Ebbitt Grill* stood on F Street, half a block from the Treasury Building, which in turn stood across the lawn from the White House. Rather more federal security in the vicinity than would be ideal. The nearest parking was in a garage across the street, half a block further away.

Inside, the restaurant was all old oak beams and check tablecloths, with assorted animals or parts thereof dotted around the walls. A long bar with old-fashioned stools, and a large marlin hanging over it, squeezed the customers' tables into two rows along the opposite wall. A second bar area upstairs was dressed with ferns, which struck Lethbridge-Stewart as being of no use to anyone.

Now they could sit in the back and come up with a solid set of distractions, in increasing order of severity. If they could force Rosenberg to a specific table in the row nearest the bar, then depending on where he positioned his case, either a person passing in the aisle or one sitting at the adjacent table could grab it at the right moment.

Perhaps Nina for the table. Olivia was more stable in her improbability ability, but in other respects she was more of a wild card. He didn't want her acting on suspicious impulse.

So. Olivia would be positioned as lookout near the garage, notifying them of Rosenberg's arrival, and then watching out for Kramer's. She accepted this with a New York snort and a burst of muttered Spanish. Jonesy would start by holding Rosenberg's table, then either join Olivia for plan A or concentrate on steering peoples' eyes for plan B.

To sustain an incident, they needed one person per idea. If Nina triggered a surprise, Jonesy could do the detail work; making sure neither Rosenberg nor his ex-wife would happen to look away from the distraction at the wrong moment. Meanwhile, either Nina, at the table to the right, or one of the others passing on the left, would grab the papers and exit to the rear.

And David, as their resident island of apparent sanity, would be disguised as a waiter, complete with napkin over his arm, ready to move in and damp down any suspicions if the Rosenbergs (an unfortunate name in the context of espionage, Lethbridge-Stewart supposed) noticed the wrong things. Other than that, he'd need to hover in the vicinity of Lethbridge-Stewart's table in the back, where he and Nallers would be observing events. Where the others could have concealed walkie-talkies, David's would be too conspicuous.

Just over an hour now till the action would start.

Final prep. Jonesy said he could borrow a car-door unlocking tool from a repair shop down the road. Lethbridge-Stewart bought a set of binoculars for Olivia and half a dozen cheap walkie-talkies from a nearby Radio Shack, with plug-in earpieces; they were bulky and conspicuous, but they'd do.

Lethbridge-Stewart and Nallers positioned themselves at a table up the back, with Lethbridge-Stewart holding up a newspaper to hide his walkie-talkie just like a completely normal person would. With David nearby, he thought he could get away with it. Probably.

'He's here,' muttered Olivia in his ear. 'Getting out. He's

got a briefcase.'

'Excellent,' said Lethbridge-Stewart. 'Get him seated, then go for plan A.'

'But he's bringing it in,' protested Jonesy, 'he's got the—'

'Stay with plan A. It might not be in the case.'

Jonesy abandoned the table he'd been occupying, then steered the next passing customers past it, until Rosenberg settled at their handpicked table. Then he slunk off towards the parking garage to start rifling the man's car.

In person, Rosenberg was a rotund man, with thinning hair and a haphazard walrus moustache. But there was a sparkle in his eyes: he wasn't an idiot. He didn't put the briefcase to either side, he tucked it between his feet for safekeeping. That would make plan B that much harder.

Nina started pantomiming *what do I DO?* faces at Lethbridge-Stewart.

'Wait for Jonesy,' he muttered.

They managed about ninety seconds before a champagne bottle exploded at the table behind Rosenberg, and the cork ricocheted off a mounted elk head, bounced off the table in front of him, then whacked a man at the bar on the back of his skull. Rosenberg stared, bewildered. Even Nina seemed caught by surprise.

'Sorry,' she mumbled into her walkie-talkie. 'I was thinking about what I might have to do, and it did it.'

Lethbridge-Stewart cast his eyes heavenwards.

Soon Rosenberg's ex-wife – Evelyn, according to the files, a vivacious middle-aged woman – joined him at the table, looking faintly nonplussed at the waiter improvising an icepack for the victim of the errant cork. The Rosenbergs chatted amiably about their German folk-dance group, and the baby which their daughter and her husband were adopting.

'Got the boot open,' Jonesy reported. 'No sign so far. Shouldn't we be getting on?'

A burst of Spanish swearing in his ear. 'Kramer. She's here already. Pulling into the garage.' More untranslatable imprecations, barking at Jonesy. 'They set us up!'

Lethbridge-Stewart knew he was part of her *they*. And he could see Nina tensing up in panic. Unless he convinced them that he was determined to stop Kramer *right now*, this whole team would fall to pieces.

'Jonesy,' he muttered. 'Stop traffic.'

'What?'

'Accident. Make her notice.'

'Right,' said Jonesy, grabbing Olivia's shoulder as they hustled away.

He'd abandoned Rosenberg's car boot mid-rummage, and scampered out of the garage, crouching low, using the cars as cover till they reached the sidewalk.

'You heard the man,' he told Olivia. 'Let's try for a chain reaction, eh?'

Together, they *squeezed* just as the traffic light turned red.

A couple of the cars braked just a little too fast, and the cars behind them just a little too slow, leading to the *crunch* of a couple of fender-benders. One of the cars bumped forward, rear-ending the one in front. Both lanes of westbound traffic were thoroughly blocked now, as Jonesy and Olivia sauntered across the crosswalk.

When Kramer noticed, that stopped her in her tracks. She was suspicious now, and suspicion made her cautious. Jonesy saw her press against the building – looking upwards to make sure nothing could fall on her – then peer around the corner, checking for hostiles. With a mischance like that, she knew the Odds were on to her, but she'd have known that shortly anyway, when she found out the briefcase was gone. Now, her caution bought them some time.

'Right, sir, guess we're on to plan B,' Jonesy muttered to Lethbridge-Stewart. 'B for bloody fast.'

'Not yet,' said ol' Brigsy, and Jonesy's eyes bulged with frustration.

Lethbridge-Stewart refused to rush.

He waited till Olivia was in lookout position outside the door, guarding their rear, and Jonesy had taken up a seat at the bar.

'She's crossing the street,' warned Olivia.

'Now,' said Lethbridge-Stewart.

Jonesy waited until a new couple were being escorted to a table in the back. Then he got up, casually giving the trailing woman the tiniest of nudges as he squeezed past. She stumbled into her husband. Who stumbled into the corner of a table. Then tripped over his own foot. Then his hand slammed down as he fell, on the corner of the table right behind Evelyn.

Clatter, crash! The whole table flipped over. Consternation on all sides. And as David joined the throng of employees trying to restore order, Nina had thirty crucial seconds to slide under her table, scoot across the floor, and nab the briefcase.

She exited slowly, as quick as she could, and made it to the back door just as Kramer made it to the front.

Lethbridge-Stewart had already left his own seat to meet her and Jonesy by the fire exit. With Nallers and David following, the five slipped out into the alleyway.

'We did it?' Nina asked eagerly.

'Double-check,' Lethbridge-Stewart said. 'Mr Jones?' Sighing, Jonesy sat on the back steps and started quickly picking the briefcase lock. Lethbridge-Stewart went on. 'David, join us at the rear. Olivia, hold position in the front. We need eyes on Kramer.'

'She's looking around,' muttered Olivia. 'Suspicious. Going to talk to Rosenberg.'

Jonesy clutched his head in panic. 'It's not in the bloody briefcase!'

He waved a small stack of bank statements and family paperwork, clearly meant for Evelyn rather than Kramer.

Lethbridge-Stewart took a breath. 'All right,' he said implacably. 'Back to plan A.'

Jonesy stared, then with a 'gnnnnnh!' of raw frustration, he thrust the briefcase back at Lethbridge-Stewart and hared away up the alleyway, back towards the parking garage.

Lethbridge-Stewart risked peering in through the door. Kramer was standing with the Rosenbergs, eyes scanning the place. He ducked back; if she saw him with the Odds, particularly with Nallers, there'd be even more questions. But right now, having fought to keep her from getting there, now they had to keep her there.

A moment's calculation. He handed the briefcase to David. 'Return it to him. Apologise, keep them talking.'

David froze. 'What if she asks——?'

'You just found the case by the door, the thief abandoned it. That's all you know.' David still looked like a deer in headlights. 'It's perfectly normal,' Lethbridge-Stewart emphasised. 'We'll get you out, we just need the time. When you see a distraction, make your excuses and go. Rendezvous at the end of the alley.'

Shakily, David adjusted his napkin and headed back in.

Lethbridge-Stewart motioned for Nallers and Nina to follow Jonesy, and he brought up the rear. He thumbed his walkie-talkie again. 'Olivia? Give David a minute or two, then start hitting them with every distraction we haven't used yet. One after another. Keep her there, keep her reacting.'

'Okay.'

By the time they reached the parking garage, Jonesy had finished searching the boot and moved on to the car itself. He was practically bent double, still badly winded from his sprint. Nina helped him rummage. Nallers had drawn a handgun, complete with silencer, and taken up a firing position covering the entrance to the garage. Ready to write off the whole mission, by writing off Kramer as well.

'Go start the van,' Lethbridge-Stewart told him.

Nallers didn't even look at him. 'No.'

'Then give me the keys.' Nallers snorted and fished them out of his pocket. Lethbridge-Stewart hurried to the van, opened the door, then went around to the other side and opened the *correct* door, started the van, and pulled up in front of Nallers, blocking his field of fire. Nallers' face spoke volumes of short unprintable words.

Meanwhile, Olivia kept the channel open. The distracting accidents were coming louder and faster. Lethbridge-Stewart could hear a clatter, a yelp, the crash of breaking glass, the *foomp* of something alcoholic bursting into flame, more shouting, assorted running footsteps, David babbling an apology and retreating, and the muffled sounds of a high-volume near-monologue from an outraged chef.

'Got it!' gasped Jonesy's voice in his ear.

'Folder under the passenger seat!' added Nina.

'Right. Get in!' As they clambered in — Nallers professionally covering their retreat — he hit the walkie-talkie again. 'Olivia. Withdraw. Find David at the front of the alley, we'll extract you on the corner.'

If she replied, it was lost under the sound of a fire alarm.

The corner was still half-blocked by the five dented cars, all pulled over to the side of the road. Lethbridge-Stewart turned the van right just past them, giving David and Olivia a chance to climb on board. Behind them people were streaming out of the restaurant, milling about in confusion on the sidewalk. Somewhere in their midst Kramer and the Rosenbergs were still being jostled, finding it uncannily hard to make progress.

Nallers eyed the throng. 'You call that subtle?'

'We were subtle where it counted,' said Lethbridge-Stewart.

David still looked overwhelmed, but Olivia was fighting a smile as she clambered into the back. 'All right. I'll admit it. That was fun.'

Jonesy's wheezing for breath had become choking laughter. 'Mission Implausible!' he called out, still clutching the list to his chest. 'Dun, dun, dun-dun, dun, dun, dun-dun…'

'Keep it down,' warned Lethbridge-Stewart as the others verged on joining in.

Kramer and the Rosenbergs were heading for the crossing, right behind them. He raised a hand to shield his face, just in case, and watched them through the wing mirror. Rosenberg looked befuddled, Kramer on high alert.

Only Evelyn seemed unperturbed. 'Wow,' she said, shaking her head. 'That place has really gone downhill.'

'They were waiting for me,' said Kramer, as they looked out over the river back at the Watergate. 'Ambushed my contact and then had a go at me too. Very professional. Oh, they know exactly what they're doing.'

'Terrible,' said Lethbridge-Stewart, feeling bleakly flattered. 'But it occurs to me, that list might be extremely dangerous in the wrong hands. Better if no one knows where to find all of them. Not even us.'

'No one except for Bryden. And Jonesy.'

'That's what we're working on. Think of it as an exercise in non-proliferation.' And fortunately, when he left them, Jonesy and his friends had literally been rolling the list up and smoking it; he could hardly begrudge them that.

Kramer seemed to be accepting that.

'I'm sorry I couldn't help,' he added.

'Would've invited you along, but I couldn't find you.' She paused, narrowed her eyes, looking sideways at him. 'So where did you have dinner?'

'The hotel restaurant,' he said easily, which was technically true. 'I needed time to think.' Particularly about what Kramer had said the other night, about realising that you were really very good at doing something you hated.

By the time Kramer left, he knew Anne would probably be asleep. He rang her anyway.

'…Alistair? Where are you? What's happened?'

'Washington, and, rather a lot.'

Strange, it wasn't until this moment that he'd felt this conversation could be awkward. Surely Anne and Bill would understand the need to tell them nothing before he left? But now that so much had happened – without even knowing what had happened on their side – he was feeling really rather far away from her.

'I understand Bill's been busy over on your side as well,' he probed.

'You didn't even say you were going.'

'I thought it was best to say as little as possible.'

'Well, you were thoughtless and high-handed and quite possibly right.' Anne could still surprise him, on a regular basis.

'Did something happen?'

He heard her taking a shaky breath. 'I was talking with Dave and Nina, just unwinding after the explosion at Edith's… All right, long story, but the point is that I talked with them about my father. Not about the Intelligence or the classified bits, just… the dementia.'

'Doesn't sound like a problem.'

'But it *could* be.' She sounded unsteady, like she had too many thoughts jostling for position to come out of her mouth at once. 'We don't know how far this goes.'

'It's all right. None of that is relevant.'

'We don't *know* that.' And she stopped. Her need to tell him was fighting with a need to keep quiet.

'You can start by telling me what you and Bill found out at Bryden's.' And an update on what was happening with the inquiry wouldn't go amiss either.

'But that's just it. I thought you were being ridiculous about us maybe letting things slip to Bryden, of course we'd be more on the ball than that, but then I went and said stuff I didn't think I ever would—'

'I understand. Really, Anne. I understand.'

'Good. I'm sure you understand why I can't tell you what

I've found out yet.'

'…Sorry?'

'I mean it. If you're even thinking about the things I've been thinking about, you might end up second-guessing yourself, and I don't want to disrupt you, unless I'm sure. More sure.'

All right. He took a slow breath and quite consciously trusted her. 'Can you be sure in a day or so?'

'Why?'

'Because I think I'm going to need you and Bill here.' Now it was his turn to worry about how much to let on. 'Events are moving on rather quickly. I want everyone together, sharing information, before things get out of control.'

'I don't think they've ever been in *our* control.' Anne laughed shakily, then sobered, insistent now. 'I can tell you this much; *don't trust the Odds.* Any of them. They have no idea how dangerous they could be.'

CHAPTER THIRTEEN
All the Brigadier's Man

BUGAYEV WAS waiting in a corner of the complex's parking garage, a dark figure in the low sodium light. Thankfully he had resisted the temptation to wear a trenchcoat.

'Major.'

'Brigadier.'

There was an awkward pause, as each waited for the other's opening gambit. Quite frankly, Lethbridge-Stewart was tired of the whole game.

'How's my wife?' he asked. Bugayev raised an eyebrow. 'When I called you in Siberia, you made a point of congratulating me on my impending fatherhood. Showing off your sources. I haven't spoken to her today, I thought I might get an update.'

Bugayev smiled, genuinely amused. 'I hope she's well. How's mine?'

'Oh, they wouldn't tell me.' Lethbridge-Stewart frowned slightly. 'Are you actually married?'

Bugayev stayed cagey. 'Not at this time.'

'Well, I wish you the best of luck. Really, I think we could both use a drink. Shall we go someplace more private?'

Jonesy watched them from a far corner, crouching behind a Mercury the size of Montana, trying to keep the concrete pillars from getting too rubbery in the corners of his eyes.

Unsteady Eddie had fixed him up with some really primo acid – Bryden even had one of Panorama's top industrial chemists check its purity – and under of course carefully controlled experimental conditions Jonesy had administered the teeniest fraction of a dose possible. Just enough to jiggle his brain into better sensing the threads of chance weaving around all them, maybe get a picture of where to pull.

Right about now they felt like yak fur.

Whoever the Brig was talking to over there, it was like there were huge clumps of fuzzy futures attached to those moments – a carpet full of threads all feeling different ways, silky or bristly or oily. No way to see where they led, just an instinct.

Then a security guard rounded a corner in the distance. With him came a wave of ripples through the fuzz, the threads around him feeling slick and slimy, a sharp whiff of rotting cat food. Couldn't be good. *Playing by sense of smell,* thought Jonesy.

So he waved. Approximately.

The Brig Kahuna headed Jonesy's way, the other man in tow. It took the tiniest of *squeezes* to make them move fast enough. The security guard saw them, leaving their car in the direction of the hotel part of the Watergate complex, took them as nothing exceptional, and kept on with his rounds. The twinge of nausea faded, and Jonesy let out a weirdly echoey breath.

'What are you doing here?' asked the Brig.

'Spying on you,' Jonesy said helpfully. The Brig shot him a look. 'Bryden wants me to keep an eye on you and Kramer.' Brig Daddy was not amused. 'I assume I didn't see any of this?'

'I'm certain you want to stay far away from it.'

Jonesy tried to answer, but suddenly he was out of words. Cause up close to the Brig, it was all hitting him at once.

The whole garage buzzing with electric crackle; so many futures, all firing off from the tiniest of chances here and now. A delicately balanced eruption. All wildly different, the world could go anywhere from there at the slightest chance, assaulting every sense with colliding impressions… A scent of peppermint, a taste of gravy, reptile-skin and sandpaper and a shrieking wall of kookaburras…

This was what history felt like before it'd been written.

Jonesy felt around the edges, maybe he could massage it into shape, but it was just *too much,* too many ways things could go, no way to be sure which was which. And so many of those threads were running right through the Brig, a lunatic tangle of unlikely events. No idea whether he was the puppeteer or the puppet, the spider in the web or the fly, but Jonesy felt the crashing certainty that as far as where the Brig's life was going *this was still the simple bit—*

Jonesy had to close his eyes to stop the churn. 'Tell you what. I'll just go away somewhere and be really sober for a long, long time.'

And because they'd moved away, the approaching security guard didn't divert from his rounds to ask these loitering gentlemen a few pointed questions. He continued on, to notice a stairwell door for which the latch had been taped over again, even after he'd removed the tape holding it open on his previous round. And the world spiralled on from there.

'Major Grigoriy Bugayev, Captain Adrienne Kramer, attached to the United Nations. I believe your people spoke to her during the Engineers business.'

Captain Kramer had her glasses on, the large round lenses making her eyes look owlish, her face seem rounder and softer. Lethbridge-Stewart was getting a sense of how often she judged which face she had to show.

'I've swept the room for bugs, sir,' she said.

'Were you taking them out, or putting them in?' Bugayev asked drily.

'Hey, you wanna check, knock yourself out. I've got all night.'

Bugayev demurred. 'General Timarov briefed me you were very efficient.'

'That's good,' said Lethbridge-Stewart. 'I'm going to have an offer for you to make to the general, and Captain Kramer's a part of it.'

Bugayev smiled, slowly, shaking his head at Lethbridge-Stewart. 'The general is a keen player of chess, and he's somewhat charmed that you British think you're the one across the board.' He turned his attention to Captain Kramer, and Lethbridge-Stewart felt the axis of the room shift. Bugayev locked eyes with Kramer. 'Have you decided to bring Lethbridge-Stewart in on the Army's secret?'

Kramer went very still. Taking it seriously. 'Any particular one?'

'We know you've been using him as your cat's-paw all this time. Developing this new suppression technology with Bryden Industries, and letting the British deny all knowledge of it. Kramer was sent to be your handler. You've been used, Brigadier.'

For a long moment, his charge hung in the air.

'Seriously?' asked Kramer, her eyebrow at maximum. 'You think Bryden would have his goons try to kill me because I was spying on Lethbridge-Stewart *for him*? Do you even hear yourself?'

'Bryden's tried to bring me in on his operation,' Lethbridge-Stewart explained patiently. 'He wants *me* to sabotage *Kramer*. This is all getting rather beyond a double bluff.' He crossed to the kitchenette area, where he'd stashed the bottle of proper Russian vodka which Mr Friedman at the off-license had recommended, and brought Bugayev a glass. 'He specifically *doesn't* want his project to fall into the hands of the Americans. Or even ours, apparently. Bryden is for Bryden.'

Bugayev took the glass, considering. 'You must admit, the Americans would be the most likely suspects.'

'As you'll soon see, in this matter, we can't rely on what's likely.'

'Your general's trying to play chess in a hockey brawl,' said Kramer. 'There's more players than us now, and they're not even trying to win the same game. What we've got here is good old-fashioned private enterprise running amok.'

'Interesting,' mused Bugayev. When he was wrong, he didn't stick with it, noted Lethbridge-Stewart. 'Harrison Bailey with the Engineers, now Peyton Bryden… Have your capitalists now decided that nations are obsolete? So they can cut out the men in the middle?'

'They figure they can play with the big boys now. Bryden Industries is worth more than Bolivia, y'know? And your old tricks won't work on multinationals. Whatcha gonna do, start a guerrilla movement to seize his factory floor?'

'Perhaps you could invade to overturn the results of a board meeting,' Bugayev countered smoothly.

Lethbridge-Stewart cut across them. 'The real issue is what they're developing. Do you know what this technology is? Or rather, who?'

Bugayev hadn't gathered more than it was something to do with human psionics. Lethbridge-Stewart and Kramer quickly summarised the abilities of the Odds, leaving out their family tree, or anything that could identify them en masse.

'We know the KGB already has files on some of them. Look for the name Elsa Mittelberg, possibly Elsa Mittelberg Jones.

East Berlin, 1945.' Lethbridge-Stewart paused. 'One of their number would very much like to know if she is all right.'

Bugayev gave him a sceptical look. 'And you not only want them out of Bryden's hands… you say you don't want them in your own governments' hands either?'

'Picture an atomic bomb, but the bigger you built the bomb, the more unstable it got,' said Lethbridge-Stewart. 'Only a fool would conduct an arms race with weapons such as that.'

Bugayev smiled with old Russian weariness. 'You and I both know enough fools, Brigadier.'

'Yes, we do,' he said pointedly, and Bugayev seemed to turn inward, going quiet. 'I'm not even talking about mistakes in judgement. We both know, we've already had nuclear alerts triggered by solar flares, auroras, even a moonrise. A single electronic failure in the wrong place can take us to the brink. Do we really need even more of an element of chance?'

Kramer sidled up, joining in. 'You guys are always saying, the only reason you developed nukes was because you were afraid we'd use ours, otherwise you'd never have gone down that path. Well… here's your chance to live up to your propaganda.'

Bugayev gave her a sceptical eye, but spoke to Lethbridge-Stewart. 'Tell me if I've got this wrong. You ask me not to take this information to my superiors… and expect me to believe you haven't reported to yours?'

'No one's got a head start,' said Kramer. 'I discovered this while I was on assignment for the UN. If I reported to anyone, it'd go to everyone. We've had to keep it on the down-low.'

'But if you take this to your superiors, she takes it to her superiors,' summed up Lethbridge-Stewart. 'Pointless, really.'

Bugayev smiled. 'The Prisoner's Dilemma. Very neat. Of course, it assumes that there is no way to cheat.'

'And that's the other part of our proposal,' said Kramer.

Lethbridge-Stewart sat down at the glass-topped table by the balcony door, pouring additional glasses for himself and Kramer. 'You know from our encounter with the Engineers, there are threats to our world which are larger than the interests of any one nation. Up to now, when you and I have worked together, we've muddled through partly on luck. You know that's not good enough.'

Kramer joined him at the table. 'What we need is an official framework to handle stuff like this. So we don't have to keep reinventing the wheel every time. Staffed with loyal domestic troops within each country, but reporting to the UN on global matters.'

Bugayev didn't raise an eyebrow; it was more of a deadpan squint. 'You think when the general objects to giving up control of these Odds, I can say, don't worry, we can give up even more control to the UN?'

'If it gives you the chance to stick your nose into our business too,' said Kramer. 'You don't have to trust us if you can check up on us.'

'*Doverjajte, no proverjajte,*' said Lethbridge-Stewart, approximately. 'Trust but verify, isn't that the saying?' Bugayev took his attempt at pronunciation with good grace.

'But the UN?' Bugayev turned to Kramer. 'You must know how many peacekeeping missions our people have proposed, and yours have vetoed?'

'About as many as yours have when we propose them. Am I wrong?'

'National loyalty is not so easily overcome. Look at you.' And there was still something sharp and probing behind Bugayev's eyes. 'You wear the uniform of a country which put your ancestors in chains.'

Kramer bristled. 'Well, yours'd put me in a gulag right now for asking the wrong questions, so I figure I'm still coming out ahead...'

'Please.' Lethbridge-Stewart made the word sound authoritative. He softened his tone. 'We all know the places where we don't have common ground. But if this becomes an arms race, all our people have already lost. Bryden's forces are ready to go.' He looked from one of them to the other. 'These people are civilians. Some of them are *your* civilians. The Odds don't want to be weapons, and our shared goal must be to keep them from being used.'

Kramer nodded, getting control. 'And to be ready for the next threat, whatever it is.' She met Bugayev's eyes head-on. 'This is what we all need to do to win.'

Bugayev finished his glass, leaned for a moment on the back of his empty chair. 'If it were anyone other than you suggesting this, I wouldn't even be thinking about it.'

Once again a cloud passed over Lethbridge-Stewart's face.

'I really should not be such an exception,' he muttered darkly.

'But we do have a common adversary here, in Bryden.' Bugayev sat down, looking Lethbridge-Stewart in the eye. 'If you agree to share the information you've gathered on the Odds with me, I agree to make a case for a UN body to General Timarov.'

Lethbridge-Stewart turned away to the window. A police siren had caught his attention. In the Washington night, just at the corner of his view, he could see half a dozen men being herded into police cars, arrested in the office building opposite.

'Excellent,' he said. 'Now we can begin.'

Jonesy had only made it as far as across the street from the Watergate. Still tripping the very heavy fantastic. Now all he could do was have a good long sit down, and hold on to the wall till the world stopped frying. Some trips you just have to take as learning experiences, and not in a fun way.

As the cops drove squishily away, it was like they dragged all the most solid parts of the world away with them. Leaving only cobwebs. The thinnest of strands that connected where they'd been to where they'd just gone right now. Some little tiny moment that had just happened, it had taken them right out of the book, and the world was so much less nailed down than they all thought. The status quo was status queasy.

His guts heaved, like a liquid scream. Or was it just a blob of futures all spewing out of him?

He knew. He could feel it where his liver should be. If Jonesy had messed with that security guard, or vice versa—if either way the man hadn't finished his rounds, if he hadn't been paying attention and doing his job well, he never would've called the cops on the burglars. How would that have played out, for the Brig or for everyone? No idea. Couldn't see, couldn't taste it. But the whole world was rocking, *rocking*, from such a little thing.

It was all Jonesy could do to keep the ground holding on to him. *Hold me closer, tiny chancer.*

And not just right in front of him, oh no. Now he was zooming out, crashing, spinning, his brain racing down all the threads which led out of the now, everything going on right now for miles around. All the stuff people thought was so unlikely, that was just one good chance away from happening.

Old Rosenberg and his wife…? Their daughter and her husband had just adopted a baby boy. The ex-Atomic-Energy-Commission professor who Kramer had pumped for info about nuclear near-misses…? His daughter and her husband-to-be had just given up a baby boy for adoption. The two families lived less than five miles apart, but they had no idea. God only knew how many times they'd already passed each other on the highway. Way down the web, Jonesy could feel the shadow of how they could meet one day, how much that would mean.

There was a hole in time right nearby, like a mouth, and she was laughing. How could she not? All these threads running through her, tying into an incredible bow which only she could see.

Jonesy rolled over, eyes to the pavement, as if the concrete could keep the world out. But he wasn't just seeing what was possible, oh no. He was feeling what wasn't possible anymore. All the little gossamer threads of chance he'd torn right through, with all his kicking and flailing over all those years. The ones that could've kept Nigel off their radar and alive, kept Daddy Walter where he could see him. And not just the chances attached to that little blob called Jonesy… That couple who Nallers killed. The trigger-happy bloke in New Delhi. Even Aziz in Ankara. All their futures swept aside like cobwebs.

That mouth was ready to swallow him. Laughing all the while.

'I kept 'em safe,' he was pleading, though he couldn't tell if any sound was making it out of his mouth. 'My family. I kept my people safe.' But had he? All the dead in his way, all the dead ends he'd made for them. Even when he knew what he was doing, he didn't know what he was doing.

He could feel the sweat throbbing where he thought his forehead had been. The whole crazy tangle was spilling out around him, and he kept scrabbling for anything he could hold on to.

He raised his head, or dreamed he did, to where that hotel window had been.

And somehow, in the middle of that hideously complicated space-time event called a life, there was a simple man.

Look at him. A palimpsest wrapped in a stereotype wrapped in a neat little moustache.

If there was anything solid in all these people… it was their human nature. People would do who they were.

And I kept doing fear…

He wasn't keen on simple answers. That was Nallers' bit. And the Brig Daddy over there, he could be wrong, flawed, plain old clueless, and perfectly square in every dimension. He could go the wrong way. But he wasn't acting out of the wrong feelings. And that felt so much better than being Jonesy.

Jonesy was crying, he could feel that much now, and the sobbing meant he must be breathing.

His best self was all in other people. Used to be in Nigel. Maybe now he could find it in what Brigadier Alistair Lethbridge-Stewart was reaching for.

Maybe it really was as simple as a security guard just doing his job.

CHAPTER FOURTEEN
Unity

THEY WERE halfway across the Atlantic when Bill broached the subject. 'So, are you actually going to call him?'

Anne shook her head, tight-lipped.

'He's practically in the neighbourhood. And he might be just the one to make sense of this—'

'What good would that do?' She waved the sheaf of notes she was still putting in order. 'All these years of work my father did, on the intersection between psi and technology… as far as he's concerned, he never did it. He doesn't have a hint of all those years because he never lived them.'

'He's still got his marbles, you know. Just not the specific ones you want.'

'He barely even knows me.'

Maybe later, she thought. Maybe when she had more of a grip on what was happening. But the Odds had taken her down such a rabbit hole… The last thing she needed right now was to get to know an Edward – no, Ted – Travers who had no memory of her.

How could that make anything make more sense?

It was nearly midnight their time, almost 7pm locally, barely twenty-four hours after the call, when they finished the drive straight from Dulles Airport to Alistair's hotel.

Stopping to freshen up would only waste time, and would just be papering over the cracks anyway. Anne had caught a glimpse of her eyes in the plane bathroom mirror; that look wasn't going away until they got what she'd discovered under control.

Already hard at work at the table in the living area were Adrienne Kramer and a man who had to be the elusive Major

Bugayev. He took a break from snapping documents with a miniature camera to shake her hand.

'Tanya says hello to you,' he said. 'And *especially* to you, Captain Bishop.'

'Of course she does,' Anne snorted, thinking of the Russian agent who had become almost a friend after their jaunt to the alien planet of Dulkis. A friend who was forever trying to hit on Anne's husband. At first it had annoyed her, but now Anne just found it amusing.

Bugayev smiled wryly; *what-can-I-say.* 'She's a deviant, but she's very good at it.'

'Good job at Bryden's factory,' Bill put in. 'We would never have succeeded in our own break-in if we hadn't had you to blame it on.'

Anne was feeling less forgiving. She didn't want to disrupt things, but she had to say something. 'My friends Edith and Dave Plummock…? You nearly gave them a breakdown.'

Bugayev sighed. 'And my friends got bullets through their heads. None of us covered ourselves in glory.'

Lethbridge-Stewart stood at the head of the table and briefed them. 'I want you to know, what I am doing here is completely unsanctioned. The group of us in this room are acting independently, non-aligned with any of our national governments or armed forces at this point. Aside from a few people at the UN like Captain Kramer here, who are also sworn to secrecy, no one else knows the extent of the problem. So, we're to serve as an international taskforce with the expertise to handle it.'

'Course, I want to get us formally organised,' added Kramer. 'Call us Department X, or Division Zero, or something. But for now…? We're so secret even we don't know what we are.'

They added their contributions to the pile on the table. Bill had brought their entire dossier on the Bryden family, including the information he'd gathered at the factory. Kramer, through her channels at the UN, had got Bryden Industries' overseas financial records, and the delegation from Barbados had delivered the architectural plans for Bryden's refinery there, in case they needed to investigate the Odds at their next stop. And Bugayev had provided a report summarising the records the *Byeliye Volkiy* had obtained on the KGB's psi experiments relating to probability, and the individuals involved. He promised the full records would be shipped to their embassy by diplomatic pouch within the next forty-eight hours.

'All the records the KGB is willing to share with our Army,' he said, with heavy irony. 'I can make no assurances beyond that.'

And now it was Anne's turn to brief the others. She looked to Lethbridge-Stewart and hesitated. 'Some of what I've discovered relates to classified official secrets.'

'Use your discretion,' said Lethbridge-Stewart.

She raised an eyebrow, and turned to Bugayev. 'How familiar are your forces with what we call the London Event?'

'An extraterrestrial incursion. Origin unknown. Biochemical warfare aimed at depopulating the area, some reports of robot drones as ground troops.'

'Not quite as unknown as all that.' Anne took a breath. In for a penny, in for a very personal pound. 'Our first encounter with the entity known as the Great Intelligence dates back to 1935, and Professor Edward Travers' journey to Det-Sen Monastery in Tibet. And yes, he was my father...' She trailed off; Bugayev was gaping with astonishment.

'*Jobanyj v rot*,' he blurted. 'Weikuang.'

Anne blinked. 'I'm sorry?'

'The CID in China. Years ago they... had reason to call our army's experts in over an incident. You're saying this... entity was behind the London Event?'

'Undoubtedly,' said Lethbridge-Stewart. 'We've had further encounters.'

He could see the chessboard behind Bugayev's eyes rearranging into a whole new shape. 'The Chinese Peoples' Liberation Army recovered various artefacts from Det-Sen after they reclaimed Tibet. Have you heard about Weikuang?'

Anne frowned. 'Environmental disaster? Industrial accident. The poisoned Earth...'

'I'm sure the Chinese would be very interested in an exchange of information on this Intelligence,' he said, with unexpected excitement. 'And they may have a lot to contribute as well.'

Lethbridge-Stewart turned to Kramer. Her face showed quiet triumph. 'Fourth vote.'

'We can hope.'

But for Anne, it wasn't reassuring: after years of convincing himself that somehow the Great Intelligence was *known* now, that it was understood, once again there were even more pieces of its puzzle which they had no idea about.

Anne took a deep breath. 'One of the abilities of the Intelligence was that even though it could loosely be described as a psionic force on the astral plane, it was able to interface with electromechanical objects through the power of its mind. Turning its will into direct control. We were able to jam or interfere with it at short range… but we never knew how it did it.'

Now from her suitcase, she produced a small, cobbled-together control box and a half-disassembled silver sphere full of shiny wiring.

'These were in my lab. When I started testing with Dave and Nina… they lit up like a Christmas tree.' She touched the control box. 'This was our own attempt to jam one of the Intelligence's control spheres… and this was Bryden's control box for Weatherballoon.'

A second control box joined the first.

'They both used the same frequency range. We all saw the effects of the Odds using their abilities, the RF interference… They're literally on the same wavelength.' She took a slow, shaky breath, squaring herself up. 'And then there's Weatherballoon itself.'

Again, the suitcase, and a strip of plasticky fabric. Then a close-up microscope photograph, showing its interwoven filaments.

'It's plastic, but not just petroleum-based. There are other natural polymers woven through it, giving it more tensile strength and flexibility. See those patterns on each strand…? Like a fungal mycelium, all connected through it.'

More microscope shots, closer and closer. More detail on the lighter filaments slithering through the darker plastic, branching like tendrils or veins. Lethbridge-Stewart leaned closer, squinting at the detail.

'Look familiar?'

Anne could see it hitting him like it had hit her: that shudder of *I know that shape.* Chaotic but not random, following a pattern which a human eye couldn't make sense of. Like the meaning in a tangle of neurons.

Was his heart thundering like hers?

'A chemical breakdown confirms it.' She met Lethbridge-Stewart's eyes. 'It's plastic made from the Web.'

She saw the realisation sinking in. Everyone knew it was bad, but had they grasped *how* bad?

She held up the most close-up photo for Bugayev. 'This… stuff was the physical form of the Intelligence on Earth. And the man who's running the Odds is building it into his new plastics. He's using Intelligence technology… which the Odds themselves just happen to be compatible with.'

Kramer was staring at the scrap of plastic fabric like a rat on the table. 'Is it dead?'

Anne half-laughed, nervously. 'Inert, yes. But dead? What does that even mean with this thing?'

'But what's it for?' Lethbridge-Stewart thought quickly. 'Bringing the plastic to life?'

'No, I think the plastic is just a distribution medium. But the Web can hatch from it; it's infested, like cockroach eggs. If it got worldwide distribution, and then triggered somehow…' She threw her hands up, shaking her head. 'Truth is, I don't know. But it's there, and it's all connected. Bryden, the Intelligence, the Odds.'

'I thought the Intelligence was… bound? Trapped somehow in our world, cut off from the… astral thing.' Even after all these years, the mystical angle still slid right off Lethbridge-Stewart, and to be fair it barely made sense to her either. 'How could it be doing this?'

'Time doesn't mean anything to this *thing*. That's one of the few things we actually do understand about it. We already know it's crossed its own timeline somehow. If it was trapped here, now, who's to say it couldn't have planted the keys to its escape centuries ago? Just waiting for those keys to move into position.'

'What do you mean, centuries?' asked Kramer.

A tight breath. Anne was keeping control, but almost vibrating with the effort. Bill reached out, put a hand on her shoulder, and she squeezed herself hard into shape.

'According to Dave and Nina, Jonesy traced the Odds' family tree back to a little village near the border between India and China… or rather, Tibet. In around 1735.' She fumbled through her notes for a page torn from an atlas. She pointed to a small dot, an inch or two from where she'd drawn a large red X. 'Which means, this Oddfather originally turned up within walking distance of the first moment of known contact between a human mind and the Intelligence.'

'Jonesy did the East too, didn't he, sir?' Bishop put in quietly.

Anne looked up, meeting each of their gazes in turn. 'We don't have the whole picture yet. But they arrived in this world with the ability to manipulate it, in much the same way as the Intelligence itself did, at the same point. We know they can cause people to not notice things, not talk about them… a null space around events. You know yourself the Intelligence can do that. And they've been spreading ever since. As I said. *Worldwide distribution.'*

Bugayev and Kramer were staring, slowly realising how much they didn't know. She pressed on.

'They might not even know. But it's the most likely answer. The Odds, their entire family tree, have been pawns of the Great Intelligence all this time.'

And Lethbridge-Stewart was just staring frozen at her. He wasn't letting the idea slide off him and getting on with it; no, something hard and impenetrable had slammed down over his eyes.

'No,' he said.

'What do you mean, no?'

'I mean it's nonsense,' he barked. 'There's no way the Intelligence could do that. They'd know, they'd have to.'

'There's no reason, when have its victims ever——?'

'It's fanciful. Conjecture.'

'Are you seriously telling me it's a coincidence that they——?'

'Every damn thing about these people is a coincidence,' he snapped. 'Why shouldn't it be?'

'It does sound unlikely,' Kramer put in dubiously. 'But for them, doesn't that make it more likely?'

'Why are you refusing to even consider it——?' Anne attempted to try again.

'I won't accept it,' said Lethbridge-Stewart, far too intensely. 'And I won't treat them as the enemy. They are our *citizens.'* He looked from Anne to Bugayev and Kramer. 'Ours – yours – the world's.' He turned his glare back on Anne. 'They came to you for *help*, Dr Travers.'

He sounded so firm, but there was something wild-eyed underneath. Anne could just spot it in his stare. Something had set him off. He was only thinking of reasons to say no after he'd decided. But why?

Bill tried to take a moderate tone. 'But if there's something bigger going down, sir, they could be the key to—'

Lethbridge-Stewart cut him off. 'One crisis at a time. Our immediate problem is getting the Odds away from Bryden. If we derail his plans, we derail whatever the Intelligence has going on as well. If anything.'

'It's more than that, though,' Anne blurted. 'We need to *understand* what it's—'

'No, we have to *stop* it.'

'Which is why we have to know! Alistair, do you really think I'd say the Odds can't be trusted if—'

He glared at her, inexplicably relentless. 'I've believed many things over the years, but this is *fantasy*, Dr Travers. Give me something we can use, or nothing at all.'

For a moment she was speechless. She'd seen him do something like this before; it was his weakness and his strength, shutting out the nuances of the inexplicable to focus on the bits he actually had to deal with. But he always did deal with them. Now he was refusing even to consider it.

He turned away, leaning his forehead on his hand, pinching hard, like he was struggling to focus through a headache. 'I know you have personal reasons to feel strongly about people having been suborned by the Great Intelligence. But we cannot allow our personal situations to interfere with what we need to do. We cannot.'

It felt like a slap across her face. For a long moment she, and everyone else, was silenced.

Bugayev shook his head ruefully. 'This spirit of co-operation truly inspires me.'

Kramer, as usual, tried to pull them back to business. 'Okay. Can we at least agree that we have to investigate Bryden's connection to the Intelligence?'

'Of course,' said Lethbridge-Stewart, still looking ashen. 'That's within the remit of this taskforce.'

'I have to say,' Bugayev put in, 'if you want to go beyond these unsanctioned meetings, and establish a formal collaboration between our countries... Dealing with this Intelligence may seem like a stronger reason.'

Kramer pursed her lips, wryly. 'Unsanctioned Non-aligned Intelligence Taskforce,' she mused. 'I could work with that.'

'Taskforce,' muttered Anne. She could feel herself smiling, that corrosive sarcastic smile she saved for moments when she knew the conversation could head nowhere good, but they were going there regardless. 'You make it sound so official.' She turned to Lethbridge-Stewart. 'Like you actually have some kind of authority over the people you say you want to collaborate with, but whose advice you're refusing to listen to.'

Bill looked pained. Probably trying to find a foxhole to dive into before Lethbridge-Stewart opened his mouth again.

The phone rang. Silencing them all.

Anne looked from one to the other. There couldn't be a long list of people who knew where any of them were. None of them likely to be good news.

Cautiously, Lethbridge-Stewart answered it. 'Hello? Yes. I see. Yes, I understand. Of course. At once. Goodbye.'

He hung up, then turned to the others, quietly now.

'Peyton Bryden has just invited me over for dinner,' he said. 'Right away.'

CHAPTER FIFTEEN
(Dis) Unity

THEY'D HAVE to continue working on their plan of attack in Lethbridge-Stewart's absence.

As he left, Anne took Kramer aside.

'Is he showing enough cracks for you now?' she murmured.

Kramer shrugged slowly, uncertain. Anne couldn't shake the feeling that she'd just seen a man bend as far as he could: to the point where he could only revert to type or snap.

But why now?

'Have I told you how we found out about the Odds?' Bryden asked him over a lobster bisque.

Bryden had invited him to a hotel suite in Rosslyn, just across the Potomac, on the Virginia side of the border where they allowed skyscrapers. Thus, rather defeating the purpose of the whole design of Washington DC. From the huge glass picture windows there, Bryden could look down on the whole seat of democracy as beneath him; they weren't quite as high up as the Washington Monument, but the angle gave you a clear sense that you yourself could rival it.

'It was my uncle, Sir Meredith Bryden. All those years he was making his name in the trenches, he thought he had a charmed life. The number of bullets that just missed him... But it turned out it wasn't his life that was charmed, it was the man standing next to him. His batman. Lance Corporal Dickie Tarpeter. Bit of a shambles as a battler, to be honest, but when Uncle worked out that he was his personal good-luck piece, and some of his luck had rubbed off on him somehow...'

'I trust he was well rewarded,' said Lethbridge-Stewart, thinking nothing of the sort.

'Never got the chance,' said Bryden, tucking into his

chateaubriand. 'Poor man made it out of the Great War without a scratch, then pricked his thumb gardening and got blood poisoning. But he became a family legend to us Brydens. Uncle was a strong believer in doing the impossible, and he was sure there were other men out there like Dickie. And he stayed in touch with dear old Mama Tarpeter… And then young Jonesy came calling, trying to trace his family tree.'

'And Jonesy led you to the others.'

Bryden nodded. 'And eventually to you. He really thinks you're something special, Lethbridge-Stewart. Personally, I didn't think you had it in you, but lately I'm beginning to see what he means…'

Lethbridge-Stewart nodded, patiently. He kept waiting all through dinner for the first shoe to drop, let alone the other shoe. Instead, Bryden's staff had served him the sort of fare a villain would serve James Bond before trying to bisect him with a laser beam. Rather too rich for his taste, but still, the wine was good.

'What exactly do you have in mind for me?' he finally asked.

'All in good time.' Bryden sat back, well-fed and contented. 'First, we do need to settle the matter of your loyalties.'

Clearly Bryden was all set to start a good game of cat-and-mouse, but Lethbridge-Stewart couldn't stand either role. 'If you expect me to act against Her Majesty's Government…'

'Oh, don't you worry about Her Majesty's Government. Or Her Majesty herself, come to think of it. You know, I still wonder if that family doesn't have a bit of Oddness in it themselves, do you think? It would explain rather a lot of this past century…'

'Nevertheless,' said Lethbridge-Stewart, and let the word hang there.

Bryden gazed out the window. 'Captain Kramer remains unembarrassed.'

There we go. 'Neither Kramer nor her superiors ever mentioned the subject,' said Lethbridge-Stewart. 'I could hardly tell them there were no such thing as Odds if they didn't seem to be aware of the Odds in the first place. That would rather raise the question.'

Bryden gave him a hooded-eyes look. 'Very smooth,' he said airily. 'And how are you planning to expose me to General Hamilton and your superiors? While still protecting your own skin, of course.'

'I have to say, I'd very much like to know the answer to that.'

Bryden smiled, and it didn't reach his eyes. 'Do you really think they'd support you? After what you've already done?'

'I don't know what you mean.'

Bryden motioned to someone over Lethbridge-Stewart's shoulder.

'I'm deeply disappointed in you, Lethbridge-Stewart,' said the voice of General Hamilton.

He froze. Hamilton himself was pacing up beside him, heels clacking crisply on the marble tiles. A low menace in his voice which took Lethbridge-Stewart right back to his days at Sandhurst, when Hamilton would haul him in on the carpet as a cadet. He was in full dress uniform, and crossing the room to stand next to Peyton Bryden.

Very carefully, Lethbridge-Stewart put down his spoon. 'General,' he said formally. 'I didn't know you were in town.'

'Evidently not. Or you wouldn't have been conspiring with a known Soviet agent.'

'You did rather blow Bugayev's cover back in New York,' Bryden put in amiably. 'Still, you weren't to know the staff here were already keeping an eye out for you. We were curious about your partner, and the general ID'd him.'

'I told you not to involve the Americans,' glowered Hamilton. 'You involved them anyway. I told you to keep a low profile before the Soviet enquiry. I find you helping the man at the heart of it infiltrate the office of a British national.' He bore down on Lethbridge-Stewart, relentlessly. 'I thought you had respect for Queen and Country. Clearly I've been mistaken.'

Lethbridge-Stewart felt his back stiffening, defensively. 'Sir. I don't know if you're aware of Mr Bryden's involvement in—'

'Oh, I'm aware. Why did you think I kept telling you your investigation was a waste of time?' Lethbridge-Stewart stood up, reflexively at attention, receiving the dressing-down as if he were back on the parade ground. 'We've known about the Brydens' pet project for years. But the more questions you asked, the more you risked the rest of the world finding out about it. That's why we told you not to keep digging.'

'We, sir?'

'Oh, the people who matter.' Bryden was sitting back, trying not to relish this too obviously. 'We're all friends in high places, you know.'

'Am I to take it that the Odds are being used as an official government—?'

'Don't be a fool. Of course it's deniable. Bryden's developing this all on his own. But if anything ever comes of it, he has agreed to make them available to our nation as we need them. Because he understands loyalty. In a way which I now severely doubt you do.'

So much for Jonesy, then. So much for all of them. Bryden's offer of independence to them had been a sham all along. And the old school ties had Hamilton trusting in Bryden's loyalty to the Crown, turning a blind eye, with no idea just how blind.

'There may be larger issues in play, sir. A global threat. The Great Intelligence—'

'No alibis,' barked Hamilton. 'No what-ifs, no conspiracy theories. If you wanted to be listened to, the time for that was *before* you exposed one of our most secret assets to both the Americans and the Soviets.' His eyes were ferocious. In all these years Lethbridge-Stewart had never seen Hamilton on a battlefield, but at this moment he believed he could kill a man out of raw anger. No way he'd listen to the truth right now… even if Lethbridge-Stewart were sure what the truth was.

'You do understand I had no idea about your… arrangement, sir.'

'You shouldn't have needed to.' Hamilton bore down on him, and Lethbridge-Stewart found himself instinctively straightening. 'You've spent too much time crossing borders lately, you've forgotten who our enemies actually are.'

Hamilton slowed as they came eye to eye; there was a look in his eyes now which Lethbridge-Stewart hadn't seen in nearly twenty years. A furious disappointment. Somehow that rattled him more than anything.

'How many generations of Lethbridge-Stewarts have served our country? And now you. Dammit, man, what would *Fergus* say?'

His great-to-the-fifth-grandfather's name was like a whip-crack across his face. Lethbridge-Stewart lowered his eyes. There were no words.

'Fortunately,' Bryden put in smoothly, 'you've got an immediate chance to redeem yourself.'

'Yes,' glowered Hamilton. 'If Bryden is right about you, you yourself could be the single biggest strategic advantage our nation has seen since we invented the longbow. That, right there, is the reason you aren't being court-martialled already. Do not mess this up.'

This was madness. 'Sir, you don't seriously believe that I'm one of these, these—'

'I have no idea. And, unlike you, I'm not afraid to admit it.' Even though they were more or less the same height, Hamilton was still able to tower over him. 'Even as a cadet, you were always convinced you were right, and the only reason you still have a career is because you usually are. But today you are very wrong indeed.'

He looked at the general's condemning eyes, knowing he was supposed to be feeling shame. Instead, it was his own hollow sense of disappointment. All these years he'd known Hamilton to have a keen strategic sense of the larger battles going on in the world. Now his focus on those battles were actually blinding him to the ones even bigger than that.

Hamilton crossed to the end table, where the phone sat. 'Now. You are going to call up the foreign agents you're collaborating with and terminate your arrangement immediately. That is a direct order. Your investigation is over.'

'Sir.'

'And then you are going to work with Mr Bryden to determine whether you're one of these Odds or not.'

'Is that also an order, sir?'

'Of course not,' snapped Hamilton. So, he still wasn't willing to put the Odds on the record, then. 'But if you return to the United Kingdom without his approval, I'll see that you're brought up on charges over the information you've fed to the Soviets. Is that understood?'

'Yes, sir.'

Slowly, Lethbridge-Stewart walked to the phone. There had to be some card left he could play. Any card of any kind.

'If I turn out not to be useful to Mr Bryden, sir, I trust I will be allowed to return to my duties? I don't want to be dispensed with the way that Nigel Plummock was.'

The general didn't recognise the name.

'A freak accident,' Bryden said smoothly. 'He blames me.'

'You're wasting time.' Hamilton stood by Lethbridge-Stewart's shoulder as he dialled the phone. 'Do not explain, do not justify, tell them nothing.'

No cards left.

He could feel Bryden's smile prickling on his back.

'Oh, it's *never* all over,' seethed Kramer, looking at Anne. 'No way in hell.'

The call had come while they were working out the best way to infiltrate the Panorama complex in Barbados, by land or by sea. Anne had taken the call, and had to break the news to the others.

'He sounded like he was under orders,' she said. Her own voice sounded shellshocked, she noted from a long way away.

'Which means we're blown,' Kramer muttered. 'Someone above him knows. So not only am I compromised, probably everyone I work with too.'

They'd already scattered across the room; Anne and Bill huddled by the phone, Kramer pacing like a caged tiger, Bugayev sitting wearily at the table, staring at the useless intelligence.

Kramer turned, trying to address them all as a group. 'We all know this is too big to let go, right? Way too many stupid and dangerous people are waiting to get a hold of these guys. On every side.'

Bugayev said nothing.

'We don't have a choice,' said Bill. 'He ordered me back to base ASAP.'

'I never imagined he'd give in,' murmured Anne, dazedly. 'That's the oddest thing of them all.'

'Doesn't mean I'm going to.' Kramer swept the papers together into a pile.

Anne could almost see the slow-burning fuse to her anger. Nowhere near exploding yet, but she didn't want to be around when it did.

'I suppose there's not much we can do now, officially,' Bill suggested. 'But if you need to contact us in the UK…'

Kramer stopped, stared at them. Eyes narrowing behind her glasses. She walked up slowly towards them, quietly piling up words with every step.

'The way I figure it, someone must've blown our cover. Someone who knew about Weatherballoon, and the Odds, and us meeting here. I can think of one likely suspect. One guy who's been to Bryden's factory. On his own. Multiple times.'

Bill gaped, looking staggered. 'Now come on, you don't think…'

'Oh, I do think. You shoulda spotted that by now.' She looked at Bill and smiled mirthlessly. 'Blackbird's got a bite, doesn't she?'

She turned away to leave them, only to hear the door already clicking shut. Quietly, while they'd been arguing, Bugayev had stood up and melted away like a ghost.

Hamilton didn't let him out of his sight till the others had all gone.

When Lethbridge-Stewart got back to his hotel room, they'd cleared away all the evidence as well. It was as if nothing had happened, when so much almost had.

He rattled vaguely around the room, at a loss. He felt concussed, like after the car crash.

Maybe Hamilton was right. Perhaps these decisions really were outside his authority, and his duty lay in defending the realm rather than anything so overambitious. He could remember Hamilton's lectures at Sandhurst, the clarity of the principles he'd driven into all the cadets. Perhaps the general's unofficial arrangement really did outrank his own unofficial arrangement.

But the more he tried to give up, the muddier and more sordid he felt. Not that that gave him any sign of where else he could go from here.

Finally, when the time-zones aligned, he phoned home.

'Hello?' Fiona's voice was tiny and tinny. He could hear every one of the miles between them.

'Hello, darling. Is everything all right, where you are?'

'Hmm. Not bad. Nothing much to report, sir. Working on an armistice with Pennington over the elm.'

'And the little one?'

He could hear her grimace. 'Doing backflips, all night. I swear.'

At that moment he wanted to hold onto her as hard as she always held onto him.

'Fiona,' he murmured, and hesitated. 'I'm going to have to stay away for a while longer. I don't know how long. And I don't know if I'll be able to be in touch again.'

'Oh,' she said. He was hoping she wasn't coming to dread

these calls. 'Do you have to go right now?'

'Not until the morning. My morning.' He was no good with words, he really wasn't. 'Be strong.'

'Never you doubt it.'

He didn't know what else to say. She let out a long hollow sigh. 'When will it all be over?'

Part of him wanted to say it already was.

CHAPTER SIXTEEN
Chance of a Lifetime, in a Lifetime of Chance

THEY HADN'T even checked into their hotel yet.

By the time Anne and Bill drove across town to their much less lavish room, their body clocks were pushing 4am. Anne fell back on the bed, not even bothering to undress.

'I'll see about rebooking our tickets in the morning,' Bill managed. 'No one'll hold a good night's sleep against us.'

'What's the use,' she said faintly.

He lay down beside her, fully clothed, on top of the bedspread. Arm draped over her, holding her close from behind.

'Nobody wants us to save the world this time,' she murmured, eyes closed.

'I could just change one ticket,' he said gently. 'They can't order you back home. You're on your own time.'

'Kramer won't even want to talk to me.'

'Perhaps if I'm not around.' He looked rueful. 'I think I blotted my books with her.'

What would be the point? They were all here because they trusted Alistair. Without him, there was more to divide them than bring them together.

'They'll know I stayed here. It's obvious why. They'll ruin both our careers over it.'

'Well, you could make it clear you're staying for another reason.'

'What, then.'

She felt him hesitate. 'Your dad.'

Flinch reflex. 'He's not my father, he's… there isn't a word for it. Just another kind of oddity.' She was mumbling, the words unfiltered. 'I barely even know him. I'd have to build a whole new relationship with him.'

'Don't we all have to do that anyway, once we grow up?'

She scowled, but it felt like a release. 'Don't you go all Arts and Humanities on me. That's not why I married you.'

The infuriating thing was that it was the obvious answer. The younger version of her father had at least some knowledge of the Great Intelligence; he had history with Kramer, and could act as a go-between if needed. It made perfect sense.

Morning.

It was just her and the phone now. Bill had left for the airport; he'd made his case, but he knew her better than to think he could argue her into finishing that number she'd left half-dialled. She'd have to argue herself into it.

Oh, she was fine at finding a rational approach to dealing with the unknown, maybe even the unknowable, she'd built a whole career out of that... but in cases like these she slammed into an undeniable truth which still completely failed to make *sense*.

The only truth that mattered was *the world took your father away, then gave him back broken*. It left her with a man with her father's face who never knew a daughter. And to him, he wasn't even broken.

But no matter how many jangling echoes Ted's face and voice set off in Anne's head, she would work with him, because the need to come together in the face of that unknowable void was far more urgent than that which kept them apart.

'Hello,' grumbled her father's voice through the phone. 'Travers.'

She took a deep breath and began again.

Once she got to New York, they lasted a whole two hours before she wanted to throttle him again.

She'd arrived full of ideas, digging out the Weatherballoon circuit diagrams, and the bits they'd reverse-engineered of the Intelligence's control sphere, to try to work out how it and the Odds made the link between their minds and the physical world.

Ted just waved all that away. 'That's your field, not mine.'

But you taught me, she wanted to say. Her father had taught her everything he knew about electronics... Everything he'd learned in the years after his return from Tibet, all the years which were completely missing from the man before her. Could this backdated, divergent Edward Travers even read a circuit diagram?

Instead, he'd retreated to his books, there in the back of the bookshop he now ran on Tenth Avenue; a dark place packed with the philosophical, the scholarly, the mystical, and the wilfully obscure. He kept moving from shelf to shelf, rummaging and collecting, while she grasped at straws.

'Different realities created by different choices,' she murmured. 'The Intelligence reaching into its past to safeguard its future. Putting you on a different path than before, like it put Alistair and his whole family on one.'

'Wasn't the Intelligence, girl,' Ted said. 'I have explained this. I was pulled away and split in two by this.' He waved the ring on his hand, and the crystal embedded within.

He was right. Blaming the Intelligence still made sense to Anne, though, after all it was a cave imbued by the Intelligence that initially sent him forward in time. And if that hadn't happened, he'd never have needed to travel backwards again, and thus wouldn't have been split in two...

'Fine,' she said. 'Nonetheless, we still have the Odds, making choices on a level we can't really choose on...' She screwed up her whole face with frustration. 'There's a pattern here, I just can't make the connection into something *real.*'

'Never mind your theory,' he said bluntly. 'You've started from the wrong end.'

'I started from the evidence.'

He snorted. 'But you didn't stop there, did you? What you're saying, it's too all-inclusive. Intricate for the sake of it. You're aiming to get everything to add up together. But maybe only some of it adds up, eh? Maybe some of it isn't part of it at all.'

So, you're saying my theory makes too much *sense,* she thought to herself. 'All right, we'll start from the data we got from the hardware...'

He still wasn't satisfied. 'You can't reverse-engineer the Intelligence's aims from its tools,' he barked; never mind that her father had spent decades trying to do exactly that. 'You have to understand it first!'

His tone hit her with a child's memory: her heart jumping as she heard her father's voice taking a bite out of someone in the other room. Never her, at that age, but she knew even then he was a real bear of a man when provoked. He'd had to be, he'd said years later, because of all the folks who wanted to take a poke at him: the mad anthropologist who thought he could really find the abominable snowman. But for years, when she was young, he'd protected her from that.

This Edward Travers was not a gentle man. Perhaps that's what having her had brought him. So perhaps this one had never learned to soften or doubt himself.

Softly, softly, then.

She breathed in through her teeth. 'All right, then… Where would you begin?'

'In here,' he said, digging through a sheaf of notes, and grabbing books from a back shelf. He was looking for a specific reference to something, but resisted explaining until he had it in his hand.

'You never used to wear this much tweed, did you?' she observed, watching him work. 'Not even in the old photos.' The younger Edward Travers had prided himself on being a working anthropologist. He'd always looked much more comfortable in the field in an anorak or grimy trousers, than dressing up as a gentleman.

'It's for the customers,' he muttered dismissively. 'Oh, they love the old-fashioned British eccentric. The young people – the latest round of flappers, whatever they are – they think I'm positively retroactive. It was all the rage in Swinging London, apparently.' He hmmph'ed. 'My London was far too solid ever to swing.'

'So, you're leaning into the caricature.'

'What else can I do? Got to cover my ignorance somehow.' Without looking up, he waved a hand at the books surrounding him. 'Thirty-odd years of context, new knowledge. I could spend the rest of my life just catching up.'

'A man out of time.'

'S'pose.' He frowned. 'Hardly fit in then either. Ah!'

He jabbed a finger at the pages in the two open books before him: cross-checking an anthropological book on Tibetan Buddhism against a translated religious text, both with lengthy hand annotations.

'Just because it's called an Intelligence doesn't mean it's *rational*,' he said. 'It's got some of the traits of an enlightened human mind, but most importantly it's still driven by hunger, by this profound need. The shadow of Sunyata, they called it, a sort of great Unintelligence which can dominate even a mind like that.' He turned his sledgehammer glare on her. 'So that's where you're going wrong. You're thinking like a strategist, but it's an *obsessive*. It's driven. It does what it *must*.'

Sounds to me like you're making the Intelligence in your own image, she thought.

'All right, then,' she said, rather sweetly. 'Now let's go back, and look at the data, and you can tell me what you think the Intelligence would want with—'

'No, now you're coddling me.'

'Oh, for—!'

He raised a finger, interrupting her. 'You got used to mothering him, didn't you? Humouring his moods, waiting for him to see sense. Because his brain went soft and you were the sensible one, am I right? Well, I'm not him. Don't shrug it off; *listen* to me.'

She tightened. But somewhere in that growl, she heard a hint of something pleading. And she tried her best to unlearn the past couple of decades.

'Driven by hunger,' he said. 'A devious mind, but a simple heart. Whatever it's doing, feels simple to it, if not to us. What's the nearest piece of the pattern? What does it want?'

'It needs to escape.'

'Well, what kind of unlikely things would it need for that to happen?'

She didn't have an immediate answer, but she saw something in the question. Another burst of memory: she was sixteen, her father was first teaching her about electronics, he'd been encouraging her to ask questions, and she still remembered the delighted look on his face when she'd asked one which made him say, 'Do you know… I honestly have no idea.' Something about whether it was possible to turn radioactive decay straight into an electrical current, since they were both just moving electrons. But they'd batted the question back and forth, and she could see the idea unfolding in his mind as well as hers.

That man was still in the room with her right now too.

'I'm not sure,' she said. 'But what if…'

But he wasn't playing along. Every time she thought she was making a connection, he slapped it down as an unsupported flight of fancy.

'For heaven's sake,' she finally exploded. 'The bottom line is, we have all this evidence that the Intelligence has been—'

'No, we don't.' That stung her. 'That's what I'm saying. It was there, yes, but there's no evidence of a *plan*. It might not even be the one in charge.'

'But if the Intelligence created the Odds—'

'*If* it did. Even that doesn't mean it's part of a masterplan. You keep saying the Intelligence created me, but I was a complete accident. Always was.' He scowled, turning inwards. 'All the way back to Tibet, I just blundered in.'

'So far as we know.'

'*No evidence.* Don't get paranoid, girl.'

She snorted. 'That's rich coming from Mad Travers.'

Now that stung him right back. He levelled a glare at her, with a pointed finger for emphasis. 'The things you've studied, if they're not calling you Mad Travers by now, you're doing something wrong.'

'Oh, I'm just quieter about it.' And they were off, getting each other's backs up. It was doubly infuriating, because she knew this didn't have to happen; they'd already proved years ago that given a big enough crisis she and he could work together just fine. But apparently this wasn't life-or-death enough yet for them to let it all go. 'Honestly, Fa— Ted. You didn't care about evidence when you thought they were all out to get you. You *loved* having enemies, it energised you. Gave you someone else to blame for anything that went wrong, whatever the evidence said.'

She still remembered the back-page newspaper clippings from mum's scrapbook: 'Mad Travers off for Tibet'. As a child her blood had boiled too, at how unfair they'd been. Only with a grownup's eyes had she been able to see how much of his Society's scepticism was down to his own combative attitude. He'd relished the fight, really, and doubled down on his expedition out of sheer spite.

And years later she'd talked to one of his early financiers, and the phrase he'd used was 'conniving swine'. Her father had had no compunction about telling people whatever suited him. In Tibet, she'd learned, he'd let a man (the Doctor, no less!) be blamed for murder, even after being pointed to evidence that he couldn't have done it, just for long enough to keep a perceived rival out of the way… She'd had a stark moment of realising just how much his obsessions could blind him.

Well, not this time. If he didn't want to be her father, there was nothing to stop her from telling him what she thought he was.

She kept her voice level and hard. 'You're so sure you know this thing, but you can't see where it ends and you begin. It's not your personal bloody ID. It's not limited to the bits you know. So don't tell me it can't be right when it's just that you don't like the answers we're getting. There is *something* there that makes this all make sense. Whether it's simple or complex, I don't know, but it is our *job* to grab this problem by the throat and shake the truth out of it! All right?'

Ted Travers was just looking quietly at her. 'Were you like this as a child?'

She stopped in her tracks, speechless.

Now his voice was gentle. 'So angry at the universe for not making sense. For not being fair.'

More memories, unbidden: hot childish tears, her voice a desperate keening whine, and Father's wavering voice trying to gently explain why Mama wouldn't be coming home, ever, ever, ever.

There was no way he could possibly have known that. 'How…?'

'I was the same way,' he admitted. 'If I couldn't see the sense in the world, it was infuriating. Terrible tantrums. Even now, I suppose.' And it was true, he'd been like that until his dying day. 'So hungry for truth.'

'It's worth holding on to,' she said quietly.

'But perhaps some things only make sense locally, not globally.' He spread his hands, indicating the two of them: their whole mad twisted lives. The two of them in that room.

The last thing she'd expected from this was insight. Maybe there only were a few pieces of this that made sense. Maybe that was the only way to make sense of it at all, in fact, not to try for a coherent Theory of Everything…

Oh good Lord, she thought, *an enemy who thinks in the same all-encompassing way you're thinking, who's responsible for everything that's going wrong around you? Honestly, Anne, you're both textbook cases.*

She sank into a chair, on the same side of the table with Ted, sitting almost shoulder-to-shoulder. 'That's my problem. It's not that you and he are too much alike. *We're* too much alike.' *Probably more so than Father and I ever were,* she added. *After all, I never knew him at your age…*

'Pair of stubborn old goats,' he echoed.

She took a long moment, then tried to push herself into goat-wrangling mode. 'All right,' she said, ever so gently. 'Let's start over. Look at all the evidence I brought, and see if any pieces make sense with—'

That finger was raised again. 'Watch the coddling. Remember now. I'm a big boy, who's—'

'—who's still got a full bag of marbles,' she chorused along with him. He blinked. She looked levelly at him. 'He said that too. Pretty much every time.' She gave him a completely raw look. 'Clearly, he liked the phrase, he just never remembered he'd already used it on me.'

Now it was his turn to look punctured. 'I think it's the first time for me.'

For a long moment, they both sat there, cursing the darkness.

He murmured, 'I'm still on course for it, aren't I.'

'What do you mean?'

Slowly, he sighed. 'I've resigned myself that one day the Intelligence will be the death of me. Won't mind going out fighting. But do I even get that choice?' He shook his head, tapped his temple. 'What are the chances that this, this pudding in here will go soft on its own, rob me even of that?' He turned to face her, to really look at her. 'You've seen it happen.'

Could that be it? He didn't doubt himself, but he doubted this other life he knew so little of…? Even with his own choices, if they really were choices, he had to wonder if the chances would break the same way.

'We don't know,' she murmured. 'You don't know it'll happen to you.' Something caught in her throat. 'He didn't even know when it was happening.'

'But I've been warned now. Well in advance. Both me and him, we were touched by the Intelligence in Tibet. After all, we were the same person then. And the Intelligence waited for him… It'll wait for me, too.' He paused, squinted, musing. 'Perhaps I'm a second chance.'

'For yourself, you think?' she said gently. 'Or for it?'

And for a moment, the big old bear looked tiny. 'I've no idea.'

She looked at him, and suddenly shook her head, and heard herself saying 'No. Either way, it's one for you.'

And it made no sense, but dear God she *wanted* it to make

sense.

Unsteadily, she drew a breath. 'And he had me to look after him.'

He shook his head, fussily. 'You've already lost your father. I can't ask you to go through that again.'

'He didn't ask me to go through it the last time. I did anyway.' She managed a shaky smile. 'But I'll tell you what. If I tell you to take your meds, you take your meds, all right?'

He took that with good grace. 'Promise.'

It took ages, but at least it *felt* like they were making progress.

They still had no concrete evidence, but Ted's reading of the texts was at least allowing him to set up hypotheses which she could test or knock over.

Finally, an awed whistle from the front of the shop grabbed their attention. A thirtyish black man – plainly dressed, solidly built, a cherubic swagger – was surveying the display books. 'Damn. That is one solid collection of weird.' He was looking like he owned the place, which irritated the man who *did* own the place. 'You the great white yeti-hunter?'

'Great white yeti *finder*, I should hope,' Ted said gruffly, sizing the man up. 'And who might you be?'

'Oh, just a go-between, goin' between,' the black man said with a cheshire-cat grin. 'Friend of yours wants to meet up, cause something's going down. Says she's looking for some great intel.'

Anne smiled, equal parts amused and prickled. 'This is Adrienne Kramer, isn't it?'

The man looked at Ted. 'Who she?'

'*She* is Anne Bishop,' said Anne. 'Adrienne knows me. We'll both be there. And tell her not to worry, it's just us.'

They met in a lounge at JFK Airport, in a swooping terminal building full of gleaming white curves and canopies. Kramer looked like she'd been burning the candle at both ends with a blowtorch.

'I've been checking all flights to Barbados, from here and DC, playing Spot the Odd,' she said. 'Looks like they're all down there now. The good news is, Lethbridge-Stewart went with them as well.'

'That's good news?' asked Anne.

'Gives us a target,' said Kramer. 'Maybe an ally on the inside. Maybe.'

'So how do we find out what they're up to?'

Kramer shrugged. 'I was hoping you could tell me. And soon. Cause… I also spotted a Russian national flying from DC to Seawell, that's Barbados. Name no one's heard of; passport looks like Bugayev.'

'He's going in.'

'Yeah.' Kramer took a slow breath. 'So, looks like I'm going in.'

'You're joking.'

'We started planning it before it all went south. Infiltrating the compound.' Kramer shrugged, looking only slightly out of her depth. 'It's gotta be done. Got Vern here and a few of his boys to back me up.'

'Gotta assume they'll be shooting at you,' said Vern, gently concerned.

She gave him a wry smile. 'C'mon. I can hit the broad side of a barn, so long as it's not moving.' She turned to Anne and Ted. 'But I could use some brains in the vicinity too. How're your visas looking?'

'Terrible,' demurred Ted. 'A constant source of frustration.'

Anne couldn't see anything to stop her going. She steeled herself and nodded an okay. 'But we have no idea what we're getting into.'

'Yeah, well, that's why I'm here,' Kramer said. 'Anything you got.'

Now it was Ted's turn to hesitate over his answers. 'We don't know for sure. Don't know a blasted thing, really. With so many of those Odds in one place, they could get up to almost anything. But if it is the Intelligence, the way I know it, and it wants them all together… There's one possibility that comes to mind.'

He turned from Anne to Kramer, and his eyes were reflecting something that chilled him, which only he could see.

'Hunger.'

Anne shivered as it hit her. 'They're being harvested.'

CHAPTER SEVENTEEN
Random Chants

OM. OM. *Om. Om.* Pack up your troubles in your old kit bag and *om, om, om…*

That sound had been pounding on and on for days now, echoing off the warehouse walls. A couple dozen of them, sitting in a circle, hands linked like a séance, keeping the moment going. Him just one part of the loop. Swapping in and out at the start and end of his shift. The relentless plod of the chant, an endless industrial throb like the refinery machinery in the compound just outside.

Om. Om. Om.

He'd never imagined enlightenment being so blastedly dull.

Wasn't he supposed to be hallucinating or something? He thought this sort of thing was supposed to give you mystic visions, show you the way forward or some such. His nephew, Owain, had tried to explain it before, but even then it had all sounded like nonsense. And now, when he tried to clear his mind, it came up with nothing more poetic than that blasted flower, opening over and over again, with each beat of the *om*. Honestly, things went more squiggly when he closed his eyes after staring at a bright light. If this is what the hippies were on about, they could keep it.

Your mind's wandering again, man. You know what to do, just note that that's happening and go right back to your basic mental image. Visualise a peaceful blue sky, just like Jonesy taught you. But under the sky, there was still that mucky churn of bubbling thoughts, never quite breaking through to the surface; all the thoughts he *should* be thinking, instead of just sitting here and going along with it all.

There should be a plan. Should be a strategy. But every time he tried to pull those half-hatched ideas to the surface of his mind, that *om* kept crushing them to powder. Impossible to focus, impossible to settle, even on the chant itself.

To him it felt like the sound of giving up.

He'd always thought of himself as having a disciplined mind, but when surrounded by the absence of anything but that one thudding sound it was astonishing how much his thoughts jumped around. Nothing to do, nowhere to go, no clear way forward, the same four walls around him. All that was left to grab his attention from moment to moment was the inside of his own head.

The blue sky. Everyone think of a peaceful blue sky. Hold it, focus it, *squeeze* it. Nonsense like that. Not very authentic as Buddhist meditation techniques go, Jonesy had said, but it gets the job done. What job? Jonesy said it was to get them all in sync. For what?

Om. Om.

About every two or three minutes another Odd arrived at their designated positions in the circle, tapping the shoulder of the person they were replacing at the end of their scheduled meditation shift. Arrival and departure times staggered through each hour, for minimal disruption to the mental workflow. His own shift started at 9:12am. They practically had to punch a timecard; they each did six sessions across a twelve-hour day, one hour on then one hour off to recover. Jonesy, and his other closest acolytes who he'd trained to run the circle and 'direct its energy' when he wasn't there, did two hours on the trot. And after hour twelve they just smoothly transitioned to the night-shift crew, who did exactly the same thing, and the *om* kept circling the clock until they took it back over the next morning.

How many days had it been now?

No idea. Good Lord, he had no idea.

Honestly, neither an actual North Korean prison camp nor an Iron Curtain brain-scrambling centre had left him feeling as *vague* as he did now. Back then he'd been able to hang on to his sense of duty. But now the man who gave him his sense of duty had ordered him to co-operate. So, what now?

Even on his breaks he still felt the *om* echoing, in the thrum and whine of the refinery's machinery. A distant scream in the canteen, a rumbling pulse in the streets of the complex. He and the Odds were nearly confined to barracks, in an accommodation block built inside the fences, kept away from the business end of the refinery's workings. There was some green space near the perimeter, plenty of time to socialise, but no real escape inside from the grim steel and concrete, the vague petrochemical stink. Not the way he'd hoped to see an island paradise.

And Nallers' sniper eyes, always on them. Jonesy's tormentor was head of the security detail assigned to them all: the man blocking every locked door. The one making sure there were always guards on the perimeter, always someone within earshot. Sharp beard, sharp eyes, blunt instrument. And the worst kind of ex-soldier, one who had got out of his time in 23 SAS(R) not a respect for the principles of military service, but merely respect for his own ability to kill. Oh, he could see it on Nallers' face: a sledgehammer's pride in his ability to push the world and make it move, and to hell with anything else.

Bryden at least had afforded him some privileges befitting a brigadier's rank; on his breaks he was allowed to use the executive beach. A small but highly secured back gate led into another fenced-off patch of woodlands, and a winding track down the slope into a pristine pocket of Caribbean coastline. If you looked the right way and kept the refinery out of view, you could imagine that the world around you was completely unspoiled.

It was there that he'd found Peyton Bryden, industrial visionary, lying on a cheap sun-lounger with a large martini by his side. Looking the right way. Suit trousers rolled up, shirt half-unbuttoned, not a care in the world.

'Ah, Lethbridge-Stewart, how's it coming along?'

His head had still been throbbing from the echoes of the chant. 'Waiting for the other shoe to drop.'

'Hmm?'

Blue sky was all very well, Lethbridge-Stewart explained, but he was still waiting for Bryden to assign them to do something real. Something that would give him some idea what all this was actually in aid of.

But Bryden had just looked away, squinting at the horizon. 'You know, Lethbridge-Stewart, there's barely been a cloud in the sky since you all started chanting. In fact, we've checked the radar. There hasn't been a single storm brewing across the whole of the Caribbean in all this time. I think it's going rather well, don't you?'

You're wandering again. Get back to the sky. The blue sky isn't a metaphor for anything, you're actually making it blue. Or are you? All this time, all Jonesy's earnest teaching and crack-brained philosophy, and he had no idea whether all his sitting and thinking and *omm*ing were doing anything at all.

'You're like stabilisers,' Jonesy had said. 'The high-improbability folks in the circle are pedalling the bike, you're keeping them from falling over.'

'Am I really? There's no way to tell.'

And Jonesy had shrugged. 'Well, you're making me feel better at least.'

Jonesy had wandered off, looking hollow-eyed. Whatever those drugs were which Bryden's doctors had put him on, to enhance his perception in the circle, outside of it they seemed to have left him vague and sedated. As if the fight had gone out of him. Or perhaps it was like he said, about when he couldn't save Nigel: a force pulling him towards normality and inaction which even he couldn't overcome. This place made the intolerable routine.

Now that Bryden had them here, he had their identities, safely locked in the records room. If the Odds ran, he could find them, as surely as he'd found Nigel Plummock. That threat would outlive him too: if Bryden himself perished in an unexpected accident, or Nallers in an entirely expected one, this compound was packed with employees who would take over smoothly and without question; they'd keep pursuing the Odds for as long as they thought there was value to be extracted from them. Strange to think that Bryden's will could outlive his body. The line between Bryden himself and Bryden Industries had never seemed less clear or relevant.

'There was a thread,' Jonesy had told Lethbridge-Stewart, one night in the dormitory, as they prepared for another night of dreams full of *om*s. 'A line of choices, that gets us through all this somehow. I can still feel it… But I can't find it.' The fight had gone out of him. Or perhaps it was himself the fight had gone out of, and Jonesy had just picked up on that.

He should be searching for the plastic. Was it done here in the refinery, that whole Web-laced concoction? How did it fit into Bryden's plan? But whenever Lethbridge-Stewart so much as looked at one of the electronic security doors leading into the main buildings, there was Nallers, a glowering shadow just at the edge of his eyeline. He needed a strategy, and nothing was coming together. Thinking was like wading through treacle. Hard to see a way forward from the endless circling *om*.

He should tell Jonesy about the plastic. Get him to open a few doors and look. But how would he even begin to explain what it implied? Try to present it rationally, the idea that they had been used, that *we* had been used, that *I* had been… No. His whole mind shuddered like a struck gong at the thought. It couldn't be real. No. No. *Om.*

Om. Om. Bryden *(om)* has only got one *om*… yes, well.

'So, what exactly is all this for?' he'd finally asked Bryden, on one of his beachside escapes. 'Are you planning to sell good weather to the highest bidder?'

Bryden had looked, surprised, then thoughtful, as if he were working out a price list. 'No, it's much simpler than that for now.' He was walking along the edge of the surf, trousers rolled up, casually soaking his toes in his private ocean. 'A bunch of those greenie scientists are doing a big study of weather patterns in the Caribbean, all this summer. They're claiming that oil and coal are causing more storms through global warming, or is it cooling, I don't know, their story changes every year. Anyway. Won't they be surprised when their data shows nothing of the sort. A nice thick layer of doubt over their story… Could set them back years.'

'I'm not sure what your interest is in all that.'

An isn't-it-obvious raise of his eyebrow. 'Well, it's always good to be useful to the Seven Sisters. I talked about it with them at one of our lunches; they were all grumbling about the study, and I thought, you know, everyone talks about the weather but no one does anything about it.'

This was the first glimpse Bryden had given of who else was backing him.

'The Seven Sisters?' Lethbridge-Stewart had asked, as neutrally as possible.

'Well, the whole cartel, really.' Bryden had spotted an interesting shell in the surf, picked it up, then discarded it into the waves. 'You know, Exxon, Mobil, British Petroleum – Shell – the seven majors.'

'So. A favour for your petroleum suppliers,' Lethbridge-Stewart had concluded, almost disappointed. 'For your plastics.'

'Of course,' Bryden said casually. 'Imagine what it would

do to their share price if people believed that nonsense.'

'If it's nonsense, why do you have to go to all this trouble?'

And Bryden gave an angelic smile. 'Oh, it's nonsense *now.*'

It all sounded so tiny and petty, put like that. What was that phrase Kramer had used about men like him? *Born on third base, can't steal home, so he tries to buy the baseball diamond.*

'General Hamilton seemed to think you were doing it for Queen and Country.'

'Ah, the old school tie.' Bryden savoured the sea air. 'Oliver thinks old loyalties are the be-all and end-all. I see them more as a starting point. We can't be afraid to explore opportunities beyond them. Don't you agree? Well, obviously, otherwise you'd never have fallen in with Kramer and Bugayev.'

'I don't understand.'

'Hamilton's a good man. Unfortunately, we need a great one.' Bryden was outright courting him now. 'Someone with an international perspective. A strategist. Someone who has a direct understanding of what you people can do... And a sense of the possibilities.'

'Are you offering me a job?'

'You already have a job. I'm offering you a promotion. Even a position on the board.'

He hadn't given an answer.

But then there was Jonesy, who'd started twitching the moment he'd told him about it. 'Come on, mate, I'm not even an evil genius and I can still see what he could do next.'

'I'm sorry?'

'Well, it's the reverse of what Dr Travers wanted to do with Dave, isn't it? Any time anyone tries to study something scientifically? Anything at all? You can skew it. Make 'em get laughable results. Or inconclusive ones. Or just the results you want. Think about it. Election polls. Pollution levels. A world where you can never even check any kind of facts if Bryden's mates don't want you to.'

That thought kept swirling around and around in his head. Relentless as the *om.* If he'd learned one thing from Anne and all her stubbornness, it was that science had to lead, and people who respected truth followed where it led. Science was their intelligence service in their battle against an unknown universe, and an army was only as good as its information. If Bryden could skew even the biggest pictures... Truth itself becomes malleable. Like half-melted plastic.

'Imagine a world where it no longer matters whether a butterfly beats his wings.' Jonesy shook his head, just barely, as if scared to move now. 'My God, what have we done?'

Lethbridge-Stewart had seen such a look on Bryden's face back there on the beach, as he'd rambled on. So complacently ruthless. 'That's the trouble with those international bodies, the scientists, all those thinkers,' Bryden had said. 'They're so reality-based, they're stuck in it. While they're all cautiously and carefully trying to understand the world… we get on and change it. Move fast, break things. And then they're just left trying to cautiously and carefully understand what we've done.'

It had been that same look Lethbridge-Stewart had seen on Nallers' face – an unthinking pride in his own ability just to push.

Bryden really didn't know what he was doing. But then, neither did Lethbridge-Stewart. And he couldn't rely on the cavalry to get him out of this; the cavalry had told him to collaborate.

Perhaps this was as far as he should go. He could just resign. Chuck it all in and try being a father for once. He and Fiona had such important things to do. If the army would turn on him like that… No, that was madness. But a madness that wouldn't just go away, any more than this blasted pounding *om*.

Jonesy had tried to snap him out of it, one night in the dormitory. The chanting still echoing faintly from the warehouse next door. Staring with those glazed grey eyes, trying to pass on whatever strength he still had.

'I can't find the thread, but you still can.' Jonesy had grasped his hands, unguardedly, and he'd flinched. 'Don't let go. Just be who you are.'

But who the blazes was that now? A brigadier without a brigade, a soldier without an army behind him, a husband without his wife. (Goodbye to Barbados, farewell old Times Square, it's a long, long way to Craigentinny but my heart's right there…) Trust your instincts, Jonesy had said. But his instincts had brought him right into this mess.

So hard to get a grip on any of it. No, it wasn't like he'd forgotten who he was. But there were so many bits, things he'd let slide out of his mind over his life. James, that first kiss with Jemima Fleming, the child he'd been back in Bledoe. So far away.

Some of it the Intelligence had made him forget… Was that why he could still believe he was an ordinary man? Was it still whispering to him even now?

Perhaps that was what he could feel, roiling under the surface of that relentless *om* in his head. A sign of how hollow this world he'd imagined was… This was Bryden's world, where corporations were people and society wasn't even a thing, a man of the world whose whole world was himself.

Om.

Something to do.

Om.

Ideas bubbling up below his surface, like globules in a lava lamp. He couldn't see inside them, but he could feel them willing him. Time to move. What would he do? He knew he would know when he got there. Time to move.

He felt it swelling as he waited, *om, om,* until the tap on the shoulder released him from the circle. He stood, *om,* feeling like he was floating. The world distant, fisheyed, the *om* echoing on through him. He walked through the concrete streets into the main office block, coasted up the steps to Bryden's wood-panelled sanctum. Vaguely he saw the receptionist wave him through.

Bryden looked up, faintly curious. 'Yes, Lethbridge-Stewart?'

He knew what to do. He just sat back and let his body do it. 'It is time, Bryden.'

From a long way away, he felt the words falling slowly out of his mouth, dragging and rasping.

Om.

'The moment has come. Take me to my Web.'

CHAPTER EIGHTEEN
All In

BRYDEN RAISED his eyes from his desk. Careful and controlled now.

'Do I take it I am addressing the… creature known as the Great Intelligence?'

'You know me, Bryden. It is time for me to act. Take me to my Web.'

It all felt so easy, just to be still. Let the voice fall out of his mouth, the words like drool, without his brain getting in the way.

'That may be difficult,' Bryden said cautiously. 'The only samples of actual Web we obtained never left our laboratories in England.'

'You have been using it. Spreading it.'

Bryden stood, spreading his hands, backing away. 'That's our own synthetic variation on your, ah, substance. We reverse-engineered it, we wanted to use its unique tensile properties in our plastics, but our version can't recombine, it can't grow. How did you find out about—?'

'Do not question me,' he rasped. He advanced on Bryden. Every step felt like he was falling and then catching himself. 'You have my Web. Bring me to it.'

Bryden smiled, his nerve beginning to fray. 'I'm afraid it's useless to you. Now, if you're looking for some sort of, ah, license agreement—'

He bore down on Bryden. Growling.

'What have you done with my body?'

The door banged open behind him. He started to turn, but a brick wall hit him and his face smacked into the carpet, he twisted, but a body bore down on him and Nallers' face was scowling into his. Gun to his temple, ready for a headshot.

Peyton Bryden exhaled, steadying himself. He stood over

Lethbridge-Stewart, his face leaning in from above, upside-down in his vision. Visibly shaken but asserting control.

'Now, I'd prefer it if you'd leave this man's body, he's rather useful to me. So, I'll give you thirty seconds to do whatever you have to do to go away.' Nallers jabbed the gun in for emphasis. 'But I want you to know, we knew you might try to return one day – and *we are prepared*. Do you understand?'

'Good Lord, man,' Lethbridge-Stewart said hastily. 'You didn't really believe all that, did you? Honestly. I thought I was rubbish.'

'Oh, you *didn't!*' exclaimed Jonesy. He nearly fell off the picnic table he'd been sitting on, in the bare concrete basketball court in the recreation quarter. 'So, what did Bryden say?'

'He was not amused. In fact, he's bringing General Hamilton down here to beat some sense into me.'

'Could be a good chance to beat some sense into *him.*'

'My thoughts exactly.'

Still, that about wrapped it up for the Great Intelligence theory. The gathering of the Odds had been a pet project of the Bryden family, the development of new plastics had been a minor ongoing venture for a completely separate R&D team at Bryden Industries, and pretty much the only person who was aware of both was Peyton Bryden himself. Who, if he were an agent of the Intelligence trying to distribute it around the world, had just proved himself to be a completely rubbish one. The use of the plastic fabric which had so alarmed Anne on Weatherballoon…? A complete and utter coincidence.

'Like I said, we get that a lot,' Jonesy said.

And, apparently, they'd got it in ancient history as well. He tried asking Jonesy more about the Oddfather's arrival, and his own travels to Tibet, but Lethbridge-Stewart could never place either of them closer than about fifty miles away from Det-Sen. Astonishing in the grand scheme of things that they could have been that close with no connection between them, but that's all it was. Just being weirdness magnets again, as Jonesy put it.

He had no idea whether Anne would be relieved or disappointed. Clearly, she'd feared the idea of an intelligence controlling everything, but she'd got her teeth into it as well. That way at least there would be a pattern to discover, sense to be made. But he hadn't liked the sense she seemed to be making of him. And for him, it was rather more comforting to accept that this world was just one damned thing after another, and the best he could do was deal with them as they came.

And the actual conspiracy was such a petty, tawdry thing. Jonesy seemed to have more idea of the potential of Bryden's use of the Odds than Bryden himself did. Terrible things were bound to happen eventually, but the man making them possible had the barest grasp on what they could be.

'I've been trying to get the message through to Bryden,' Jonesy said, sitting and smoking disconsolately. 'About Nallers having killed Nigel. But he doesn't want to know.'

'Plausible deniability,' Lethbridge-Stewart said.

Jonesy snorted. 'More than that. All his type are the same. Anything that's inconvenient to him, it's just not happening to him. It's somebody else's problem. Nallers is the bloke he pays to make problems like that go away. And then he pays other people to make Nallers' problems go away.'

'How much do you know about him?' asked Lethbridge-Stewart.

'Bryden?'

'Nallers.'

Jonesy shrugged. 'Bugger-all, really.'

'I told you we pulled his files. Edwin Bryce Nallers. Late of the 23rd Special Air Service Regiment, Reserve. Honourably discharged, just. Second son of Ronald Nallers, and Felicity Bryden.'

Jonesy just stared for a moment. Then he laughed, a cracked, weary sound. 'Well whadaya know. He's just been protecting the family too.' He sprawled back on the picnic table, staring blankly at the sky. 'All those rich bastards. Bloody Cosa Nostra. Behind every great fortune there's a crime.'

'It's a common attitude,' said Lethbridge-Stewart. 'At least you've got some idea of a bigger picture beyond your own people.' He paused, pointedly. 'You and Captain Kramer.'

'Oh, come on,' sneered Jonesy. 'You think her lot give a damn about—?'

'All this time you thought she was working for the CIA, she was risking her own position for the good of the world.'

Jonesy just rolled his eyes. 'You don't really think—?'

'She was investigating you independently. Like me. I helped her cover you up to her superiors myself. And yes, this was *after* she knew you'd tried to kill her.'

Jonesy blinked, and a whole series of expressions flitted across his face, before he finally settled on rueful embarrassment. 'Well, I'm a berk, aren't I.'

'Frequently,' said Lethbridge-Stewart. 'But not at the moment.'

He had to be fair. Jonesy was still reflexively disruptive, pointlessly mystical… But Lethbridge-Stewart couldn't fault the way he looked after his people. The times he'd seen Jonesy reassuring Nina, as she spun through a spiral of anxious thoughts, or communicating in broken Punjabi to a family who barely understood where they were but trusted him with their lives… Well, he'd never make an officer in any army Lethbridge-Stewart would recognise, but Jonesy made an excellent herder of cats.

'We still need a way to get you all out from under Bryden,' Lethbridge-Stewart went on.

Jonesy sighed. 'Long as there's money to be made? He'll never back off.'

'You said there was a thread through this.'

Wearily, Jonesy threw himself back on the picnic table, shaking his head at the sky. 'Why d'you think I said I need you to spot it? If there were a chance in front of me, I could grab it. But there's too many choices between here and there, I can't see the way through… The thread just led me to you.'

Good on tactics but weak on strategy, thought Lethbridge-Stewart. The man was still intolerably… No, that wasn't it, he was *tolerably* erratic and sloppy. And it was surprising how much randomness Lethbridge-Stewart could take in his stride when he had to, really. Like Kramer had said; whatever it takes to win.

Whatever it takes, he thought.

'Jonesy,' he murmured. 'Once General Hamilton gets here… there might be a way.'

The night Hamilton arrived, Lethbridge-Stewart was still on his meditation shift. He clocked off at 8:12 precisely, replaced in the circle by a similarly low-key Indian man called Haresh for the night shift.

At 8:27 he crept back in, with a wide-eyed and anxious Unsteady Eddie in tow.

Looking as brisk and business-like as he could in front of the bored security guard, he strode up to the circle, where David and Nina were sitting next to each other, their fingers intertwined as they kept the chant echoing on. Lethbridge-Stewart nodded to Eddie. Eddie tapped David on the shoulder. David, surprised, not expecting to be relieved for another forty-five minutes, nevertheless yielded his position in the circle to Eddie. Nina looked on, bewildered, throwing anxious eyes at Lethbridge-Stewart, not daring to break the chant to ask. He prised her fingers loose from David's, then planted her hand on Eddie's. He could see the jolt of panic hitting her like an adrenaline rush. But he gave her nothing, looked as forbidding as possible.

Before he dragged David away from her, he leaned down to mutter harshly in her ear.

'Whatever you do, don't think of a storm.'

Jonesy was waiting outside, to fill David in.

'We're making a move,' he said. 'I'm going back in to run the circle.'

'Find more of the high-improbability Odds who are off-shift,' Lethbridge-Stewart told David. 'Get them to take the place of the low-improbability ones like Haresh. Swap them in one at a time. We want the stabilisers off.'

David looked even more dubious than usual. 'You sure you know what you're doing?'

'Absolutely not. No one in this entire operation knows what they're doing, and we intend to make that extremely clear.' Lethbridge-Stewart stalked off towards the administrative block, where General Hamilton would be waiting. 'And tell all of them I *do* want them to think of a storm.'

He was a bit more ready for it this time.

Bryden clearly wanted him to feel like he'd been called into the headmaster's office. But seeing Oliver Hamilton in civilian clothes, flushed in the unaccustomed heat, was more like realising that your headmaster was really just a middle-aged man with his own troubles at home.

He could still give him a thrashing, though.

Lethbridge-Stewart took great pains to point out that outside of that whole impersonating-an-alien-intelligence incident, he'd been giving Bryden an exemplary degree of co-operation. Bryden couldn't actually fault him on that. No, they still couldn't say conclusively whether he was an Odd or not, but then being conclusive about them was hard by definition, wasn't it? And fortunately, Hamilton had actually grudgingly understood the reason why Lethbridge-Stewart had pulled the stunt he had, beyond *it seemed like a good idea at the time.*

'Oh, *really*,' snorted Bryden, pacing his own conference room in frustration.

'If he'd been right, you know what a catastrophe it would have been,' said Hamilton.

'But he *wasn't* right.'

'It's not our job to take things for granted, sir,' said Lethbridge-Stewart.

'You could have just *asked*, man!' snapped Bryden.

'Could I?' Lethbridge-Stewart left that hanging there for a minute. 'When we're dealing with a threat as beyond our knowledge as the Great Intelligence, we must make sure that no one's been compromised.' Hamilton nodded. 'We have to be sure of everyone's motives.'

Suddenly a plant administrator pushed open the door. 'What is it, Michael?' Bryden snapped.

'Ah, excuse me, bit of a flap on, we need you down in Operations—' And he hastily escorted Bryden out by his elbow, leaving Hamilton and Lethbridge-Stewart alone.

'Well,' said Hamilton in the sudden silence.

Now or never, thought Lethbridge-Stewart. He kept his voice formal, deferential. 'I've been thinking very seriously about what you asked me last time, sir. About what Fergus Lethbridge-Stewart would think.'

'Well?'

Lethbridge-Stewart squared his shoulders. 'If he were alive today, I think he'd be most astonished to learn that we were no longer at war with the French.' He met Hamilton's eyes, as firmly as he could manage. 'The world has changed, sir. It's still changing. And I think you should be more concerned with how Bryden wants to change it further.'

Thunderclouds formed on Hamilton's horizon. 'I told you, man, if you don't co-operate—'

'I am co-operating, sir. And I am reporting to my superior

that Bryden's methods and his goals don't align with our own. The Odds are unstable, but he's already pressed them into service – and not for us.'

'Ridiculous. He assured me—'

'He told you what you wanted to hear, sir.'

'Unlike you, I suppose?'

Lethbridge-Stewart shook his head. 'He told me what he *thought* I wanted to hear. He assumed because I was willing to work internationally, that meant that I thought the same as him. He's not interested in the national interest.'

'You're hardly in a position to lecture me about someone else's doubtful loyalties, Lethbridge-Stewart…'

Lethbridge-Stewart remained undeterred. 'Do you know why we're here, sir? In Barbados?'

'Privacy,' said Hamilton. 'Away from oversight.'

'I mean why this refinery is here, sir.'

'Do tell.'

'Taxes,' said Lethbridge-Stewart. 'Did you recognise Michael?'

'Who?'

'The plant administrator. One Michael Bryden.' Once again Kramer had spotted the key details in the files. 'Their forgotten son, so far as Inland Revenue is concerned. His residency is split between Barbados and the Cayman Islands. And Peyton's transferred most of the family assets to his name, to keep the tax money out of Her Majesty's hands. No doubt including the money he's getting from a consortium of seven multinational oil companies, who are funding these experiments with the Odds for their own benefit.' He saw the surprise hit the general's face. 'Every step of this project has been engineered to keep the benefits flowing to him, and not to us.'

Hamilton glowered defensively. 'He should have briefed me. The security implications—'

'Are of no interest to him. Peyton Bryden's idea of being a citizen of the world is to have responsibility to no country at all. To hell with Great Britain, he wants a greater Bryden.'

Hamilton was turning away, trying to think, but Lethbridge-Stewart kept closing in.

'And you're trusting this man to do his patriotic duty.'

'You're being damned impertinent, Alistair.'

'Talk to him yourself,' said Lethbridge-Stewart. 'Tell him

I tried to warn you about his deal with the Seven Sisters, but it actually sounded quite good to you. See how much he tells you then.'

Hamilton was wavering. Careful not to push it. *Remind him of your duty, your loyalty, play the straightest bat you can.*

'Sir. You assigned me to the Fifth Operational Corps after the London Event because we both believed that there are forces out there which are more dangerous than nations. Some of them are right here on Earth.'

'Surely you don't mean Bryden—'

'When he's using the Odds? Very much so, sir. He could effectively give nuclear capability to the highest bidder.' And if he'd timed things right, before the night was out Hamilton would be seeing the destructive abilities of the Odds first-hand. 'If the corporations are not acting in our interest, nations must stand against them.' *And sometimes,* he stopped short of adding, *we must stand together.*

The conference room door banged open. Bryden himself stood scowling in the doorway.

'You've got some explaining to do, Lethbridge-Stewart. I want you down in Security. You too Hamilton, you'll want to see this.'

A CCTV freeze-frame in the security command post. A black-clad figure caught slinking out of the back of a Panorama semi-trailer, dashing for the edge of the pool of light in the loading bay. Zoomed in on the shadowed face: Captain Adrienne Kramer.

'Good Lord,' said Lethbridge-Stewart.

'Oh, you've been co-operating,' grated Bryden.

'I assure you I have no idea what she's doing here.' Lethbridge-Stewart could feel Hamilton's eyes on him, accusing again. 'You know I've had no contact with her since then, you made sure of that yourself.'

'And you didn't arrange this in advance?' demanded Hamilton.

'How could I? I had no idea I'd be—'

'Well, you've got a chance to prove it,' snapped Bryden. 'Stop her.'

Nallers' voice crackled from a radio. 'We don't have eyes on her. She's been leading us a hell of a chase.'

'Right, Alistair,' said Hamilton, fixing him with a glare. 'Given what you knew when you were working together, if you'd been planning a break-in, what would you have done?'

If Lethbridge-Stewart prevaricated even for a moment, he'd lose any chance of convincing Hamilton of his honest intentions. 'Find the Odds. Make contact with some of the ones we know, try to get intelligence on what you were doing with them. Residential quarters. Secondary objective, investigate the plastic—'

And Bryden was already barking orders, directing Nallers and his men to the Odds' barracks. He and his underlings kept scanning the scattering of CCTV monitors for any trace of Kramer.

Which was good, Lethbridge-Stewart thought, because it meant that no one was noticing the background of those CCTV views: the thick cloudbank gathering offshore, clearly visible in the moonlight through the perimeter fence.

So long as Bryden kept expecting Lethbridge-Stewart to betray him with Kramer, he'd be more likely to be blindsided by the Odds' action, and not to suspect his involvement. Hamilton too, really. The Lethbridge-Stewart they knew had built his whole career on stabilising dangerous situations… The last thing anyone would expect would be for him to deliberately make things *less* stable. Lean into the chaos.

He wasn't afraid of the oncoming storm. He was prepared to handle it.

So long as he could last long enough to get to it.

More voices on the comms channel. 'Simmons here, sentry at 4J. I've spotted the intruder, seems to be heading for the pipeline.'

'Well get after her!' Bryden leaned into the mic. 'All units, converge on 4J.'

'Hang on,' murmured Nallers. 'I've got her here, at 2F. Looks like there's another man with her. Halt or I fire.'

BANG! Lethbridge-Stewart jumped. Nallers hadn't even raised his voice for his 'warning'.

'Did you get her?' asked Bryden.

'Nah. Pursuing.'

'But 4J? We may have another hostile,' said Bryden.

'Could be Bugayev,' Hamilton said quietly. 'If the Soviets get their teeth into this…'

Rather more chaos than one had wanted, thought Lethbridge-Stewart.

'Shit!' shouted Nallers. A blast of static, or was it a burst of steam? 'Damn woman opened one of the pressure valves.'

Bryden was clutching the back of a technician's chair. 'Well close it!'

'Working on it. All units, if you're not converging on 4J, try 2E.' They could hear Nallers' glower through the radio. His voice was murderously flat now. 'Permission to be sick of this shit, sir.'

A pause. Bryden bowed his head, pinching between his eyes, as if he had a migraine. 'Just get them out of my way.'

'With pleasure, sir.'

Bryden wheeled around, then jabbed a finger at Lethbridge-Stewart. 'Tell me you don't know anything about this.'

'I sincerely don't, Mr Bryden.'

'Then get out of my way. Hamilton, watch him. Get your man back into line.'

Adrienne Kramer crouched among the pipes, breathing hard, gun at the ready. Cursing her desk job, she wasn't built for this, but it's gotta happen. Too many lives at stake.

If she died here what the hell story were they gonna tell Donald? Sir Colin and UNION had better have a convincing story for her superiors, about why she went off to some hotspot. What country was Donald going to end up blaming for taking her away?

Vern crouched behind her, covering their rear. 'Good a place as any to keep them busy,' he said. 'You split, they won't know we've split up.'

Her breath caught in her throat. 'You sure?'

He beamed. 'Never. But I'll keep 'em moving.'

She raised her walkie-talkie. 'You keep in touch.' Oh God, she wanted to leave him with a smile. 'Hope to god you're a better shot now than in the old days, *Assassin*. Don't forget, I know where your bodies aren't buried.'

He clapped her on the shoulder and turned away. She took slow breaths, rallying her nerve: *they shot first, they'll shoot again, you know you gotta be ready to take them out. This is the real thing. It's what all that practice on the firing range is for.*

You can do this. You can beat the odds.

Nina, clinging to the hands on either side of her, feeling like a telephone wire full of screaming calls crackling down her line.

Don't think of a storm, don't think of a storm, but she can feel it lurking around the back of her mind waiting to pounce, the more she tries not to imagine the clearer it gets. It's like being on the world's tallest rollercoaster and there's no brakes, and then there's no rails, and then there's no coaster…

'They're going to kill her, you know.'

'He didn't say that.'

'Nallers will, and Bryden will turn a blind eye. And then you'll turn a blind eye.'

'That's enough.'

Lethbridge-Stewart could hear the first rumbles of thunder now, here in the conference room. The moment closing in. Hamilton wouldn't meet his eyes. Hamilton was trying to think, but that's the last thing he wanted to give him. No more time to rationalise it away.

'All to protect a project you've kept from your superiors, which Bryden has already betrayed to international conglomerates.' He paused for emphasis. 'Not the sort of thing you'd want them to hear about at my court-martial.'

'I said enough!' Hamilton turned away, pulling tight, grasping for his sense of duty, if not principle. 'Whether Bryden is double-dealing or not, we need the Odds. If not to stay ahead, then to stay in the game at all.'

'They will murder her, and they'll get away with it. Because you've kept this whole project unauthorised and unaccountable. Why have you never made this operation official?'

Hamilton shook his head, pained. 'Bryden didn't want the complications.'

'Then there's no one who can hold them to account but you.'

He put himself right in Hamilton's eyeline. Now he could see how the man who'd taught him at Sandhurst had ended up here. He'd kept this in the grey area because he could convince himself the rules didn't apply. Everything around the Odds was marginal, flexible, unlikely. Everything could bend. But Hamilton was also the man who had drilled into him the principles which should guide an officer in the first place. That if some things couldn't be done the right way, they shouldn't be done at all.

'I can salvage this, sir. Let me find her.'

'Out of the question.'

'Sir, you are asking me to do nothing to prevent the murder of an allied officer.'

'I'm telling you to protect the interests of your country. *Do not interfere.*'

Hamilton's mouth was set in a determined line. Convincing himself it was necessary not to know any better, even though he did.

Lethbridge-Stewart drew himself to attention, held himself there, meeting his eyes.

'You'll have to make it a direct order, sir.'

Hamilton stood there, eyes blazing. The thunder rumbled, on and on.

'Damn you,' Hamilton snarled. But he turned away, shoulders slumping, and Lethbridge-Stewart knew not only that he had won his battle, but that Hamilton had won his own. 'Go.'

CHAPTER NINETEEN
100 Little Brigadiers

IT WAS in the moment. Not that moment, of course, the next one. All the next ones, really.

We were all grasping hands in the circle… It's like holding a high-voltage line. Your heart vibrating in time with the current. Across the circle, I'd locked eyes with Nina; she was all wide open with anxiety, hands clutching onto strangers. She was panicking and, of course, she was thinking about the storm. And that was feeding that first ripple of chance, a tiny wrinkle of wind in the sky… which I could catch, and *squeeze* into a bigger one, then an even bigger one. And all the extra high-improbability Odds that we'd swapped into the circle – Oddular modular, eh? – they were amplifying the instability. And once it was wavering enough… that whole steady rhythm of their thoughts that had been tamping down any storms… out of step, now it was like a wave machine for the sky. Everything out of phase, the power pouring in; the butterfly effect about to sting like a bee.

I was pulling the storm towards us. A thousand tiny nudges, the one little chance that could lead to something bigger, spinning it round and round into a mini hurricane. The thunder running right through me. I was getting flushed, gasping with my own sense of, well, possibility. I don't want to know what my *oms* were sounding like.

I'd never been able to do this before. But with the whole family behind me? Holy mother of God it felt good.

And I could see them all! The guards in the alleyways of the complex, running round a maze; trails of them ahead of where they were, where they could be about to go. I'd worked out there was a flap on. I could even spot Kramer losing the guys who were after her. I could focus in, see her hiding among the pipelines, focus a different kind of way, see all the Kramers who were about to be. Squint hard enough and I could see a whole web of where she'd go over the next few minutes.

But if I reached out to try to give her a nudge... I could feel it all wobbling under me. I had to keep a grip. I couldn't push anyone out of danger, not without letting go of the reins of the storm. It was like running on a treadmill and counting your paces. Takes your brain and your body to do it... but at least you can still see.

So, it was all down to the brigadier.

I could see him: pressed flat and upright against the admin-block wall, gun at the ready, eyes scanning for guards. Feeling the wind whipping up round him, the time trickling away. Doing what he's meant to do.

How do I explain what I could see?

Imagine him breaking into a hundred pieces.

A hundred hims, all overlapping and blurring right now, all at the start of the paths he could be about to take. Each one containing a whole lot more different ones within it, that'll branch off down the line, but these are the big ones.

And a hell of a lot of them, I can already feel how they'll go sour. It's hard to make sense of if you're not in my head, but with the storm whipping up and the wind squalling and the rain like darts, it's like every sense is cross-wired right now. And most of the futures I can see bound up in him taste like blood and metal and rot.

But at least one doesn't.

If he can be that one.

He moves. Left/right/straight-ahead. Already the futures are peeling away. A couple go left and I can already feel how they'll end – those hims will never find Kramer, everything goes to hell, there's explosions and destruction and none of us walk away.

Almost all of him go right, cause he knows what he's doing.

A hundred little brigadiers, looking for their fate. Couple take a wrong turn, then there's ninety-eight.

He's in the shadows, slipping past the residential block. Far as he figures, Kramer didn't make it to her main objective – him – so she'll try her secondary one. The refinery floor. Hide out inside, find out what she can about that plastic. She was just at the pressure valves near 2F, so he knows which door she's heading for. He can cut across and get there.

But he ducks back under the eaves. Nallers left men on guard outside the accommodation block. And Nallers is with them. They're clustered round the side of the building… crouched round a box at the base of the wall. Calling in.

'Sir, it's definitely an incendiary device. Could blow the whole building.'

I freeze so hard I nearly let go of the storm.

Oh God, half my people are in there. They're really gonna kill us all, just to keep us out of Bryden's hands. So much for Kramer helping us out. But Kramer didn't even get to the building. Someone else planted it…? Who?

But my grip is slipping. I've got to keep the *om* going, like breathing, hold on to it cause if there's any chance of us getting through it this is the only way…

Nallers' radio just squawked at him, and he's answering. 'Defuse no, remove yeah, gimme time.'

Nothing I can do. Nothing the Brig can do either. He slips round the corner, his cloud of possibilities all close together. Ninety-eight presents all about to happen. I focus in on the leading one.

In all of them, no way of escaping it, he's creeping towards the corner as Kramer inches towards it from the other side. He's brisk, business-like. She's crouched, taut, terrified.

He steps out. Stands startled in front of Kramer.

She recoils. So does her gun.

I nearly scream. There's a hole in his head where his left eye should be, he's falling backwards and smacking in a heap on the pavement, and I don't know if there's enough of him left to see the anguish on her face as he dies.

That's one.

The one next to him gets shot in the throat. Same effect, but slower and more agonising, and Kramer is still fighting to stop the bleeding when one of Nallers' men puts a bullet in her own brain.

The one next to that one, the bullet catches him in the shoulder, they make it through a gasping conversation, and I get a glimpse of him leaning on her as she half-carries him away. But they're too slow, they'll never do what they need to do in time, and I can feel the howling winds and the big bang lying in wait for them.

Another, and another. All the different ways a bullet can tear you apart, over and over.

Nineteen of him, shot.

But all nineteen of them are sliding out of focus, and finally it clicks that those are the ones that *haven't* happened. Just chances peeling off into the distance of never-was. Seventy-nine Lethbridge-Stewarts *weren't* shot. They pulled back round the corner before Kramer's finger clicked on the trigger. Maybe three of them, she never fired, but in all these chances his reflexes still kicked in. He's still alive, and he's still alive cause he's good.

Seventy-nine left.

'Kramer!' he barks. His words, it's like they're swamped with reverb, all the other possibilities, only becoming clear in the moment after they're spoken. 'What's your objective?'

'Stop Bugayev.' They hurry off for the cover of the pipelines. 'We came down here to see if we could get me in, get to you. Then he came down too, loaded for bear, so we had to move fast.'

'You know he set a bomb?'

'We guessed, yeah. You?'

He gestures at the swaying whistling branches just beyond the fence. The wind is whipping up, the first fat raindrops smacking into them. 'That storm… The Odds. We destroy this place, we convince Hamilton and Bryden that the Odds can't be stable.'

'Yeah, well his pre-emptive strike is pre-empting your pre-emptive strike.'

They move, a cloud of him and her all spread out and rippling.

'They sighted him in another sector,' the Brig tells her. 'They thought he was you. Our best chance of stopping him.'

'Got it. Sir…? It's good to see you.'

That's the last thing she says before the bullet tears through her from behind. Through one of her. The stragglers of her had been just far enough behind for Nallers' squad to catch sight of her, and get a shot off or chase them down. Fifteen, sixteen more of her and the brigadier get spotted, and zigzag off in a bunch of directions. I see them die in the alleyway, or in a cul-de-sac between buildings, one brigadier makes it for several minutes and only gets shot near the perimeter fence. But sixty-three of him are stealthy enough that they're both still alive, and they're the ones who stay real. Call it instinct, call it luck.

Whatever that one sweet future is, it's still in there.

I look ahead of them, seeing if I can spot this Bugayev. A black shadow in a wetsuit, hiding among the oil tanks in the storage depot. Crouching down, planting another bomb. Cutting the Gordian knot there, getting rid of the Odds and all Bryden's plans at a stroke. He must be so proud.

Can they find it in time? I can't see how. But that pesky tang of hope hasn't gone away.

The wind is beginning to whirl. The first fat drops of rain hitting closer together, spattering in sideways. The perimeter fence rattling in the growing gale. I can't stop the storm now even if I wanted to. But it's not going to hit its peak until after the timer reaches zero.

I can see the Brig and Kramer barrelling towards the oil depot. They've worked out that Bugayev's not likely to stop with one bomb, he'll want to cover his tracks. It's the most likely target.

If the tanks go up now, the wind will send the burning oil whipping all through the complex and beyond. A firestorm, a fire-front racing through the forest, across the island, faster than the rain. A chance we'd never seen coming. And now it's even odds.

Bugayev's ready to make a break for it. Back to the beach, the way he must've come in. He'd have been out of the range of a blast there. But even he hadn't bargained on a windstorm, of course the weather was clear when he started out. And now he's hearing footsteps…

He crouches in cover, raises his silenced gun. No blur on him. The chances of him being any different than he is are pretty much none.

The sixty-three brigadiers and Kramers are scattering around the depot, all searching their own paths. Cautiously checking for fields of fire. Oh, if only they were all real, they'd have the place searched in no time. But only one of them will actually happen.

Fifty-six of the brigadiers don't get shot right away.

Nine of those only survive because Bugayev takes out Kramer first.

Four of them, Bugayev never fires. He waits 'til they pass,

then runs hell-for-leather for the security fence by the beach while they search for the hidden bomb. I don't know whether he makes it clear of the firestorm, or whether he burns with them. Those are the first chances to fade.

The other brigadiers and Kramers, they're all scrambling for scraps of cover. The firefight takes seconds, or minutes, depending on which one you focus on.

My head's racing, I can see all of this in an instant. I still can even now, it's burned into my head like the world's biggest freeze-frame. Chances taken and missed. Whole futures rising and falling on the tiniest turns of corners.

Four of the brigadiers get shot by Bugayev. Five of him get shot by the security guards who get there three minutes later, and wade into the whole mess guns blazing. One of those dies putting a bullet through Nallers' heart; that one almost feels satisfying except I can still feel us all screaming in the firestorm when the bombs go off six minutes after that. Kramer gets killed thirty-five times, Bugayev fifty-one, twenty-two of them by the brigadier himself, his hand steady, and cursing the road that led them there.

Forty-three brigadiers to go.

In five of them they kill Bugayev, then run out of time looking for the other bombs. Everyone burns. In six more, they abandon the search for the bombs, run back to alert us, and start trying to evacuate everybody. Three of those get killed by security before they can even start. The other three get to us in the warehouse and get a breakout started. Some of us don't burn. He does, because he's still inside trying to get the others out when it happens. With me beside him.

Altogether, I die sixty-seven times. All of them full of fire and wind and rain and lightning and screams. Even now I can still feel those deaths hurtling towards me like a freight train.

That leaves thirty-two of him who find the bomb in time. Three of whom get shot while hurling the bomb over the perimeter fence. Four others get shot a bit after.

So, in twenty-five of those chances the brigadier walks out of there alive, with or without Kramer, with Bugayev dead or gone. They've got rid of the other bomb, and he's still able to help us try to escape when the storm hits. In four of them we fail, he's discredited if not killed, and after all that we end up back under Bryden's thumb. The rest... We get away, scatter into the shadows. And the world goes on just like it was.

To my tiny little eyes, that'd look like a win. Twenty-one out of a hundred; a victory against the odds.

All those possibilities dancing before my eyes, and I'd never have spotted a bigger picture in them.

Twenty-one out of a hundred, and in the end none of those twenty-one is real.

Because the one that becomes real and solid, is the one where fifteen seconds into the firefight, Brigadier Alistair bloody Lethbridge-Stewart lowers his gun, and bellows into the howling wind.

'Grigoriy! For heaven's sake, man, there's another way!'

CHAPTER TWENTY

Rolling Thunder, Rolling Dice

THUNDER CRACKED the sky, louder than the gunshots.

'You hear that?' shouted Lethbridge-Stewart. 'That storm didn't exist an hour ago. The Odds are about to break out of here. You don't need to destroy this place, they're about to do it for you!'

No answer from the shadows by the tanks. He squinted, couldn't spot Bugayev.

Kramer joined in. 'Lemme guess. They briefed you to take out Bryden and keep the Odds out of anyone's hands? By any means necessary, right? Well, it's *not* necessary! They want to get the hell out of our hands too!'

'They're civilians, man,' shouted Lethbridge-Stewart. 'Take your people home.'

Finally, Bugayev's voice, echoing from somewhere. 'How do I know you won't—?'

'We'll all go with them! You can watch us every step of the way. We can work out the security once we're out of here!'

'Trust but verify, right?' added Kramer.

Silence. He and Kramer huddled behind the corner of the building, raindrops whipping them in the eyes, over and over. Glancing around for any sign of Nallers' men, as the seconds dragged on.

A hand waved from the shadows. It was followed by the rest of Bugayev, holding the deactivated lump of plastic explosive.

'I had no choice,' he said sardonically. 'You talked so much, I wouldn't have had time to get clear.'

The storm didn't so much break as fall like an avalanche. Building up steadily and relentlessly beyond all reason. The rain had already been pelting them in the oil depot, wind tearing through their clothes, but by the time they got back to the alleyway it had gone from scattered heavy droplets to a steady downpour, and then to sheets of stinging rain.

Within minutes, by the time they got back to the residential block, it had increased on the standard British weather scale from *a fair bit* to *quite a lot* to *good Lord.* Lethbridge-Stewart, Kramer, and Bugayev leaned into the gale, forearms up to shield their eyes.

At least the security guards had retreated in confusion to somewhere less wet. And Nallers had disposed of the first explosive device. Wide-eyed faces were peering out of the main door to the accommodation block. Kramer headed for the building to take charge, but Lethbridge-Stewart stopped her.

'We need Jonesy!' he shouted.

They slogged across to the warehouse, where the circle of Odds was still hard at work chanting. He motioned to Kramer and Bugayev to wait, and they huddled just outside the door. Lightning flashed as he hurried in, and the rumbling thunder echoed around inside, filling the cavernous space, blending with the relentless *oms.*

With the other two out of sight, he hurried up to the guard on duty inside, as if carrying an urgent message. Once he was close enough, it took three punches and a convenient brick wall to lay the man out. A quick wave, and Kramer and Bugayev joined him.

Kramer was squeezing the rain out of her drenched hair. 'Not exactly how I thought the day was gonna go,' she told Bugayev. 'You?'

'I did think less rain, more explosions,' he conceded.

Jonesy had his eyes screwed shut, sweat standing out on his face, as he urged the two dozen others on to keep the rhythm. God only knew what would happen if they startled him. Hesitantly, Lethbridge-Stewart touched him on the shoulder.

'Oh, thank God,' Jonesy gasped, without even opening his eyes. 'You're real, you did it. You really did it.'

'Yes, well, we've made a start,' said Lethbridge-Stewart.

Jonesy drew his hands together, linking the hands of the people on either side of him, then sprang to his feet out of the circle. Skittering around the place, terribly distracted, his mind in a thousand places at once. 'Not a minute too soon. We just took out the records office. We should be ready to go.'

'You're controlling all this?' asked Bugayev. He was trying not to let his eyes widen too noticeably.

Jonesy shook his head, staring twitchily. 'Way past that point! We started this, we can't stop it. All we can do is steer the worst away from us. If we're lucky.'

'Right.' Lethbridge-Stewart made the introductions. 'Kramer, Bugayev, Jones. Now you all more or less know each other, so, we either work together or get killed.'

Jonesy stopped, gave Bugayev a sideways look. 'Hang on, how many minutes ago did you just try to blow us all up?'

'But I didn't,' Bugayev said simply. 'How much time do we have?'

'And what's the plan?' asked Kramer.

'We evacuate,' declared Lethbridge-Stewart.

Bugayev looked askance. 'In a tropical storm?'

Jonesy grinned dangerously. 'Oh, we're gonna walk between the raindrops, and we're taking you with us.' He raised his voice, calling out to the circle of Odds, shouting over the howling pounding storm. 'Right folks, keep your heads where they're at, but it's time to stand up. We gotta move, we're bugging out.' He pointed to three of the bewildered folks in the circle; Graeme from the data centre, and two others Lethbridge-Stewart didn't recognise. 'You three run interference. Keep the guards busy. Do it for Cricklewood, eh? The rest of you, get your families, get your things, get everyone who's off shift, get your arses ready to move, we'll meet you with transport.'

'Three semi-trailers should do it,' Lethbridge-Stewart told Kramer and Bugayev. 'Each of us takes a third of them. When we hit the main road, we scatter. That way no one of us can possibly take control of the full force of Odds.'

Jonesy nodded, pointedly. 'And all you've gotta do then is get everyone on a plane back home. Their homes, not yours.' His eyes gleamed, and Lethbridge-Stewart could see the lightning in them. 'If you try anything funny...? Just remember we outnumber each of you at least thirty to one... And we can make your lives *so* complicated.'

The circle of Odds was breaking apart, shuffling towards the door, their minds clearly still half on something else, some still muttering 'om' under their breath. Lethbridge-Stewart spotted Nina, twitching, clutching her own hair.

He turned to Kramer and Bugayev. Kramer was shouting into her walkie-talkie, confirming that Vern was still operational. 'You go with Jonesy to the loading dock, get them the transport.'

'You're not coming?' asked Kramer.

Lethbridge-Stewart shook his head. 'We have to make sure Hamilton and Bryden know this is because the Odds are so unstable. Otherwise, they'll never let them go.'

Bugayev nodded, soberly. 'I'd wish you good luck, but luck seems to be the problem.'

As Jonesy led the other two away, Lethbridge-Stewart swore he could see the rain bending around them, leaving them almost dry. No such luck for himself.

He splashed through the torrent flowing between the buildings, rain bucketing into his face, aiming his path diagonally so he could manage to move in a straight line.

Almost to the admin building. The annex at the end was on fire, smoke whipping out the window to be lost in the gale, the result of that lightning strike they'd seen, heard, and felt earlier. A direct hit for Jonesy there, right on the records rooms. The only known copies of the full list of Odds present were lost in that smouldering ash.

He fought his way to the main door. No lights inside. He banged on the glass, hanging on to the handle, until one of Bryden's minions scuttled out to let him in.

Bryden, Hamilton and the others were huddled in the hallway, where there was just barely enough light to see. Beyond them lay the darkened security operations room, every screen and microphone dead. Bryden was pacing, caged, at a loss. *A literal power failure*, thought Lethbridge-Stewart.

'Where the devil have you been?' demanded Bryden.

'With Jonesy,' said Lethbridge-Stewart, breathing heavily. Making it back there had been much harder work than he'd thought. 'We were trying to get control of the weather again. It didn't work.'

'Oh, I'll bet!'

'We did both warn you, Mr Bryden, the Odds are inherently unstable.' Lethbridge-Stewart made his words as firm and clear as possible. It might not convince Bryden, but at least it would reach Hamilton. 'You've gathered so many of them in one place, something was bound to go off-balance.'

'But it was all going so well!' Bryden shouted. There was something childish in his voice; the tantrum of the hereditarily powerful. How dare reality not live up to what he wanted.

'That's exactly the problem,' said Lethbridge-Stewart firmly. 'You held things under control for so long. The more you push, the harder the backlash when it snaps the other way.' He was paraphrasing one of Jonesy's wilder theories about how it all worked, but coming from him it would sound authoritative.

Bryden scowled, but Hamilton seemed to be buying it. 'What about the American?' He'd picked his words carefully in advance.

'She and the Russian have dealt with each other. I saw it happen.'

'Oh, how very convenient, isn't it?' snarled Bryden.

Hamilton rounded on him. 'Nothing about this is even slightly convenient, Mr Bryden. Now we're sitting on an international incident over this, and the resources you promised us are useless!'

Lethbridge-Stewart kept his voice deliberately level and practical. 'Mr Bryden, I don't know what mumbo-jumbo you've convinced yourself of this time, but I assure you I am not in control of the situation.' Which was technically true. 'None of us are. All we can do is ride it out, and try to minimise the damage.' He turned to head away. 'Now. Best to stay indoors, and away from any windows or electrical equipment until the cyclone passes.'

'What are you going to try?' asked Hamilton.

'Damage control, sir. Jonesy's theory is that if we scatter the Odds over a larger area, we may break up the improbability vortex and the storm will dissipate.'

'Improbability vortex?' scoffed Bryden. 'Stay where you are. I won't have you sabotaging anything else.'

'Let him go,' Hamilton muttered. 'He can't do anything worse than you've done already.'

'Sir,' acknowledged Lethbridge-Stewart.

He turned to look at Bryden, who stood mute with fury. What was it the man had said back in New York about a career-limiting manoeuvre?

'Bad luck, old chap.'

But as he turned and hurried back towards the door, he saw Bryden wresting a walkie-talkie from one of the security men.

'Give me that. Nallers? Never mind the generator, leave them to work on that. I want you to look in on the Odds. If they're doing anything suspicious, stop them. Stop them hard.'

Oh, thought Lethbridge-Stewart, and pushed twice as hard through the storm.

Jonesy was crackling. All that time he'd felt there was no chance, suddenly everything was possible.

He jiggled the lock on the transport manager's office – this one's for you, Mum and Dad – and he, Kramer, Bugayev, and Vern snatched handfuls of lorry keys from the pegboard. They each ran to the parked semi-trailers, kept trying keys until they got three of them started, flung the others aside, and pulled up outside the accommodation block.

A small squad of guards was braving the storm, but the three boys from Cricklewood were putting up a hell of a defence. Arms flung forward like amateur wizards, twisting and grimacing, they'd conjured up a whirling waterspout from the ocean side of the storm and sent it barrelling through the complex. It had picked up some fish along the way, along with other debris, and the guards got blown off their feet and pummelled with flying fish to boot. Was Nallers with them? Oh God he hoped so.

The family were streaming out of their barracks now, a chaotic swirl of suitcases and questions. Kramer took charge of splitting them into three groups, Bugayev and Vern opened the rear doors of each trailer and started helping people in. Jonesy made sure they counted every one of them in. There should be one hundred and two of them, not counting him and Lethbridge-Stewart.

What was taking him so long?

The waterspout wasn't as steady as Jonesy had hoped. Now the Cricklewood three were haring back the other way, the swirling storm in pursuit. No sign of the guards, though. He tried to reach out, give his people a hand, but there was just too much going on at once. Maybe he could nudge things a bit, but the cyclone was way too big to steer, really all they could do was hold on and keep the worst away from them.

He herded them into his trailer, then gave his final instructions to the crowd of Odds squeezed inside. 'Okay, so when we hit the road, circle up, focus yourself on keeping the rain away from us. If we can go at a good clip, we should be able to get clear of the main storm, but that depends on you, all right?' He repeated the spiel at each trailer door as he closed and locked it.

At the wheel of their own lorries, Kramer gave him a thumbs-up and Bugayev a quick salute.

That only left Lethbridge-Stewart.

Where had he got to? Jonesy *pushed* a bit with his mind, nudging the worst of the wind and the rain away, so he could safely walk. Stepped out around the corner, looking for any sign of the man.

'Don't you damn well move.'

Nallers.

The thunder rumbled obligingly. Jonesy let his hands hang out, showing he was unarmed, but tightened up in his head like a gunslinger.

Nallers was aiming a bloody speargun at him. Cocky bastard had worked it out, found a gun that couldn't possibly blow up in his face. Even if the trigger jammed, he could still just stab him in the throat.

They stood facing each other, Nallers' gun levelled at Jonesy's eyes. Jonesy, the rain swirling around him, none of it daring to touch him. Nallers, drenched, but just not giving a toss. The immovable object.

'Tell 'em to stand down or I put this through your neck.'

'I told you that won't work.'

Nallers didn't even blink. 'I'll take my chances.'

And any other time, he might be able to *squeeze* it somehow. But his head was so full of storm. Only so much he could handle at once.

Jonesy kept his voice cool. 'Edith says hello.'

Nallers blinked. 'Who?'

Oh, for——!

'Nigel's wife? Remember her, you even fixed her heater?' Nallers really didn't, he just looked puzzled at the irrelevance of it all. 'You really don't give a shit, do you?'

'Not a one.'

But Nallers wasn't gonna fire just yet, not with two officers who he thought were CIA and KGB in the cabs of the trailers behind him. There was still a chance.

'You've never actually dared to take me on, have you? Cause

you might just lose.'

Nallers shook his head. 'What you do, that's not winning, that's just cheating.' He gestured with the gun, still keeping it levelled at Jonesy's head, and smiled like a wolf. 'I win.'

Jonesy gaped. 'You really mean that?' Nallers really meant it. 'Even if I beat you it was cheating? I kill you but it doesn't *count?* Aw, so what if you're dead, you died knowing you were right!' Just like every bloody idiot soldier who ever died for the wrong side, sure it was right because it was *theirs.*

Jonesy was building up a good head of steam, the storm swirling in his brain, squeezing and spiralling and feeding every bit of fire he had into this one charged moment. Winding himself up more and more. 'Like you never cheated a day in your life to get where you were. Like you didn't cheat the odds just by being born to the right dad. Like that makes it right and natural for you to, to…' He ran out of breath before he ran out of rant, had to gasp some air in to recover. Finished it croaking in the rain. 'To kill Nigel. You, you…' No final punchline, he'd run out of words.

Nallers had waited, relentlessly, like he'd known he would, just to twist the knife. 'You done?'

Jonesy drew and let out a huge slow breath. Not collapsing, controlled. 'Not quite…'

And he smiled the smile he'd been saving up for since the day Nigel died.

'…about four more seconds.'

The charge was building, every little chance he'd been stirring up was sparking into place, little unlikelinesses building to bigger ones as he grabbed hold of the sky, and he had just a moment to savour the look starting to cross Nallers' face: the first inkling that in fact he'd been terminally thick.

Three. Two. One.

Flash.

Lethbridge-Stewart saw the first flash, but not the last one.

He'd been battling his way through the wind and the rain, knowing that simple geography would mean that Nallers would get there first, working on strategy for when he caught up. Bracing for battle.

Ahead he could see the headlamps of the lorries, and a Jonesy-shaped figure scuttling across the pools of light, disappearing just out of view around the corner of the accommodation block.

He slogged closer, and the sky lit up, arc-light white seared on his eyeballs, over and over like a whole chain of fireworks. He stumbled with the thundercracks, his ears ringing. But he dragged himself onwards, too much at stake to stop now, got to get them to safety...

All his muscles were turning to soup. Wiry vibration of electricity conducted through the ground and water, no one jolt enough to kill him at this distance, but shock after shock jolting him out of rhythm, trying to freeze him on the spot—

He crumpled.

Face down on the pavement in the rain. Light and wet playing over him, headlights, far away at the end of a long tunnel. Then a confused sense of movement, getting carried, metal door slamming and a crowded space full of people. An echoing motor, moving floor he was lying on. And then that endless inescapable *om*.

He had to get up. They all needed him. He had to—

CHAPTER TWENTY-ONE
Near Life Experience

PEACE NOW. Far away and blurry. Just a rhythm carrying him along, rocking him gently.

He still felt the urge to fight, but there was nothing to fight with, or for. It could wait. He'd never been good at resting, but at the moment he had no choice.

There was still something in the haze surrounding him, slowly coming into focus. Just a single flower. That ever-opening rose that had kept filling his mind in all those meditations. But it stood here closed, unfulfilled, caught between the in-breath and the out-breath. On a stem of ragged thorns that could rip you with its touch.

All rather poetic for him, but it felt like the good kind of poetry. Like Kipling, it had a clarity to it, a sense of purpose.

The more the rose filled his view, the more he felt the words which belonged to it; ideas hovering around as if drawn to its pollen. Impulsive. Idealistic. Never gives up, never gives in. Never cruel or cowardly. Yes, these were words worth reaching for. Though often caught up in violent events, he remains at heart a man of peace…

Lethbridge-Stewart flinched. No. This rose wasn't meant for him. He wasn't a man of peace, at best he was a warrior who chose his battles wisely, most of the time at least. He was who he was, and he wasn't ashamed. But if peace was what they were after, at best he would be doing the wrong things for the right reasons.

But this time, hadn't he brought his fellow warriors together to avoid a war? In the name of fighting a greater enemy, yes, but he had steered the world away from a battlefield today. Perhaps in that world of peace, he could be said to be in it if not of it.

He wasn't that man. And he knew he never would be. But wouldn't it be good if *someone* was?

Perhaps that was the way. If it was him and this rose, then he was the one to build a garden around it, and keep it safe. He'd defend it, and tend it, and with his help who knew how it would grow? If he, and Kramer, and Bugayev – if he and *Fiona* – if they could bring into this world something greater than themselves, really what else could they ask for in life?

Somehow that made sense. Which, in the realm of things he'd been dealing with lately, made it rather precious.

Now he could see that rose, the whole bush it branched off from, safely rooted in his back garden. He looked at it, and he wondered how high it would get. Somewhere behind him Fiona was in their home, life was going on.

He reached out for the rose. The petals felt too subtle for his coarse fingers, the thorns did sting but only for a moment. Perhaps the rose needed his blood to thrive.

He could hear a baby crying.

He had eyes again and they were open.

A room. A hospital room. Lying on his back and aching like all hell. A small and spartan hospital room, a careworn Anne sitting there with a magazine. His ears ringing hollowly, still working out how not to be deafened, in the silence left after the last of the thunder and lightning and *om*.

'Anne… what are you…?'

'Oh, thank God.' She hurried over to him, reached for his hand, but thought better of taking it. There were a fair number of bandages and dressings on him.

What in heaven had he just been thinking about? No matter.

Once they'd established the basics – he was in hospital in Bridgetown, still in Barbados; all their people had made it out alive – she explained that he had mild but widespread electrical burns, they'd take a few weeks to heal fully, and the doctors would want to check that his brain hadn't been scrambled.

'Too much to do,' he rasped.

Anne shook her head; Kramer and Bugayev had been managing rather well without him. Technically he couldn't say he'd been struck by lightning, because the charges had all been conducted through the ground, so he'd been spared the worst of them; he had either been very lucky or very unlucky, neither of them was sure which.

'Apparently, they found the body that did get struck. Seventeen times.'

His lip curled. 'Nallers.' Of course.

But what was she doing here? 'Ted and I came down with Adrienne, to try to get in to reach you. He's gone down a different path, in investigating the Intelligence. A little more... mystical, fantastical. Not having thirty years of bad memories of people scoffing at you will do that. You can get a little wilder. I think it's helped him to be believed.'

'Wasn't the Intelligence,' Lethbridge-Stewart managed. It still hurt to talk. 'Never was. Bryden's web was... synthetic, all along.'

It took her a while to take the idea in. Once she did, her shoulders sagged with relief. 'I never thought...' If anything, she seemed wryly amused. 'I should've known. Chaos looking like order. It just seemed to be the most likely answer. I missed one of the basic rules of science... it's not just the bits that fit your theory you have to look at, it's the ones that don't.'

'It did make sense.'

'But there's always more than one theory out there. Just in case your first one doesn't actually match reality.' She let out a breath he hadn't known she'd been holding. 'Oh, Alistair. Welcome back.'

The nurse came in with a pitcher of water and plastic cups. It was surprisingly hard to raise the cup to his lips without spilling it on his face. His whole body felt like tenderised meat. Anne moved up to help, but he managed. He nodded, letting her know he appreciated the gesture.

'Working with Ted's been quite an adventure,' she said drily. 'Never mind the family stuff, even. Before with my father, I just blamed it on him getting old and crochety, but now? He's not senile at all, just... difficult. Brilliant, experienced, pig-headed. Expects people to follow his lead without question. I'd be going out of my mind... if I hadn't had years of practice, working out how you and I could meet halfway.' She raised her own cup of water in a toast. 'To learning experiences.'

Later Kramer and Bugayev joined them, fresh from the airport.

They seemed quite relaxed for two people who'd been shooting at each other last night.

'Commie bastard won't even let me buy him lunch,' said Kramer.

'You know how it is. Ten years from now, someone finds the receipt, it's proof I was an American asset.'

With each of them keeping an eye on each other, Jonesy keeping an eye on them both, and Vern and some of his boys keeping an eye on the scattered Odds, they'd spent the day at the international airport changing the assorted Odds' return ticket dates to get them home as soon as possible.

'I'm sorry I couldn't be there to manage it,' said Lethbridge-Stewart. His throat hurt less now, and he was sitting up in bed.

'You already did your bit,' said Kramer. 'We just had to fill in the details.'

Bugayev gave a sideways smile. 'It seems you're a very effective leader when you're unconscious.'

'Yes. Quite.'

They'd also notified General Hamilton that he was alive and in hospital, and left with Anne before Hamilton arrived to avoid any awkward questions.

When the general did arrive, he seemed genuinely concerned about Lethbridge-Stewart's health, and made it clear that due to the changes in the situation, he was welcome back in the UK as soon as he felt well enough to travel.

'We do have a difficult matter to deal with, though,' he said. 'The question of how we handle the fact that we were responsible for a natural disaster on foreign soil.'

Lethbridge-Stewart noted the *we*. Oliver Hamilton wasn't usually so transparent: he was trying to convince him that they were both in this together. 'I was only here because you told me to be, sir.'

'Quite.' He could see Hamilton shifting on the spot, running through his options. Suddenly his ability to threaten a court-martial didn't look so attractive, not when the under-the-table deal he'd been aiming to protect had gone so spectacularly off the rails, and he'd directly tried to stop the collaborative international investigation which ended up pulling him out of the fire.

'I see no reason to make any report on the matter whatsoever, sir,' Lethbridge-Stewart said, and gave Hamilton just a moment to start to relax. 'On one condition.'

'Which is?'

'That you do what we should have done years ago.' Even just sitting up in the bed, he found himself drawing himself upright, as proud as if he were in full uniform. 'Push for the creation of an independent UN task force, to handle matters like these internationally. Say it's because of the Engineers if you want. But make it happen.'

General Hamilton was silent for a long time, his features hardening into a glower. Searching for a strategy to escape, gradually grasping that all his retreats had been blocked.

He stood, pacing away from Lethbridge-Stewart, towards the foot of the bed. His voice flat. 'You do realise the whole reason you made brigadier... the whole reason for the Fifth Operational Corps... was entirely to prevent this.'

Lethbridge-Stewart nodded. 'Nevertheless.'

Suddenly Hamilton was blurting his thoughts out, almost rambling. 'Don't you see, man. The UN had already started to get its claws in, it was all Gilmore and I could do to shut them down in '67. That fool Farquhar was all ready to hand our defence over to his snaky little backers...'

'Quite. And then you handed it over to Bryden.'

He saw how that stung, and he regretted it. He wanted to win the argument, not humiliate the man. The very thought that it was possible for him to humiliate Oliver Hamilton hadn't even occurred to him.

He softened his tone. 'I know there needs to be a balance. Would you trust me to do a better job of finding it? Sir.'

It took a long moment for Hamilton to resign himself. 'You never do stop thinking you're right, do you, Lethbridge-Stewart?'

He allowed himself a slight smile. 'Only when I am.'

There was one more arrival before visiting hours ended. Jonesy.

He'd brought flowers – Lethbridge-Stewart wasn't sure how to take that – and a sheepish smile. 'Really sorry about all this,' he said. 'I didn't know you were in range.'

'Just bad luck, I suppose,' Lethbridge-Stewart said pointedly.

Jonesy took the hit. 'It kind of got away from me, yeah. It's just, that was the only shot I'd have at Nallers, y'know? The man was a sucker for puncturing someone's monologue.' He settled in the chair Anne had left, leaned it back at a sharp angle till he was propped against the wall. The man seemed congenitally incapable of just sitting normally. 'So, how're you healing up? Hair still standing on end? D'you give shocks to the nurses every time they touch you?'

'Certainly not.' Lethbridge-Stewart shifted tack, spoke respectfully. 'For someone who doesn't know what you're doing, you did a good job getting your people to safety. Very commendable.'

Jonesy shook his head, sat down on the edge of the bed. His eyes were far away. 'Power failure on the east side of the island. Three hundred houses flooded. Four dead, not counting Nallers. Six if you count Ronnie and Jeanette… Oh yeah, Bugayev told me all about them.' The names didn't ring a bell, but that might just be the pain medication. 'Makes you think, doesn't it.'

'With what you and Bryden were messing with, it could've been far worse,' Lethbridge-Stewart said firmly.

'I know that, I felt it. I'm used to being able to squeeze the chances my way, but… We started something bigger than us. Bigger than we could stop. Chance doesn't mean control.'

'I think we were extremely lucky.'

'I don't, and I hope I never do.' He stood up, shambling around the room. 'That's why I'm getting out. Before I start accepting acceptable losses.'

Jonesy looked haunted. Before he'd been revelling in it all; now his face showed signs of having learned that chaos was bloody exhausting.

'I was talking with Dave and Nina, just now,' he went on.

'How are they?'

Jonesy met his eyes. 'She thinks you were cruel.' Closing in on him now. 'And cowardly. She said you should've just told her to think of a storm.'

Now it was Lethbridge-Stewart's turn to be sobered. 'With her, I didn't think that would work.'

Maybe not, said Jonesy's face. 'She and Dave don't want to work with you or Dr Travers anymore. Can't say I blame her. I think we all just want to lie low for a while, be forgotten about. If they'll let us.' He settled cross-legged on the end of Lethbridge-Stewart's bed. 'Maybe you should try it too, mate,' he said gently. 'Sit back for a while. Smell the roses. Be a Nigel.' He shook his head, looking inwards. 'I never could, but you'd make a good one, if you try.' A pause; he shrugged. 'Anyhow. Wait 'til you've got your bouncing baby bundle of germs under control before you take any more chances.'

It might be wise, Lethbridge-Stewart thought. *It would certainly be easier.*

'Perhaps once the new international operation gets set up,' he conceded. 'First, we need to make sure nothing like this ever happens again.'

A shadow of the old Jonesy's smile. 'Well, if there's one thing we Odds are good at, it's non-repeating phenomena.'

'There's a space in it for you, if you're still willing. Find out the answers about how you work.'

'There's a chance,' conceded Jonesy.

About as much chance as me sitting back and staying in my garden, thought Lethbridge-Stewart. But a chance was a start.

Now Jonesy was leaning forward, propped on his hands. 'And, y'know, I've been thinking, about you being one of us. Maybe… you're not. Cause none of us are much like you, really. But you know how I said, we can rub off on you? Well maybe somewhere, in all that secret stuff you've done, you ran into another of us. Not one of us kids, maybe a full-blooded one. A granddaddy of all the oddities. Someone who could warp this world to fit him. And maybe, just maybe, you soaked up a little bit of his nature into your own. Just enough that you can deal with it all.'

There's always more than one theory, thought Lethbridge-Stewart. And this one didn't try to twist him into some kind of free-floating agent of chaos; just an orderly man who could still recognise the value of working with the chaotic ones. Something more rare and valuable, he supposed. 'I rather prefer that idea.'

'Oh yeah, you're that determined to be normal, aren't you?' A long pause; Jonesy shook his head, vaguely awed. 'You're just going to forget all about it, aren't you? Put it out of your mind. All the big things you deal with… they don't change you.' He pondered for a moment. 'But maybe the little ones do.'

'What do you mean?'

Jonesy shrugged, let his musing out half-formed. 'I don't think it was Nallers killing Nigel that changed me. It was Nigel and Edith having me over for dinner in the first place. If not for that… well, what are the chances, really?'

His thinking didn't quite make sense to Lethbridge-Stewart, but that was all right. It didn't have to. Sense was waiting for him back home, in the garden and the nursery, in the look in

Fiona's eyes just before she came out with a turn of phrase which reduced him to laughter. All those small things.

'I should go,' said Jonesy. 'Got a ticket booked to the ends of the earth. But I just want you to remember.' He stared into Lethbridge-Stewart's eyes with the wisdom of a survivor. 'You've been touched by something weird. But you can deal with it. That's who you are. You're the one who deals with it.' All his affectedness dropped away. He reached out his hand to shake. 'We're all better off for knowing you, Brigadier.'

Lethbridge-Stewart shook his hand, and Jonesy froze, vibrating, as if being electrocuted. Startled, Lethbridge-Stewart let go, and Jonesy mock-collapsed, then grinned at him. 'Thought you might like to get a little of your own back.'

Lethbridge-Stewart allowed himself a half-smile. Jonesy meant well.

'Yes, well. You don't need to underline that I've been touched by something odd.'

Finally, finally, everyone else in the world had finished with him. He dozed until the nurses came with dinner, then dozed again afterwards. Finally, the times came into alignment, and he dialled that endless international number.

'Hello?'

'Fiona?'

'Alistair?' Her voice sound frayed, wound a bit too tight. But just hearing it again was enough to undo that last knot of tension in him. He let out a breath he'd felt himself holding for weeks.

'We're safe, darling... we're safe.'

CHAPTER TWENTY-TWO
The End of the End of the Beginning

'**THIS IS** the last time,' he murmured to Fiona, as he finished dressing in front of the mirror. He adjusted his uniform jacket and drew himself up to his full height. 'I promise.'

She rolled on her side, sullenly, resenting being awake.

'Sprout kept me up half the night again,' she mumbled, eyes screwed shut. 'Haven't had a proper sleep since… When did I stop sleeping on my stomach?'

They'd long since picked a name for him, or her, and backup names just in case, but Fiona was still superstitiously refusing to use them until the baby actually arrived. As if she were hedging her bets, guarding herself from any lurking mischance.

'It's only an overnight,' he said gently. 'I'll be back before anything happens.'

'Mmhm.'

What else was he supposed to say? He wasn't nearly enough of a romantic to know.

'Soon be over,' he said, but she just shook her head sleepily. As if she were bracing to carry this child for the next twenty years, as if the next stretch of their life was to be endured rather than enjoyed.

On an impulse, he slipped out to the nursery, to retrieve the sketchpad she'd abandoned on the bureau. Looked at the nursery animals on the walls, still not quite finished. She'd run out of energy a while back, all her strength was going to protecting herself. Or perhaps she'd gone off the whole idea of the room as their child's sanctuary, after that night he'd seen Jonesy out its window. She wouldn't say.

He placed the sketchpad on her end-table, in case she felt like it.

Such a shame she was feeling so poorly, on the day when

everything was coming together. The culmination of months of tedious and undramatic work: all those trips away, New York and Paris and Geneva, supporting an undertaking so much bigger than his own efforts.

Pride and joy, he thought. His duties were his pride, and she was his joy. Perhaps one of the reasons he loved her was that she could make him feel not like himself. But he'd been very himself lately. The world required it.

And that was Bryden's sin, to serve his family and to hell with the world. He might still be making a mistake, but at least he wouldn't make the same one.

He sat on the edge of the bed. Gently, he ran a hand through her hair. 'I love you.'

'Love you,' she muttered into her pillow.

He paused, awkwardly, by the door. 'I'd never leave if I didn't know you could manage on your own.'

She raised her head, flatly, to meet his eyes. 'You're right. I can.'

The staff car pulled up outside the bungalow, it was Corporal Wright behind the wheel.

'Still driver, see,' he said with a wry smile, miming a steering motion.

'Some things never change,' said Lethbridge-Stewart, getting in.

'Actually, sir,' said Wright, 'I volunteered for this. Asked specially.'

'Good heavens.'

'Least I could do, all those years of you not getting me killed.'

Or having you killed, Lethbridge-Stewart thought fleetingly, but said nothing. That wasn't fair of him. Wright had had his moments, but he'd proved himself over the years.

'There's still a place for you if you want to apply for a transfer to the new force.'

'I don't know, sir.' He was doing that wide-eyed thing again. 'Once my time's up, I think I might get out of the army, do something less risky. Like juggling dynamite.'

'Really?' Lethbridge-Stewart raised an eyebrow.

'I mean it, sir. These past four years, I'm lucky I made it out alive.'

Lethbridge-Stewart gave him a thoughtful look through the rear-view mirror. 'Yes… You have led a bit of a charmed life, haven't you, Corporal?'

'Oh no, sir. A charmed life, I'd never have been within a mile of you at Holborn in the first place.'

'Fair point,' conceded Lethbridge-Stewart.

The Fifth Operational Corps would continue on without him; Walter Douglas had got his chair, and a promotion, to handle strictly domestic matters. For now, the skeleton crew devoted strictly to UNIT would get custody of the Hercules air transport, and the mobile HQ van they had trialled back in Peel. But eventually, a battalion's worth of men would be following Lethbridge-Stewart to the new outfit.

'I suppose none of us would've made it through, if not for you,' said Wright. 'You done right by us.' They drove on in silence for a while. 'But me and Cerys, sir… it's getting serious. Reckon maybe I should do something where I can look after her more. Make sure I'll be coming home at night.'

'Very commendable,' said Lethbridge-Stewart. This was the first he'd heard of Cerys, so he added a 'Congratulations.' But his thoughts were on Fiona. 'You haven't told her anything about your work at the Fifth, have you?'

'Oh no, sir. More'n my job's worth, ain't it.' A flicker of a proud smile. 'I wouldn't even tell Captain Kramer.' He stared out the windscreen. 'But Cerys knows I had men killed right next to me. Really, sir, what kind of a life is that?'

Lethbridge-Stewart nodded, soberly. As far as Fiona knew, his new role for the UN was mainly a consultancy; he'd hoped that would lift the shadow he'd seen over her, since the day Jonesy brought his job to their home. If that wasn't enough…? Perhaps he'd tell her that he'd arranged to transition to a civilian job. Better a small lie than that constant gnawing worry, surely. She should believe that there was such a thing as peacetime in this world, rather than war just outside her view.

Perhaps the only way to nurture that flower in his garden was to keep it in the dark. Rather the opposite of what one was supposed to do with flowers. Never mind. He was no good with metaphors anyway.

They were pulling onto the airfield now. The Hercules transport sat on the runway, and Wright turned smoothly up the ramp into the belly of the bird. *He's actually a rather good driver*, thought Lethbridge-Stewart.

'But if you want to do something worthwhile… the door is still open.'

The newly-minted Brigadier Walter Douglas met him in the Herc's Ops room. They'd already done the formal transfer of command for the Fifth the other day, shortly after his promotion, so this was just a matter of Dougie transferring the Herc to him in return.

Dougie looked sharp; the new insignia suited him. It was how Alistair had always aspired to look himself, every inch the straight arrow, even if much of the general staff now thought he was pointing in the wrong direction.

As far as the officers and civilians in charge of his inquiry had seen it, his new posting to UNIT was an exile; as far as they knew, a largely ceremonial post with a skeleton staff. Hamilton had just quietly arranged for him to be exiled to exactly where he could do the most good.

'An amicable divorce,' Dougie said as they finished the formalities and signed the necessary forms. 'You get the cars, I keep the house, and you can borrow the children when you need them.'

'And the bank accounts are in good shape,' added Lethbridge-Stewart. On top of everything else, Hamilton had turned his capitulation to the UN into an accounting dodge; the money from the UN would neatly replace the loss of funding from Bryden Industries, as that relationship was swiftly wound up. The deal meant they'd actually be paying some of Douglas' bills, in exchange for access to his men as needed.

He may be a pariah now at UNIT, thought Lethbridge-Stewart, but a necessary one. Like Kramer had said: the best way to vex your enemies was to make yourself indispensable to them.

He looked at the new brigadier; Dougie had played it all very smooth, and still by the book. No one could fault him for siding with a superior officer over his CO, particularly given the things he hadn't known, and still didn't know. No doubt there were still things which needed to be said, but now didn't seem like the time to say them. Perhaps it never would be.

Now Dougie was meeting his eyes as an equal again, properly, for the first time since Lethbridge-Stewart had made major before him. 'Well, Alistair, I suppose that's that. Anything you need, within reason, don't hesitate to ask.'

Lethbridge-Stewart smiled slightly. 'And you shouldn't hesitate even if it's not within reason.'

'You do realise this is your Mad Mitch moment,' General Hamilton said flatly.

They were seated in the passenger section, high above the Atlantic. Even if Lethbridge-Stewart had blown out one of the plane's windows at 30,000 feet, the atmosphere inside would have been only marginally chillier.

'With respect, sir, I don't think that's entirely fair. Colonel Mitchell's actions in Aden had public repercussions for the forces. I've done nothing to embarrass you.' True, he too had done an end run around orders, put high command over a barrel... but never for glory. His or the Empire's.

Hamilton shook his head; it wasn't that. 'Above a certain rank, your job stops being to win battles and becomes to win wars. Mad Mitch never rose higher, because he'd showed he lacked that perspective.'

Lethbridge-Stewart remembered admiring the man's boldness, as a young officer. But in the end, they still withdrew from Aden, as they had always aimed to, no matter how much the *Daily Mail* wanted Mitchell to singlehandedly retake the whole colony.

And now Colonel Colin Mitchell (Ret'd) was railing in Parliament against Britain joining the EEC, and doing for the whites in Rhodesia what Kramer's friend Vern was doing for the blacks. Still an object lesson there, though not the one Hamilton had intended: no matter how much one valued tradition, one should never become yesterday's man.

'They don't declare wars in this theatre, sir. You know that.' He made one last attempt to bridge this new divide. 'Sir... you know I was right.'

'But for the wrong reasons. You weren't looking to protect the interests of the United Kingdom. That makes you useful, effective... But not reliable.'

So, to Hamilton and the top brass, he was a dangerous maverick, to Jonesy he'd just been a company man at heart... Perhaps he needed to have a chat with Captain Kramer, about how to function with a foot in two different worlds.

'Am I going to get the same treatment as Peyton Bryden, sir?' he asked.

'Well, we're not quietly cancelling most of your contracts,' said Hamilton. Though International Electromatics would no doubt be pleased with that bit of the fallout. Word had it that Hamilton had also told Bryden that any sign of reprisals against the Odds for Nallers' death would cost his company major financial reparations to Barbados, and had been surprised at how quickly Bryden had disowned his late nephew as a loose cannon. Apparently, Bryden family loyalty only travelled one way. 'But you won't be getting the same support as before. If you only knew how many times I'd already had to protect you... Ah well. That's Billy Rutlidge's problem now.'

So, it was over. Hamilton would stand by his side at the UN signing ceremony, flying the flag... but twenty years of being treated as a prize pupil had come to an end. Ah well. Time for a new phase of life anyway.

'I hope there won't be too many secrets kept from us, in the name of the national interest,' he said formally. 'The new taskforce is supposed to be the primary force worldwide for dealing with the unknown. It would be embarrassing for Britain if something turned out to be known after all.'

'You keep doing what you're good at, Alistair.' Hamilton paused, his eyes still hard. 'I'll make sure you stay there.'

Anne smiled at Edward Travers. 'One more chance...'

He shook his head dismissively and went back to arranging his bookshop window display. 'Bunch of stuffed shirts patting themselves on the back over canapés? I'd rather gnaw my own arm off, you know that.'

She'd stopped by Ebon Books on her way to the UN plaza, just to see if he'd reconsidered her invitation to the inauguration ceremony. But he'd rather focus on running his shop, and tending the annex full of esoterica in the back.

'Besides,' he went on, more gently. 'This is your day, not mine. You don't need me hanging around.' Such a frustrating old goat, even now. He still couldn't grasp that at long last, she *wanted* him there. 'Researching the Intelligence; in the end it had nothing to do with all this.'

But it pushed me to bridge the gap, she thought. *Here's to unintended side effects.* 'Even so, you belong with us. Once the new outfit is up and running, Adrienne wants you on staff as a consultant. Special projects.'

His face creased, an unfamiliar wry smile. 'Working for you, eh? Do I get to pick which project?'

'I'd have thought it was obvious.'

A thoughtful look. He stopped, then sat down, musing, in one of the overstuffed reading-chairs he'd dotted around the back of the shop. A quiet question. 'Anne...? Did you ever ask me why I went to the East in the first place?'

She smiled ruefully. 'You had to prove yourself right.'

'Oh, that's not why it mattered.' For once his face was completely unguarded, even gentle. 'It was the yeti itself. The whole idea of it, since I was a child. If I'd just wanted to find some exotic predator, I could have tromped all over Africa like everyone else. But something this large... and it's *peaceful?* Even timid?'

It wasn't his face that got to her; it was that he had a young man's eyes. Not having thirty years of bitterness over people scoffing at you would do that. As far as he was concerned, he had told his story to Alistair and immediately been *believed.*

'This thing was my Shangri-La on legs. If I'd really found them, I'd probably still be out there, living amongst them like that Fossey woman.'

And then you'd never have had me, thought Anne. The thought should unsettle her. But the echo of joy on his face... Was there a core to Edward Travers, an essence of his best self which had somehow survived everything he'd been through... and that core didn't include her life at all? What was left of him, with no memory of her whole lifetime, seemed more whole than she'd ever known him. She couldn't fear that.

His face darkened, as he slowly shook his head. 'But instead, I found this... hungering *thing...*'

She put a gentle hand on his shoulder. Now she could see her father in that face. But had the Intelligence done that to him? Or had that hunger, that anger, been in him from the moment he started his search? Had the Intelligence just led him where he was already going to go?

He shrugged off the mood, back to himself. 'Anyhow. Get Adrienne to pay for an expedition like *that*, I'll be there like a shot.'

'Well, I'll put a proposal in. After the launch ceremony.'

She still couldn't call him 'Father'. And he would always have a complicated journey. But today marked their chance to lead them all to somewhere better.

'United Nations Intelligence Taskforce,' said Lethbridge-Stewart, as he looked at the black leather binder with the new logo embossed on it. He turned to Captain Kramer. 'Do I detect your hand in the naming?'

Kramer grinned, tight-lipped, but wouldn't be drawn. 'Well, it's not bad. Helps remind some of the big boys about the kind of things we have to co-operate over.'

'Your trouble is, your jokes don't translate,' said Bugayev. 'Try explaining to the Chinese what you mean by "Intelligence".'

'It's funny to think that this might actually be the most lasting effect of everything the Great Intelligence got up to...' mused Anne, 'And it didn't actually have any part in it.'

Lethbridge-Stewart smiled. 'Unintended consequences.'

They had a few minutes while Kramer finished gathering files for the young lieutenant who'd be replacing her, before they would head over to the official ceremony. Lethbridge-Stewart turned to Bishop, who he hadn't seen since the Bishops' farewell dinner back in Edinburgh some weeks ago. 'So how are you finding New York, Major?'

His last duty as commander of the Fifth was to grant Bishop one more promotion. He'd more than earned it.

Major Bill Bishop gave a dubious look. 'Loud. I don't think I could last the two years here, I'll be much happier once Anne and I relocate to Washington.'

'We'll all be working out of New York till they get the new HQ set up,' said Kramer. 'It's down in Southeast DC, by the sewage treatment plant, you believe that? But it's not a bad building, and once it's ready, we're down there for good.'

'Well that'll make Donald rather happy,' said Lethbridge-Stewart. 'How long do you plan to spend getting the outfit into shape, before you leave to have children?'

Kramer's eyes gleamed. 'Oh, now we're just waiting till their policies catch up. After *Schattman vs Texas*? I bet I won't even have to be discharged.'

He blinked. 'But how will you——?'

'With Ma and Aunt Mabel five miles from HQ? We got the childcare covered. And Dad's already looking forward to being

Grandpa Sarge.'

'I see you have a plan,' conceded Lethbridge-Stewart. 'I've learned not to argue with your plans.'

'Oh, we got plans,' said Kramer. She turned to Bishop and Anne. 'I'm really gonna have to rely on you two, and the other civilian specialists. The restrictions about deploying US troops in civilian environments over here... We're gonna have to do things kinda different than you're used to.'

'A free hand at last,' said Anne.

'I'm looking forward,' said Bishop. 'Assuming my apology for all that has been appropriately filed and countersigned by all the relevant department heads.'

Kramer smiled, closed-lipped. 'Couple more wouldn't hurt.'

Bishop matched her grin. 'How many times did you make Bugayev say sorry? He shot at you.'

'That was business,' said Kramer.

Major Bugayev was still browsing through his copy of the presentation binder. He raised an eyebrow. 'Commanding officer, Brigadier General Michael Braddock.'

Kramer rolled her eyes. 'What, you thought I'd be running the place? Whole reason Colonel Braddock picked up the ball for UNIT USA was to get himself a star. I'm his XO, mostly on the Operations side. Still wants me out of the field. That's gonna be fun.'

'I think it's a disgrace,' said Bugayev, to Kramer's surprise. 'In our forces, a woman of your abilities... You'd be—'

'I'd be working for you, wouldn't I,' said Kramer, smiling pointedly. 'Did I mention I'm getting a bump up to major?'

Bugayev matched her smile. 'Congratulations. I'm due to make lieutenant colonel in four months.'

'I wouldn't expect too many more promotions if I were you,' Lethbridge-Stewart said darkly. 'Working internationally will lead them to question your loyalty.'

'If he didn't question everyone's loyalty already, he wouldn't be the general,' Bugayev said wryly, but it rang hollow.

Still, perhaps it was best if he never did rise above brigadier. Stay at a level where he could engage directly with emerging threats. Win battles, so the likes of Hamilton wouldn't have to win wars.

Kramer looked at her desk, drew a slow breath. 'Okay. It's time.'

*

Bugayev waited until they were in the lift before he drew a folded paper from his pocket. 'I thought you might appreciate this,' he murmured. 'Contact details for Mrs Elsa Mittelberg Steiner. Widowed, but alive and well. Now working as a secretary just outside of East Berlin.'

Kramer smiled, tapped her binder. 'Funny about that. I've got a line on Walter J Jones of Geelong, Australia. All those in favour of getting these two back together?'

'Unfortunately,' said Lethbridge-Stewart, 'No one's seen hide nor hair of Jonesy since he went underground.'

'Leave it with me,' said Anne. They all turned to look at her. 'He still checks in on Edith Plummock, every once in a while. And so do I.'

For some reason, there was a sudden small moment of awe shared between all four of them. A sense of *now we can actually do this right.*

'Well,' said Lethbridge-Stewart. 'Not bad for a first day's work.'

They emerged into the plaza, walking from the Secretariat building towards the General Assembly hall, where the inauguration ceremony would take place. Somewhere nearby a transistor radio was blaring, that Stevie Wonder song Kramer had once played for him, about the dangers of believing in things that you don't understand. He didn't particularly agree with the sentiment, but it had a rather good march tempo. The sun was bright and the skies were clear, the pavement glinting around them. He glanced to either side, and realised that all five of them had fallen into step.

Near the door stood a small knot of large black men, Vern and Donald at the front. They greeted Kramer with raised-fist salutes – except for Donald – and big beaming grins. She gave them a casual Army salute as they passed, and looked around one last time before she and the others went inside, a smile spreading across her face as she took in a day she'd clearly never expected in her life.

'Some days, it's just right.'

'...And this is Adam Suisse, he'll be heading up the scientific section in Geneva...'

Lethbridge-Stewart shook yet another hand. The reception

after the ceremony was in full swing, and Sir Colin Crowe was bent on introducing all the new senior staff the world over to each other. 'A pleasure to meet you, Brigadier,' said the new man. Was that accent Swiss? French? 'I've heard nothing but good reports, and look forward to working closely in future.'

'Yes, no doubt,' said Lethbridge-Stewart.

Suisse had thinning dark hair, piercing eyes and a knowing smile, and the unmistakable voice of one of his UNION interrogators. For that matter, he'd spent most of Sir Colin's rather nice speech at the ceremony wondering whether his was the voice of his main interlocutor. They would never admit it, of course; now that the international arrangements were legitimate, the last thing anyone wanted to acknowledge was that they had been doing this all along.

He made his excuses and headed for the bar. The champagne was rather richer than he was used to, but this was a bit of an occasion. The main reception hall was a riot of international faces and outfits; he'd talked about saving the world, well, here it was.

Captain Kramer and her husband were off to one side, her arms round his shoulders, looking up at him with the most thoroughly contented smile he'd ever seen on her face. He left them to have their moment and joined Bill and Anne instead; they were being polite to an agelessly charming older fellow called Dr Frederick Black who was clearly angling for a job on their team at UNIT USA. Once he finally finished with them, the three spent a moment just looking at each other.

'Are you getting the "how on earth did we end up here" bit as well?' murmured Anne.

'Yes, well, we talked about starting something bigger than ourselves,' said Lethbridge-Stewart. 'This certainly qualifies.'

'Well, it's all the rage now, isn't it,' said Bill. 'Joining the EEC last week, and now this.'

'But seriously,' mused Anne. 'Look at the way we got here... What are the chances?'

But Bill shrugged it off. 'Once we actually decided to work together, we had a good shot of pulling it off. And the Brig here was never going to *not* get us standing together. He's got history with that. Since the day we met.'

Odd, he'd never quite thought of it like that. If there were anything the Lethbridge-Stewart name should stand for, uniting across old borders was precisely it. Less than a century after the English and Scots had last been slaughtering each other, a man whose family name crossed both sides had defended them both against a foreign empire. A century further on, and his own father had stood allied with the descendants of Fergus' foes against a greater threat. Now that foe in turn had become an ally in NATO against a still larger bloc, and today the nations of the world were finally taking their first stumbling steps towards common ground against even greater enemies.

Give them another fifty years, where would they be? Not that he was in any danger of being out of a job, but the frontiers he had to defend were moving further and further away from that little bungalow in Craigentinny where Fiona and the baby would live and grow. And that was as it should be.

Perhaps he was a little bit of a romantic after all.

There was a moment, and that moment was right. Every chance had come out the way it needed to. They were content. That was enough.

And then the anxious little man from the reception desk tugged on Lethbridge-Stewart's jacket. A call for him. Please come immediately.

Fiona's father. His voice tight. Rushed to hospital, he said. Early onset. Complications. Fiona was in the room right now three thousand miles away from Lethbridge-Stewart and they didn't know whether the baby would live or die.

There was nothing he could do. Not a chance.

He'd never seen this coming. No, that was a lie; he'd known there was always a chance of something going wrong and he wouldn't be there. Either way, whatever happened, he'd played the odds and lost.

And Alistair Lethbridge-Stewart could only sit and wait, outside the party, behind a desk manned by strangers in a foreign country – jacket undone, tie askew – and wonder how it only took a moment for everything to change.

The Lethbridge-Stewart series concludes in
**The Lost Son by Andy Frankham-Allen
and Tim Gambrell**

ABOUT MARSHA...

THE ROAD to this book began... well, right when it was set.

The Rosenbergs' adopted grandson, the one who would grow up five miles from his birth parents without knowing...? No surprise, that was me. Ten years later, when I was first discovering *Doctor Who* (and the Brigadier), my best friend Cary Gordon would be going to school with my biological sister, while my friend and neighbour Kevin Cherry's dad would be working half a mile from them. At the same IBM building as an Aussie named Jim Orman, who'd brought his family up for a year-long posting, including his daughter Kate. None of us knew.

That bit where Jonesy is just lying there overwhelmed by the vast web of coincidence surrounding him, leading to this moment and beyond...? Yeah, that's me, most days.

But it began more directly thirty-one years ago this year, at a one-day *Doctor Who* convention with Tom Baker and Sophie Aldred. John Peel was there too, holding court in the bar; no way to tell that decades later we'd have a surprisingly fruitful collaboration on these three books. But more immediately, that was where I met the wonderful AC Chapin, cosplaying as Ace, and the seeds were planted for my fan film *Time Rift.*

It's because of *Time Rift* that I finally met Kate Orman — years after she'd left DC — and kickstarted my writing career. And more immediately, that I met Marsha Twitty... the original Adrienne Kramer.

I remember her at an early planning meeting with the Washington DC *Who* club, shyly offering to help out with the film somehow, and suddenly finding herself reading for a co-starring role. We watched her blossom into the part of General Kramer, making it her own; a feedback loop of writing and acting which made her more and more integral to the story. And slowly, we saw what Marsha had: a gentleness, a refreshing lack of drama amidst this mob of high-drama creatives, something quiet and dependable, an off-kilter sense of humour and sudden random show-tunes.

Finally, after years of work, once the film was finished, once the dust had settled and the dramas were forgiven and the on-set love affairs had flared and died, us survivors of the inner circle were finally old and wise enough to see that Marsha was not just a member of the team, not just a collaborator, but a friend. And, in fact, *friend* went right to the heart of her nature.

That smile of Kramer's, that special whole-hearted one behind the professional mask…? That's Marsha's. It's her slow beaming look of delight at the read-through for the first *Doctor Who* novel Kate and I wrote together, *Vampire Science*, when Marsha realised that the character who'd just dramatically entered the scene was *her*.

More years. Whenever we returned to Washington, Marsha was there, whether playing Kramer again in a quick short-film reunion, or regaling us with her latest fanfic/fantasy epic, or just thrilling to the fiftieth anniversary *Who* special with us all.

And then there's a guy who read that first book, who years later became an editor himself, after a whole parallel chain of improbabilities led to *Doctor Who* not just coming back to TV, but thriving on a scale huge enough that it could support the Brigadier's own book series. Andy Frankham-Allen asked for permission to feature then-Lieutenant Kramer in *Times Squared*, a story about their first meeting. Twenty years after her first day of filming, Marsha was tickled pink just to be remembered. She still didn't grasp that of course, of course, she will *always* be remembered.

Diabetes is cruel. We lost Marsha far too young. (Since then we've also lost Itzy Friedman, who deserves a book of his own; at least we got him into the UN reception.) But since Andy wrote such kind words to Marsha's family, that sparked off the idea of giving her one more hurrah, a story which put Kramer at the heart of the formation of UNIT. It's not so much that Marsha lives on – old Adrienne is a very different person from her, far more hard-nosed – but Marsha's *influence* lives on.

We all get by with a little help from our friends. In my case, I keep being struck by how much of where I've been throughout my life is down to the people around me.

So, thank you, Marsha.

Thank you to the whole gang at Half A Dozen Lemmings Productions; not just AC, Cary, and Kevin, but Amy and Ben Steele, Kris Kramer Foley, Neil Marsh, Eldridge Brown, David Dougherty, the awesome Vern Roseman, and everyone else threaded through those years.

And thank you to Marsha's boyfriend, Donald Bennett, and mother, Brenda Brander, for insight on Marsha and '70s DC and the family meatloaf, and Donald, Kevin, and Vern for reading and approving the scenes which "their" characters played with her.

To Jason Miller for local New York knowledge and Juan Kelly for the Isle of Man (though we did have to decide that the 1972 Isle of Man TT was held a bit earlier than normal). To Laura Goodin for abseiling advice, Bill Schlichtig for military perspective, Jim Orman for messing about in boats. To the Internations writing group; Caroline Hey, Ross Leahy, Florence Cotel, Jonas McCallum, Amy Wang, and more, for valuable views from outside the fan bubble. To Vicki Kyriakakis for a reminder of how powerful writing can be.

To my grandmother, Evelyn Kaitz, with her backbone of iron and laugh that could move mountains; you too deserved a bigger cameo.

To the read-through crew: Lisa Stewart, Michael Handy, Allison Tyra, Gerard Atkinson, Rob Lloyd, Kyla Ward, Nick Whiley, Lei Na Lu, Danny Horn, for everything you put up with. To all the Helical Scan folks who might be surprised to recognise themselves in the cast. To the other *Lethbridge-Stewart* writers, not just John, but especially Rick Cross and Simon Forward, for your valuable contributions. Special gratitude to everyone from Lyn Cox to Nathan Schattman who's been in the loop, and kept us sane in these lunatic times. Even to the estranged friends along the way; I wish you peace and healing.

And love always to Kate Orman, with special thanks for tolerating the excesses of this production.

Absolutely crucial thanks to Nicholas Courtney, and everyone else who made the Brigadier such a delight.

And to this whole world-wide web of parents, grandparents, brothers-sisters-cousins, in-laws, once and future friends, and everyone else who bumped up against us in whatever tangential ways, enough to jostle us to the point where we could be here, now, as we are, making this the book that it is.

It's a good place to be. Thanks to you all.